THE GUNS OF THE AMERICAN:
THE COMPLETE ADVENTURES
OF NORCROSS, VOLUME 2

OTHER BOOKS IN THE ARGOSY LIBRARY:

Satan's Vengeance

BY CARROLL JOHN DALY

*The Viper: The Complete Cases of
Madame Storey, Volume 2*

BY HULBERT FOOTNER

*The Sapphire Smile: The Adventures
of Peter the Brazen, Volume 4*

BY LORING BRENT

*The Curse of Capistrano and Other Adventures:
The Johnston McCulley Omnibus, Volume 2*

BY JOHNSTON MCCULLEY

*The Man Who Mastered Time and Other
Adventures: The Ray Cummings Omnibus*

BY RAY CUMMINGS

Trailin'

BY MAX BRAND

War Declared!

BY THEODORE ROSCOE

The Return of the Night Wind

BY VARICK VANARDY

*The Fetish Fighters and Other Adventures: The
F.V.W. Mason Foreign Legion Stories Omnibus*

BY F.V.W. MASON

THE GUNS OF
THE AMERICAN

THE COMPLETE ADVENTURES OF
NORCROSS, VOLUME 2

W. WIRT

ILLUSTRATED BY

ROGER B. MORRISON
& JOHN R. NEILL

COVER BY

PAUL STAHR

STEEGER BOOKS • 2020

TABLE OF CONTENTS

The City of Japheth 1

The Guns of the American 109

About the Author 205

THE CITY OF JAPHETH

*John Norcross, war Lord of a western China
city, goes adventuring in search of a lost
city in the mountains of Turkestan*

CHAPTER I

MEN OF MILLIONS

"I WANT TO go there, Landess," repeated the old man, getting up from the deep cushioned chair in the richly furnished library of Henry Landess, third richest man in the world. The library, with its shelves filled with almost priceless manuscripts and books, was on the third floor of the massive stone house on Fifth Avenue, overlooking Central Park in New York.

The old Hebrew went to one of the windows and stood, staring at the myriad lights twinkling across the dark green. For all the seventy years his body carried, it was slim and erect; and his face, smooth-shaven, looked like the pictures seen in the art galleries of the Patriarchs in the time of Christ. Even the immaculate evening clothes did not dissipate that impression.

"I must go," he continued, in a moment or so, coming back and beginning to pace up and down in front of the immense flat-topped, glass-covered mahogany desk. "Oh, God of Abraham, I must go, Henry! See, twice I have started, only to be turned back. The men that I hired to take me in were cowards that turned and ran. Look!" And he pulled up his sleeve.

"See the scars where those cowards bound me and carried me back to what they said was safety. Safety! When I wanted to go on until— Once through India, and once through China did I try, only to be driven back like a dog! I am like a man possessed by devils! Money? What good is it? Millions I have, as you have, Henry; and yet—and yet—what good? What good? I want to go there and die among the sacred things. Where I can see and

The Afghans studied their prey for a moment.

touch them. It is foolish, yes, and men would call me crazy; but
I want to go. I—want—to—go, Henry."

"Sit down once more, Isaac," said Landess, gently. "You are
not crazy." Landess was old, as old as Isaac Nathan. He was slim,
frail, with snow-white hair, but his eyes were young and shone
with the unquenchable spirit of great adventure that would light
them until they closed forever.

"Why shouldn't you want to go and spend your last days
among the things you hold sacred? Sit down and rest for a
moment that brilliant brain that has planned calmly and coolly
for so many years. You can go there, Isaac. Don't you see that in
your eagerness, you have rushed headlong into certain defeat?"

Isaac Nathan sat down, a smile now on his tight old lips and
in his still keen eyes.

"That is so, Henry," he answered quietly. "I have been like a
young lover rushing blindly to meet his dear one. I should have
come to you before. Together you and I will plan—as we used to
do in the old days when we fought them all. Do you remember
the day that we cornered cotton? Then we had a fight, didn't we,
Henry? Then my brain could plan, and execute. And now—and
now? Twice I have been turned back because the men I paid
were—

"Steady!" interrupted Landess. "Get back, Nathan! It is the day of the corner—they are calling on us for millions in gold! You must help me get them. Where? Stop thinking of what has gone wrong. It is water under the bridge. Now help me plan this thing. Are you a child that must be taken by the hand—or are you Isaac Nathan, the man who for years stood side by side with Henry Landess and fought them all? Answer me, so that I may know how to proceed."

NATHAN STRAIGHTENED up in his chair, and the hand that he held palm down across the table was as steady as steel.

"I am Isaac Nathan," he said, simply. "Failure is forgotten. You have a plan, Henry?"

"Yes. I know a man who will take you where you want to go, Isaac. I do not say that he *may* be able to, or that perhaps he can. I say that this man, if he chooses, and if you live up to that time, can put you among the things that are sacred to you."

"Henry, if he can (and I know that when you say he can, he can), I will give him—but what is money to me? Whatever he wants, he may have, that is all."

"Sit back and rest, Isaac. In two days, you and I will go and ask Captain John Norcross to take you to the sacred things. My yacht is in commission. Are you ready to go?"

"Yes, Henry, I am ready. There is no one left now of my family, to bid good-by. Miriam awaits me behind some bright star; I would start to her from this place I want to go. Yes, I am ready."

"We will go then, in two days," and Landess smiled at Nathan, a gentle, understanding smile which Nathan returned. The two men, both rich beyond the possibility of even estimating their wealth, more than powerful because of their millions in every civilized country and a few uncivilized, looked deep into each other's eyes and saw there what they had always seen in times of stress or peace, partnership.

"This Captain Norcross," inquired Nathan; "who and what is he, Henry?"

"He is a Mississippian, a gentleman by birth and breeding.

A captain in the regular army, commanding colored troops. He rated higher during the war and afterward resigned the service to become a special agent, because he loves action. He is the man that secured the Alveraz emeralds for Webb; and for me he fought his way up through Afghanistan to a Chinese city on its eastern border, and there got for me something that is priceless. I would be ashamed to tell you how many millions it cost me to buy it from the Greek church."

"You bought it from the church? I thought you said that this Captain Norcross got it for you?"

"He did; but in honor, I had to turn it over to the church. I bought it from the Patriarch in Athens. Captain Norcross outwitted Carlton's agent, outfought savage tribes and Chinese War Lords, put a Manchu princess on her throne, and brought me what I wanted. As little Ch'enyaun, the Manchu princess and War Lord of Ningyuan said," Landess added with a smile, " 'My honorable elder brother fulfilled his trust.' I can only say, Isaac, that I love him in the place of the son that was not given me; and if I wanted to get anything in the world, or wanted to go anywhere, I would ask Captain Norcross to get it for me or take me there."

"You can say no more, Henry," answered Nathan, his eyes shining. "Where is he?"

"At the moment, in Pekin. I do not think he has gone back to Ningyuan. Wait, I will make sure." Landess pressed a button on the desk. A manservant came in.

"Give Mr. Richards my compliments and ask him to join us here, please," Landess ordered. A moment later a young man, also in evening clothes, entered. He was a typical New York executive, with his calm, cold young face, keen eyes, and tight lips; he was Landess's first secretary.

"You know Mr. Nathan, Mr. Richards." It was a statement, not a question and Richards bowed. "Yes, sir."

"Captain John Norcross was in Pekin ten days ago. Locate

him, please, and if still there, put him in communication with me here. Use the P.A. cable."

"Yes, sir," Richards bowed once more and went out. Inside of five minutes, the great power of millions began to function smoothly across the continent, across the Pacific, by wire cable and wireless. It was "Clear for Landess," and those three words pushed everything to one side.

"**IF HE** is there, Henry," asked Nathan, after Richards went out, "what then?"

"Why, then, Isaac, you and I will go there and tell him what you want; and he will do it, for me."

"Can we, in any way, get anything for him before we go, to save time? Equipment, men, whatever he needs?" The brilliant brain of Isaac Nathan was working now.

Landess smiled. "I think that Captain Norcross will have all that is necessary, Isaac. After he came home, most of his colored troopers stayed over there and fought for the Princess Ch'enyaun and her husband, the Manchu noble T'ang Wang. About one hundred and fifty of them. They had plenty of the equipment," here Landess smiled, "that Captain Norcross carries with him. See, Isaac, wherever this Captain Norcross goes, he is strong enough to—what did he say?—oh, yes: strong enough to shoot his way in. His men served under him on the border and in France and love him and follow him anywhere. Isaac, those are fighting men pure and simple, experts with revolvers, rifles or machine guns. Captain Norcross smiles and says they are a 'bunch of no-'count scoundrels.'" Landess leaned back in his chair. "But he loves them just the same."

"But—I started in with five hundred men the first time and—"

"Not this kind of men, Isaac. You had men who went with you for hire. Men who cared neither for you nor for what you sought. Time-servers, that is all. Captain Norcross's men—his hundred fifty—are worth many thousand of such. They go with him because he is 'de Capt'n'; and that is very different. Do not worry about it, Isaac. If he will start with you, you will arrive, as Corporal Delicate Moss says, 'wid bells on.'" Landess chuckled as the memory of the immense corporal came to him.

"Besides, Isaac," he confessed, "after Captain Norcross went back to straighten out the men he left behind, and to help the Princess Ch'enyaun and T'ang Wang in a little war, I sent him four shiploads of, shall I say, equipment, of various kinds for the city he is building."

Nathan smiled. He knew full well how Landess, with legislators and high officials at his command the world over, could ship anything he wanted, at any time and to any place.

"If he is building a city, Henry, it may be that he will not want to take me."

Landess shook his head. "No, Nathan. No matter what he is doing, if I ask him, he will take you. He is no man of mine, you understand; no man owns him. But—he loves me, as I love him. He is as a son to me." It was at three o'clock in the morning that Richards entered the library.

"Captain Norcross's compliments to Mr. Landess. He awaits orders."

"Very good, Richards. Tell him that I leave for Pekin in two days."

And an hour later:

"Captain Norcross will await the arrival of Mr. Landess at the palace of the Mandarin Kungchang."

CHAPTER II

THE LOST TRIBES

CAPTAIN JOHN NORCROSS, lean-flanked, broad-shouldered, with thin, tanned, serious face and calm blue eyes, sat in the scented gardens of the Mandarin Kungchang. He was about thirty-two.

With him sat T'ang Wang, Manchu noble of the pure blood, who wore on his hat an embroidered unicorn with a girdle clasp of jade set in rubies—the insignia of a mandarin of the first military class. He had been leader of swordsmen for Ch'enyaun.

The two cities Ningyuan and Tai-yaun in Chinese Turkestan, five hundred thousand people and a hundred square miles of territory rendered unquestioned obedience to the dainty little Manchu girl, descended in unbroken lineage from the Chieftain Nurhachu of the Long White Mountain. Her cities commanded the passes through the great Thian Shan range from Siberia and Russian Turkestan.

Norcross had aided her in regaining her city of Ningyuan a year before, when she had been driven from it by her uncle who thought to seize the power.

He had seated her once more on the throne of her ancestors and had acted as her "honorable elder brother" when she married T'ang Wang. Now T'ang Wang was governor of all the province of Kuen Lun; and he had awaited the coming of Landess with his "elder brother" Norcross.

Across the mother-of-pearl inlaid table sat Landess and Isaac Nathan.

It was easy to see that Nathan felt Norcross could bring him to his heart's desire. He sat straight, his eyes holding those of Norcross. No longer was he uncertain; now he was the man who had fought for and won countless millions. He sensed that Norcross would understand him and his longing.

"Captain Norcross, I do not know of what faith you are or whether you have even read the Bible; but it may be that you remember this: 'And the Lord hardened the heart of Pharaoh, King of Egypt, and he pursued after the children of Israel; and the children of Israel went out with a high hand.'" Nathan looked inquiringly.

"Well, suh," Norcross answered with a smile, "my people have been Presbyterians for a right smart length of time, I reckon. I did go to Sunday-school for a little while back yonder in Natchez, Mississippi, but I don't remember too much about it. That's something about the children of Israel crossing the Red Sea, isn't it?"

"That is correct, Captain. Do you remember this: 'And when Pharaoh drew nigh, the children of Israel lifted up their eyes, and, behold, the Egyptians marched after them; and they were sore afraid; and the children of Israel cried out unto the Lord'?"

"No, suh. I don't reckon I do, Mr. Nathan."

Nathan smiled. "It is not to be expected that you would, Captain Norcross. Well, at that time, just before the Lord commanded Moses to stretch forth his hand over the sea and cause the water to be divided so that the children of Israel could walk on dry land, one of the captains of Israel rebelled against Moses, saying, 'Hast thou taken us away to die in the wilderness?' And that captain, with his family, the tens of families and the hundreds, seized on many of the sacred things of the temples that had been brought with them and left the camp of the children of Israel that night, under cover of the darkness.

"This captain, who was strong in fighting men, took many sacred things with him. He took the Ark of the Covenant; and with it, Captain Norcross, I personally believe he took also the Scroll of the Mosaic Laws, the pot manna, Aaron's Rod that budded and—and— But I see that these things mean nothing to you, Captain Norcross. This captain, whose name was Japheth, led his people away from Moses, followed and harried by a strong detachment of the troops of Pharaoh, who hung on like hungry wolves, met always by the good swords of the shepherds. Japheth led his people for three thousand miles before they came to the land they settled. How long it took, that I do not know… Is it believable, Captain?"

"Yes, suh," answered Norcross.

"**HE LED** them finally up beyond Chinese Turkestan. What it was called then, I do not know. In the Kuen Lun range of mountains he built a city. I see by your eyes that you are wondering how I know this. For ten, yes, for fifteen years I have been collecting evidence; here and there, a scrap now and then from all over the world. I know that the city is there."

"It is right probable he did build him a city, Mr. Nathan. But that range is beyond even the Thian Shan. Have you ever heard of a city up there, T'ang Wang?"

"Yes, honorable elder brother. In Ningyuan, when I was still in the school of swordsmen, there were rumors that there was a city in the Kuen Lun."

"That is it!" cried Nathan, his face illuminated with an inner fire. "I want to go there, Captain. To this day, the descendants of Japheth live there."

"Why," said Norcross, a little surprised, "that ought to be right easy, Mr. Nathan. They must have some contact with the Chinese or the Tartars or Russians."

"They have had contact with no one, those thousands of Israel," said Nathan grimly. "Their city is a walled one and they hold the land for a long ways surrounding it, with the sword. No man has ever won within the city. It is the only city in the world to-day that is wholly of the pure Hebrew. They have been that since the days of Moses."

"They must be fighting men," said Norcross with a smile, "to have held their city that way against all comers for thousands of years. You know something—anything—of the city, Mr. Nathan?"

"Three times," answered Nathan, "have men been driven from the city to die; and once, a woman. She was found by the Chinese, she and her baby. They told of the city, and died. My agents have been active for years, Captain. If I could only get there I—I think they would let me in. I am old now; and I think I have reverted back to my people—back to the days when the Hebrews were a people… I want to go there and die where they still are. Will you take me there, Captain Norcross?"

"If you will, John," said Landess, softly, "it will mean much to me. Isaac Nathan has been as a brother to me, always."

"I don't quite get it, I reckon," answered Norcross. "Given that the city is there—and that they keep all outsiders from coming in—why haven't you organized a strong enough outfit to go in as far as their lines?"

"I tried to. Twice," interrupted Nathan. "The men that I hired deserted me. They were cowards who thought only of their own safety and—" His tone was growing shrill.

"Steady, Isaac," broke in the softy firm voice of Landess. "Water under the bridge, remember. Captain Norcross can take you to the lines. Yes, and into the heart of the city if you wish. I tell you that; I, Henry Landess, who have never told you false."

"That is right, Henry," answered Nathan, sitting back once more.

"Well, suh," said Norcross, "I can sure try, anyway. Let's get it straight. You want to be taken to a city that you say is in Chinese Turkestan, in the Kuen Lun range. After we get there, what then?"

"Why, then, Captain Norcross, I will ask them to let me come in and stay," answered Nathan, simply.

"And if the city isn't there, or has been destroyed, or you find the stories about their being strictly Hebrew are false?"

"Why, then, I think that—that I will die. If that is the case, will you bury me up there in the mountains, Captain, so that I may look at the city that was once Japheth?"

"I hope we won't have to," answered Norcross gently. He had looked deep into the soul of the Hebrew patriarch sitting there, and understood. "But if we do, we will obey your orders, Mr. Nathan."

"Then you will take me there?" Nathan leaned forward.

"Yes, suh, we will sure take you there," answered Norcross.

"I will go with you, Isaac," said Landess, "at least as far as the city that John has built. Once before I was invited by the Princess Ch'enyaun to come to Ningyuan, and rest."

"When can we start?" asked Nathan, rising.

"To-day, if you wish. Our men await us just over the border of India at Gilgit."

"You do not need to make any preparations, Captain?" asked Nathan in surprise, as Norcross and T'ang Wang rose.

"No, suh," answered Norcross, with a smile. "Not until we reach Ningyuan I know that Mr. Landess can hurry our passage through India, to the border. Once there we have enough men to go through. Are your affairs attended to, T'ang Wang?"

"Yes, elder brother," answered the Manchu noble, governor of a province. "If they were not, they would be put aside until we have placed the friend of the War Lord of America in the heart of his city, as the War Lord, through you, placed the Princess Ch'enyaun in her city." And the Manchu, of a race that never forgets a debt of gratitude or of injury, bowed to Henry Landess, of New York.

CHAPTER III

INTO CHINA—AND PERIL

ISAAC NATHAN STOOD with Landess, Norcross and T'ang Wang on a little knoll, some ten miles beyond the border of India from Gilgit. In front of them loomed the massive Karakoram mountains of Chinese Turkestan.

Past the knoll there marched a compact little column of big colored men dressed in army khaki, the non-commissioned officers with the yellow rating stripes of the cavalry. Leading them was a stockily-built colored man who wore on his tunic the one bar of a second lieutenant. Fifty men in the ranks, twelve mules loaded with ammunition, six with machine guns, six more with rations.

The men carried heavy order marching equipment, Springfield rifles and bayonets; Colt .45 revolvers, holstered, swung from full cartridge belts at the proper "riders" angle. They may have been infantry at the moment, but they never forgot for a moment that they were "Troop B of the Thirty-first."

Five hundred of T'ang Wang's swordsmen had already gone into the hills as vanguard, and following the column were five hundred more of the best swordsmen in all China.

It was a hard-boiled, efficient-looking outfit that swung easily past; and it was just as hard-boiled and efficient as it looked, and it may be quite a little more. The colored men had served under Norcross in the regular army on the Mexican border and in France, and had more than willingly come with him to Chinese Turkestan.

They were simon-pure fighting men, who had absolute confidence that "dis outfit can whup de world." They loved Norcross as "de Capt'n," and any one of them would have cheerfully crawled through hell naked for him. Now, as they passed the knoll, Corporal Happy Combes said to the Mobile Kid, on his left: "Ain't dat de gent'mum dat meets us heah de first time us starts back?"

"Yes, suh, dat's de one, Happy. Dod gent'mum name is Landess. Ah nevah seed de odder gent'mum befo'."

"Maybe-so on de way back us gits de chance to show 'em whut reg'lars can do," offered Corporal Combes, hopefully.

"Dem's both fightin' gent'mums," announced Buck Foster, beside the Mobile Kid.

"How come you know dat, Buck? You only got you a little bitty squint at dem when us passed," demanded Happy Combes, with a grin that showed two rows of firm white teeth.

"Dat's all Ah need, boy," answered Buck, who had been raised on the old Dinwiddie plantation in Kentucky. "Ah knows quality folks when Ah sees dem; an' Ah knows fightin' gent'mum de same. Dem gent'mum ain't like de Capt'n, but they is quality folks an' fightin' folks just de same."

"Listen to de chattah of dat ape," said a voice from the next file. "Only kind of folks dat boy knows is de kind whut brings him in to say: 'Good morning, judge, please suh.'"

"Ain't dat de truf! An' den he knows dat de ol' judge he say: 'Ninety dollars an' a hundred and eighty days, boy.'" Another man took it up; and the lines, as far as they heard him, laughed.

There were few men there who had not qualified for the Distinguished Marksman badge, and all of them could make a machine gun or rifle spit out a steel-jacketed death, as well as handle a Colt .45. They were a happy-go-lucky outfit, as colored troops are when under officers they love; and they were also a fighting outfit. They fought Chinese, Cossacks, Zulus and whatever else got in their way, with pleased grins on their black faces; and they died the same way.

NATHAN WATCHTED them file by, his eyes shining. He looked at them and then at the lean, calm-eyed man standing beside him who commanded them. If his men loved Norcross, Nathan could tell by the look in the blue eyes that Norcross loved them also.

"Are these all of your men, John?"

Nathan had dropped the more formal "Captain Norcross" long before they had crossed India.

"No, suh," answered Norcross, as they started to walk along after the column, ahead of T'ang Wang's rear guard of swordsmen. "I have two hundred and fifty more at Ningyuan. After I came back to help the Princess Ch'enyaun and T'ang Wang fight off a Chinese and Cossack attack, I decided to stay, for several reasons—one of which you will meet in Ningyuan. I lost quite a few men then and later I sent back a few of them as a recruiting party to the States; and that brought my outfit up to its present strength. Most of the men have served in Troop B of the Thirty-first Cavalry at various times and the rest had been in other troops of my squadron. And Mr. Landess here," he smiled at the white-haired man walking beside him, "has sent me everything from airplanes to trench mortars, I reckon."

"Then, when we get to Ningyuan, how long will it be until we can start for—for my city in the hills?"

"The day after we arrive," answered Norcross, gently.

"Ningyuan is on the way to your city, Mr. Nathan. You have already started."

Nathan walked along for a few minutes, silently, then looked up and smiled. "Do you know, my friends, I feel absolutely at rest and at peace for the first time in many years. You have not failed me, Henry; and I know that you will take me to my city, John."

The column went steadily forward. When Landess and Nathan got tired of walking there were mules to ride, the big colored men taking the burden of machine guns or ammunition cheerfully on their brawny backs.

The camps were made in pleasant places, and both Landess and Nathan slept soundly under warm blankets. The swordsmen were around the camp in a far-flung circle with four machine gun detachments of the colored men at each compass point to back them up, for they were in no man's land.

Neither Norcross nor T'ang Wang, experienced fighting men that they were, took any chances whatsoever. It was Chinese territory, but a fighting ground for Afghans, Tartars, Chinese, with not a few Russians and masterless men of all breeds thrown in for good measure. The revolution in Afghanistan, the continual one in China, the ever-heaving unrest in Russia and India, had thrown a hard mixture in there. It was no man's land to the nth degree, and the Chinese War Lords there held what they had by force of arms alone. There was no law, except that which was made and enforced by steel or lead.

The column moved steadily through the hills toward Ningyuan. Corporal Combes's wish that something would happen so that the "reg'lars" could do some showing, was not fulfilled.

On the tenth morning, as Norcross, Landess, and Nathan sat at breakfast, Norcross pointed to a snow-tipped peak far ahead.

"Mr. Nathan, do you see that peak ahead and on the right a little? Just below it is the pass that leads to Ningyuan. To-morrow night we will camp there and the next night we will be in Ningyuan."

Nathan put down his coffee cup and smiled. "Henry, and John, neither of you can know how happy I am. I know that soon I will be in the place of rest and quiet, among the sacred things."

A little later the bugle blew "Troop mount," and then "Forward march." Highnote, the bugler, being a cavalryman, disdained all calls but those of the cavalry; and mounted or not, he used them.

THE AFGHAN Khan watched the proceedings from an aerie on top of one of the hills. His keen eyes picked up details that most men would have needed field glasses to find.

He was far above and outside the circle of swordsmen; though if he had been inside it would not have made his fierce old fighting heart beat a stroke faster.

He turned to the three men who lay beside him. Two of them were his kinsmen, the third a fat, greasy-looking Persian. The grime on that one's broad face could not hide the fact that he was desperately afraid; and he had good cause. To be alone in the hills with three Afghans was about the same as being in a den with three tigers.

His lust for gain had driven him as far as Zaman Khan's headquarters with his story of rich pickings; but he had not figured on going farther. He went, just the same; and now, as he lay alongside, he had no special reason for doubting that once Zaman Khan got the information he wanted there would be a dead Persian in the hills shortly after.

The Persian had intended to tell what he knew, make a dicker for part of the loot, and scurry back to India. There he would wait, trusting that Zaman Khan would come through with at least five per cent of what he should promise. But after Zaman Khan had listened he had ordered the Persian on a horse.

"Ho!" grunted Zaman Khan. "They form like well-trained troops. By the beard of the Prophet! If it were not for those sons of unspeakable mothers, the Manchu swordsmen who swarm like flies around honey, I would cut him out now with what men I have. There are only a few of the black men. Look, mongrel of Persia, and tell me which of the white men is he who owns all the gold."

The Persian inched his way gingerly to the rim and looked over, screwing up his eyes in an effort to see more plainly. He knew it was up to him to point out Nathan and be quick about it also. Any show of hesitation would be classed as double dealing by the fierce, suspicious Afghans, themselves past grand masters at the art. And the slightest shade of an idea like that coming to them would result instantly in a drawn sword or dagger, which would be used just as promptly.

"Make haste," commanded Zaman Khan. "We must ride far to gather the clans. Of what good are your eyes if you cannot even see at this short distance? Better that they be plucked from your head and hung up for the ravens to pick at."

At this by no means idle threat, the Persian pointed. "That one—walking toward the little tent in front. That is Nathan, who has most of the gold and jewels of his country."

The Persian had been one of the men hired by Nathan on one of his previous tries, and had been tipped by a friend who had seen the column leave the Indian border that Nathan was going into the hills again. The Persian had tried to frame a kidnaping on the earlier trip, but had not had time. That was the reason he had come to Zaman Khan.

The Afghans studied the man pointed out for a moment or so with their camera-like eyes, taking in every detail of his appearance. Then Zaman Khan arose, after easing back from the rim over which they had been looking down into the valley.

"It may be," he said, with an evil smile, "that the Prophet Mohammed, who rests in the bosom of God, will delegate me to relieve the infidel dog of the burden of carrying so much wealth. Ride, you, to Adalis! You, to the Saddosai! Gather all who ride under my standard. We meet at the Peak of the Gods. Ride and pass my word, which is this: Laggards shall not join in the loot. Say that I, Zaman Khan, swear it by the sacred stone at Mecca. To horse, kinsmen!"

The Persian decided, as he rode beside Zaman Khan, that if he got the chance he also would keep right on riding—until he had put the border of India between him and the Afghans, share or no share.

CHAPTER IV

OFF FOR THE KUEN LUN

THE MANCHU PRINCESS Ch'enyaun sat in one of the smaller audience chambers in the palace of her forefathers at Ningyuan. With her, around the polished teakwood table, sat the lovely wife of Captain John Norcross, who a year before had been the Magyar Lady Anna Guilai, Nathan, Landess, Norcross and T'ang Wang.

The proud little Manchu princess, whose ancestors had led the Manchus straight through China to the Peacock throne, had met Landess before. As Nathan was presented to her, the velvety black eyes had looked deep, to see the white shining spirit in the frail old body.

"You are welcome to my city of Ningyuan," Ch'enyaun had said softly, as she held out her slender little hand that could also close around a sword hilt, with a grip of steel, "Not only because you are the friend of the War Lord Landess, but because you are—" Her English, taught her by Norcross and by T'ang Wang, who had spent four years in England, did not permit her to say exactly what she wished to say; so she finished the sentence—"because you are *you*."

Nathan had smiled gently at the upturned lovely little face and answered: "I am glad to be here, O mighty ruler of cities, and also glad to have you welcome me, because you are what you are."

She had smiled delightedly; and now she was sitting beside Nathan, looking like some gorgeous little butterfly in her bright silken robes that blazed with priceless jewels.

With Anna Norcross, she had heard Nathan tell of the legendary city and of his longings to reach there. He had told it simply and from his heart. Long before he had finished, both of the beautiful women were leaning forward, their eyes shining.

Both of them had been raised in a hard school; Anna by the Altai Mountain Tartars, of which her father had been *haduagy* or chief captain, although by birth a Magyar; and the princess Ch'enyaun, raised in the Manchu code. Both had brave fighting hearts that beat true in their exquisite bodies.

It was a far call from Isaac Nathan, who had fought his way up to millions in New York, to the princess Ch'enyaun and to Captain John Norcross's wife, descended from kings and conquerors of a thousand years ago. But Nathan's race was as pure-blooded, and their hearts reached across the distance to his. As he told of his tragic failures to reach his goal, Anna Norcross leaned across the pearl-inlaid table and patted one of the hands he had clenched as he lived over the days when he had been driven back.

"You must not think of it any more. My Lord John will take you to the city. And if you do not want to stay there, once you have found it, come to our city of Guilai on the mountain of Su. There you will find rest and peace."

Nathan smiled and relaxed. "That I will do; but I know, somehow, the city is there."

A palace officer came to the entrance and bowed. "You have my permission to enter, Ming Li," Ch'enyaun said.

The officer advanced to within ten feet of the table and bowed again before he spoke. "The people you summoned have arrived and await your pleasure, O War Lord of many swordsmen and cities."

"You will send them in one by one, the eldest first." As the officer bowed and backed out of the room, Ch'enyaun explained. "They are people from Taiyaun and the country as well as those in Ningyuan, who know or have heard the—I do not know the English word, elder brother."

"I reckon the word you want is 'legend'; that means story or tale of old, Ch'enyaun," Norcross answered.

"Yes, that is it. These people have heard legends of the city in the Kuen Luh range. T'ang Wang, you question them, and the Lady Anna and I will translate for the War Lord Landess and Mr. Nathan"

"And also for your elder brother," added Norcross. "My Chinese is limited to about six words."

"As was my English, John," Anna said, as her hand sought and found his, "until you taught me."

THE FIRST man in, an old gold-worker, couldn't remember much; and the fact that he was in the presence of Ch'enyaun and the foreign lords, did not help his memory very much. But T'ang Wang, his grim young face gentle for all its sword scars, as gentle as it always was when dealing with the people, led the old man slowly along. The people knew and loved the just, calm, Manchu leader of swords; and the old man finally told all he knew.

It wasn't much. His father's father had been told by his grandmother that once her father was hunting in the Kuen Lun. In trailing a wounded snow leopard he had climbed one of the high mountains and there from the crest he had looked down on a walled city which seemed to be built as a square with four mountains as the corners. He could see great temples and massive stone buildings, and thought he could see the gates in the wall.

Then, as he looked, he was confronted with men who bore swords and spears, who carried round shields of some shining metal. He knew they were not Chinese, or Tartars or Uzbegs. The leader strode forward, giving some order in a strange tongue. The hunter, seeing an opening, turned and fled and the men had cast spears at him.

"You say that your ancestor, who doubtless is at present on high receiving the honor he deserved as a mighty hunter," T'ang Wang asked, as the old man came to a halt in his wandering speech, "hunted in the Kuen Lun, O venerable grandfather of swordsmen? It has come to my mind that your grandson, Tzu

Chen, is one of the brightest scholars in the school of swordsmen."

The old man smiled at the compliment and became more
at ease. "That is true, O mighty leader of swords. The family of
Chen has resided in the Kuen Lun since the days of the Duke
Chow. My father's father was the first to leave the hills. He came
here to Ningyuan in the reign of Prince Chieh-ni, the ancestor
of the resplendent princess," here he bowed low to Ch'enyaun,
"who now rules the world."

"Where in Kuen Lun did your family of Chen live?"

"At the foot of the great Mountain of the Lower Gods, near
K'uang."

"He hunted then around the Mountain of the Lower Gods?"

"Yes, O mighty swordsman of the Manchu; and far afield.
For days he would travel in search of game. The house of Chen
were mighty hunters."

The old man was dismissed with a present and the next called.
But to what his story gave, the rest of the tales did not add
anything more tangible. It was a mass of vague fable and myth,
interwoven with stories of the gods. About all that they defi-
nitely agreed upon was that somewhere in the Kuen Lun there
was a city of some kind. Nathan, listened eagerly, offering questions to be asked, but at the finish, Norcross and T'ang Wang
looked at each other. Nathan caught the look and sighed. "You
doubt it?"

Norcross smiled. "I do not think that there is the slightest
doubt, Mr. Nathan, that somewhere in the Kuen Lun range
there is a city. But I do not think that we are any nearer to it at
the moment because of the stories we have heard. I think the
best thing we can do is to start for there and try to pick up information as we go."

"I will send all my hunters out," Ch'enyaun announced, "and
all the country people that can be spared. With the men of my
Lord John can go my swordsmen, who are also hunters. Now,
you must rest in my gardens, you and the Lord Landess, while

my Lord T'ang Wang and my honorable elder brother make ready."

"YALLER" COUDRAY, who received his nickname on account of his color and in no way on account of his nerve, which was chilled steel, made an important announcement the next morning, after Norcross had finished an inspection of all men and equipment. The big negroes stood in the four-pointed star formation with the machine guns at each point, the one- and two-pound rapid-firers, between the points. First Lieutenant Coudray had been Norcross's first sergeant in the regulars.

As Norcross walked back toward the palace, Coudray ordered, "At ease. Dere will be one hundred and fifty men detailed to go wid de Capt'n into de mountains and find a place dat Misto' Nathan wants to git to. Ah goes wid de party. De rest of B Troop stays heah and at Guilai. Half of de machine gun squads go and half of de rapid-fiah section."

From the ranks came an immediate response to this announcement.

"Us goes, Skinnay."

"Yo' stay home, Slewfoot. Yoah wife don't let yo' ramble round after dark."

"Doggone! Maybe-so us meets some mo' of dem Cussacks!"

"You ain't goin', boy. You is too pigeon-toed to climb dem hills. Ah takes de gun an' tends to the mattah."

"Yaller—Ah means, Lieutenant Coudray! Don't me an' de Mobile Kid go wid de—"

" 'Tenshun!" shouted Yaller. "Mah goodness, does yo' apes keep up dat chattah, Ah goes by mahself. Half goes an' half stays. All dem what has extra duty to work off, stays. Dat'll teach 'em to obey ohdahs 'bout keepin' clean 'quipment. What we does is dis. Us goes to de barracks an' Sergeant Deacon Yancey deals de cards. Two by two. High man goes an' low man stays. Ace high. Dismiss."

This method of deciding a delicate question appealed very much to the big colored men, and as they ran toward the

barracks, several of them tried to get near Yancey with suggestions that when their turn came he deal from the bottom of
the deck.

CHAPTER V

AFGHANS CHARGE

ONE OF THE machine gunners sat up and rubbed his eyes,
then looked about the outpost, which lay just within the circle
of swordsmen surrounding the camp. It was at the foot of one
of the mountains in the Kuen Lun range.

He looked over at the orderly camp, the tents inside the star
formation, machine guns and rapid-fire guns in place at the
points, the men sleeping in their blankets along the lines. He
could see the smoke curling up from the stovepipe in the cook
tent.

"What's de mattah wid Highnote?" he grumbled. "Ain't up
yet to toot dat blame horn! Dat nigger gittin' mo an' mo' ornery
each an' every day. Ah sees de smoke an' Ah smells de coffee. Dat
black no-'count scound—"

"You sees an' you heahs, does you?" rumbled Squint-eye
Mears, who lay sprawled out at full length, using his arm for a
pillow. "Well, iff en you doesn't hush dat bull-bellowin', endurin'
de time dat Ah gits mah beauty sleep, you *feels,* big boy. An' what
you feels is mah fist on yoah jaw."

"Does yo' try to gimme dat feelin' thing an' Ah finds hit out,"
answered Skinnay Martin, promptly, "right af'tah dat, yo' wakes
up hearin' de nurse say: 'take dis, Misto' Squint-eye!' Doggone!
One of the gent-mum am waitin' like me for dat monkey-face
to sound de come-an'-git-it. He's takin' him a walk ov'ah to
dem funny rocks. Boy, howdy, dat Misto' Nathan sure does like
to look at rock. All de time he—dog mah cats! Ah thought Ah
seed some of dem bowlders move, up yonder on de hill."

Squint-eye sat up, a bitter expression on his grim, saturnine face and in his eyes. This Squint-eye was one of the best, if not the best, machine gunners in the outfit. It was he that boasted once, "Ah cuts hair wid dat gun at nine hundred yards."

"Man," he announced, "dat tongue of yoahs is tied in de middle an' runs at both ends."

"An' yoahs is de same," put in one of the other men, sleepily. "Ah sure wishes Yaller don't detail me no more wid you apes. Dat's all Ah got to say; nevah no more."

Cheerfully Skinnay began singing:

"Nevah no mo', nevah no mo'—
Ain't gwine to get detailed, nevah no mo'.
Ridin' up to heaven in a chariot of fiah,
And sit on de knee of de—"

His singing was interrupted by a yell from Squint-eye, issued as he dived for the gun trigger. "Mah Gawd! Look comin'! *On de fiah!*"

The camp was near a little stream and as far out from the base of the surrounding hills as possible. T'ang Wang had dropped back to bring the rear guard closer up now that the column was well in the Kuen Lun. The advance screen of swordsmen was scattered through the hills in front and on both sides.

Some of them, enough to maintain an irregular line around the entire camp, were in sight. But with those in the hills, Chinese without Manchu officers, the Afghans had played the old, old hill game of ambush and sudden death. They had slipped below and around the small units, and in most cases the swordsmen had not even seen the steel by which they died. No guns were used, just the silent steel; and not one of the advance guard lived to win through with a warning.

What caused Squint-eye to yell was the first movement of the avalanche that poured down from the hills—big, bearded men with swords and the dreaded Afghan knives. Most of them were Afghans, but there were more than a few Uzbegs,

Tartars, Chinese who had fled their War Lords, and Cossacks who had deserted or been driven from their *sotnias;* also men of mongrel breeds. Zaman Khan was a warrior who welcomed all good swords to his standard, despite race or color.

As the charge started, a compact little group ran out from behind the rocks which Nathan had started over to look at. Zaman Khan, from his post in the hills, had seen the old man leave the lines and, feeling that the Prophet had dropped the ripe fruit into his lap, he had ordered forward some of his clan to capture Nathan. It was this movement that had started the rest off.

Nathan looked up and saw what was bearing down on him. Turning, he started to run, but was overtaken before he had gone a yard. One of the big men reached out for him, got him, tossed him over his shoulder, and the entire group whirled around and ran back behind the rocks.

AS SQUINT-EYE yelled and opened fire, Highnote, the bugler, had just raised the bugle to his lips to blow the reveille. Skinnay had been a little ahead of the schedule with his demand for the "come-an'-git-it" mess call. Highnote also saw what Squint-eye did, and instead of reveille, he blew "Boots and saddle—Troop mount—Charge—Commence firing," running them all together. Then, being game and dearly loving a fight himself, he started in on, "Oh, they keep the pigs in the parlor," which was the battle song of B Troop.

The swordsmen of T'ang Wang stood calmly where they were, making no effort to retreat from the howling death that was rushing toward them. They were picked men, all graduates from the school of swordsmen at Ningyuan. But they were outnumbered fifty to one, and they died in their tracks, carrying down with them double the number of their foes.

Squint-eye and the rest of the machine gun squad fired three or four rounds with the Browning and rifles which cleaned up their immediate front, then picked up the gun and ran for the lines. As they started, Skinnay saw Nathan, slung over an Afghan's shoulder, disappear around the rocks.

They just made the lines which opened up a little to let them through. So close behind them were the first Afghans that when Skinnay yelled: "Misto' Nathan's took! Misto' Nathan's took!" no one paid any attention to him; and Skinnay himself had other things to think of in trying to take care of a big Afghan who broke through the line right on top of him.

As the bugle finished the "Charge," Norcross ran out of his tent. He was in his pyjamas, but there was a cartridge belt around his waist and his heavy Colt .45 was in his hand. His feet were bare, but his blue eyes were as calm and smiling as ever. As he ran toward the north point of the star where the attack seemed the thickest, he shouted, as he passed the men on the line between the points: "Receive the gentlemen properly, you birds."

The men were on their feet, the bayonets had been snapped into place; and on all the lines between the machine guns, the gentlemen were being received with all B Troop had—which was quite a lot.

Before a round could be fired, the first Afghans had hit the line. It was the nearest to a surprise that Norcross and his men had ever experienced. One half minute more slowness in response to the bugle, and the first wave of big men, whose vital organs were protected by steely sinews and heavy sheepskin coats and quilted vests, would have flowed over the camp. They came up in great leaps and bounds; their faces, bearded to the eyes, were working with the lust for killing.

But they were met by equally big, steel-muscled men, who were just as prompt in either offense or defense. The colored men, neat and trim, smooth-shaven and immaculate in their khaki, did not give an inch; in most cases they actually stepped forward to close. The charge was made by an outfit hard to stop—but it met one just as hard to go up against.

The bayonets met the sword-blades and the knives with as hard a parry as the cut or thrust, there was a clang of steel on steel, the "Ho" of the big men as they put forth all their strength; and then one or the other went down, his place at once taken by another. It was a mad swirl of fighting for a few minutes. At several places four or five Afghans hit the line in a group and two or three colored men went down. The man does not live that can handle two fighting Afghans at the same time, unless he is using a gun at a distance. But the Afghans followed them to the ground as soon as Norcross and Yaller Coudray and some of the nearest machine gunners, who were taking care of such breaks in the line, saw what had happened.

The first wave suddenly ceased to exist and now the rifles and machine guns opened up.

"TIGHTEN UP!" Norcross shouted. "Close up!" The star became smaller as the men picked up the space left by twenty of B Troop who would never again answer "Heah" or "Pres-unt" at roll call.

Back in the hills the mullahs, the fighting priests, could be heard chanting: "The sword is the key of heaven and of hell; a drop of blood shed in the cause of God, a night spent in arms, is of more avail than two months of fasting or prayer; whosoever falls in battle, his sins are forgiven; at the day of judgment his wounds shall be resplendent as vermilion, and as odoriferous as musk; and the loss of his limbs shall be supplied by the wings of angels and cherubim."

Zaman Khan had seen his men seize Nathan and after a curt order to one or two of his lieutenants, the chief had disappeared. He knew that there was no need of his presence. Once the ball had started rolling and the mullahs began, he did not need to urge on the attack. Neither could he stop it.

All that the colored men had done was to clear the immediate front for a moment. The next wave arrived, charging into the very face of the deadly guns. Their numbers and the press behind brought them up to the lines in spite of the ones that fell. But always and ever, they were met by bayonet and Colt. The men of Norcross's outfit were now just as fight-crazy as the Afghans.

Landess had come out of the tent that he shared with Nathan and stood in front of it. It was the first time he had seen men killed in battle, and his fine old face and eyes showed the horror of it to him. He tried to locate Nathan with his eyes, thinking that he must have sought cover somewhere. He saw Norcross, his pyjamas hanging from his body in bloody threads, a smile on his lips, encouraging the men as he ran from point to point.

From where he stood, Landess could hear Yaller Coudray: "Dem apes can't clean B Troop! Stay in de line! Dat's de boy, Buck! Slewfoot—take one of dem two offen Happy!" And he saw Yaller's lightning-like play with a bayoneted rifle.

In spite of the merciless fire, party after party of Afghans hit the line. The distance over which they charged was too short, on account of the rocks on the right, and at the rear giving them cover until the last fifteen or twenty yards. Those who tried to charge on the left and in front were more in the open and few of them lived to match sword against bayonet.

There was a lull for a moment and the voices of the mullahs in the hills could be still heard, urging a final effort to wipe out the dogs of infidels, and promising reward in the Mohammedan heaven.

"Close up!" Norcross shouted. "Get those rapid-fire pieces over on that pass to the left! Strut your stuff, you no-'count scoundrels! We'll show those birds what B Troop can do. Sergeant!" he yelled to Coudray, forgetting in the stress of battle that he had made Coudray a lieutenant when the outfit swelled to three hundred men. Yaller Coudray was once more his old top-cutter and the men were B Troop. "If you see that we are going down, take ten men and cut your way out with Landess and Nathan. It is up to you to get them back to Ningyuan. Come in a little with that gun! What are you trying to do, take it all?"

The machine gun squad who had inched forward so as to get a clear half circle swing, grinned and moved back—back at least an inch, as Skinnay Martin came up to Norcross and obstructed his view of them.

SKINNAY SALUTED, for all that he looked, as one of the men said afterward, like "somepin' de cat brung in." He had gone to the ground in a wrestling match with a big Afghan, with life the stake; it had not improved his looks any, but he had the same old grin on his face.

"Capt'n, please suh, Misto' Nathan done been tooken by de wild men."

Norcross's face went white. "Say that again."

"Please suh, Ah said dat Misto' Nathan was walkin' ovah yonder by dem rocks, an' when de ruckus started, one of dem grabbed him and highballed it round de rocks wid him."

To Norcross came the picture of his wife, leaning across the table patting Nathan's hand; and her voice came clearly to his ears, above the cries of wounded men: "My Lord John will take you to the city."

Then, as if flashed on a screen, he saw Nathan's fine old face, the eyes shining with absolute confidence and happiness as the column left Ningyuan. The picture was blotted out by a wave of actual pain. He, John Norcross, late of the Army, fighter in the far places, had allowed the man that trusted him to be taken—and by Afghans.

All he was, all the military training, all the cool, clever, planning brain—everything was submerged in the one overwhelming urge of "Get Nathan!"

He ran to the point of the star fronting the rocks, stooped and picked up a bayoneted rifle. The big colored men from all the star, sensing something, were watching their "Capt'n."

Already those in the far lines had turned a little on their feet, and their rifles had dropped to "Charge bayonets." The machine gunners had stood up, their Brownings forgotten, rifles of the fallen in their hands. It was like a football team on the line, waiting to go down field at the kick-off. Every man tensed, quivering with eagerness. If the gates of hell were open in front of them, B Troop would have followed "de Capt'n" straight through them.

"Blow 'Charge,' Highnote," Norcross demanded.

But even as Highnote raised the bugle to his lips, the attack came once more from all sides. There was nothing for B Troop to do but fight where they were. The machine gunners crouched at the guns and the rifles spat out defiance, the men behind them as merciless as the men charging in. In the open, the fire would have destroyed any charge, but here, where there was cover, it was different. The Afghans reached and went over the two guns at the south point. It became a madhouse as the men rose from the guns. It was like some herd of grizzly bears in a death grapple with black wolverines.

Norcross saw the break in the line but could not reach it. He had been seen and recognized as the white leader, and the point where he was had become a mad corner of hell.

"Ain't dis some fight?" panted Happy Combes, as he came alongside of Sergeant Delicate Moss.

"Gimme mo' room!" grunted the immense Delicate, "till Ah mops up on dese cooties!"

Yaller Coudray, the Mobile Kid, Buck Foster, and Slewfoot, all big men, trained to the minute, fast as cats, stuck as close to Norcross as they could. Yaller had in mind Norcross's order regarding Landess and Nathan, but had privately made up his mind that "de Capt'n" was going also or he, Yaller, was going to be found dead as close to Norcross as he could get.

The star formation was gone now, but all over the field of battle there were rings of the colored men, like the shield rings of the Norsemen.

SUDDENLY WILD yells came from the hills and the pressure relaxed, then fell entirely away. Down from the hills came four wedges of swordsmen. T'ang Wang had arrived with the rear guard.

They had passed some of the bodies of their comrades up in the hill and had seen the mutilation that the Afghan does as a show of contempt and disrespect.

Now they came down like maniacs, destroying all living things in their path. The Afghans turned to meet this new foe, but as the colored men opened up with the rifles and machine guns once more, the hillmen, realizing they were caught between two fires, broke and fled.

Norcross's brain had cleared and he remembered Landess. He started for the tents, then he saw him standing by the cook tent. Memphis, the tall, gaunt cook, with him. In front of the tent lay the bodies of two of the Afghans. They had won through that far, to be met by Memphis, who was a fighting man as well as a cook. One he killed with his Colt .45 as they came up. The other had to swerve a little to avoid the falling body and before his sword could sweep down, Memphis had him, one iron hand on the sword wrist, the other at the throat. There had been an instant of strain, then Memphis swayed out and to the left, his hip coming against the Afghan's. The man rose in the air as he did, Memphis let go the wrist, his arm came under the shoulder of the Afghan and the body twisted. Landess, standing behind Memphis, shuddered as he saw the head loll over on a shoulder as Memphis let go.

As Norcross started over toward Landess, T'ang Wang came up.

"You are wounded, elder brother?"

"No—not seriously. Nathan is taken, through my negligence. I am going after him."

The Manchu looked at Norcross, then asked tensely, "Where?"

"Where? You do not understand, T'ang Wang. I said that Nathan had been captured. The man that trusted me, I allowed— He has been taken to the hills," Norcross went on, calmer now. "I will take as many men as I can, consistent with the safeguarding of Mr. Landess, and go find him."

"It is not your fault to grieve over, O Lord John," answered T'ang Wang. "My swords are to blame. They were the outer guard and they failed to keep it."

"You are delaying me, T'ang Wang. All the words in the world cannot alter the fact that he has been taken from me. I failed him, not your swordsmen. Sergeant Coudray, detail a party of—"

Norcross looked at the colored men left on their feet. Of the one hundred and fifty that left Ningyuan, there remained only some ninety-odd. The rest lay on the ground, wounded or dead. "Detail twenty-five men to go into the hills with me. You will remain with the rest to taken care of Mr. Landess."

"O honorable elder brother," T'ang Wang said quietly, as Norcross turned, "your grief has led your clever spirit far along paths clouded with mist. No small party can go into the hills for hours yet and live. The Afghans and the mongrel dogs with them are running fast now. Let them clear and—will you grant me five minutes now, before you go? Then I will also go with you, elder brother."

NORCROSS LOOKED at the proud Manchu noble that he knew loved him, and steadied himself. "Yes, T'ang Wang. Now the clouds have cleared away and I see clearly once more."

"I know that you do, Lord John. It may be that we can get some information that will enable us to strike quickly."

He pointed to a wounded Uzbeg near the lines and gave a curt order to the swordsmen who stood behind him. Two of them pounced on the wounded man and dragged him to T'ang Wang. The Manchu thrust his fierce, scarred face to within an inch of the Uzbeg's, who tried to cringe back.

"Who led?" T'ang Wang snarled, in Pushtu.

"Zaman Khan," answered the Uzbeg promptly. He owed no loyalty to the Afghan; and if he had, he would have told, just the same.

"Take him back," T'ang Wang ordered, then his eyes went to the piles of wounded and dead. An Afghan was sitting up, holding a shattered shoulder. Again T'ang Wang pointed and issued an order. The Afghan did not cringe and draw back as had the Uzbeg. He did his best to reach a sword; and failing that, he tried to kick and bite. But he was brought to T'ang Wang and held there.

"Lord John, this man will know where Zaman Kahn left the horses. It may be that he will not give the information willingly.

I will send him behind those rocks with some of my men. When they return they will know all that he knows. It is for the Lord Nathan, elder brother."

Norcross did not have to be told what was going to happen to the Afghan unless he told, and very quickly. But that "for the Lord Nathan" made the decision for him.

"Tell him first that if he speaks he will be spared and sent on his way," he answered curtly, as he started for his tent.

The big colored men, engaged in giving first aid to the wounded, watched the Afghan being carried away, with cold eyes.

Before Norcross had washed and, with the help of Skinnay Martin, bandaged the not deep cuts on his chest and arms, T'ang Wang entered.

"The Lord Nathan was the object of the attack. Zaman Khan had received word from some source that the Lord Nathan was the rich man who had tried to go into the hills before. Zaman Khan promised the men that helped him the looting of the camp and a share in the ransom. As soon as the Lord Nathan was captured, Zaman Khan withdrew with some of his tribesmen. For which," T'ang Wang added with a grim smile, "he was cursed by this man, who is one of the Afridis, not of Zaman Khan's family. After a little, surprisingly little, persuasion, because of that fact, he told of where Zaman Khan left his horses, which is far from here owing to the footbridges to cross. He also drew a map of the way. Zaman Khan plans to take the Lord Nathan to his stronghold near Ghanzi."

Landess came in the tent.

"John," he said, gently, "I do not want you to consider me for a moment. Take all of your men and the Lord T'ang Wang's swordsmen, I will keep up if I can, and if not, I will sit on the side of the path and await your return with Isaac Nathan, or whatever death may come."

He stood there with a simple dignity that reached the Manchu noble and Captain John Norcross as nothing else could.

"We will find him, Mr. Landess," Norcross answered. "It will not be necessary that all the men go. A small, picked party can do much more in the hills. He will be with you once more very soon. We will draw back into the hills a little ways, and make a camp that—that will not be surprised this time. There most of the men will wait, with you."

CHAPTER VI

AFGHAN PRIZES

NATHAN HAD MADE no attempt to struggle as he was lifted in the Afghan's brawny arms. He knew it would be useless and would sap what strength he had. As the man carrying him ran around the rock, Zaman Khan, who had come down from his post, snarled an order for him to carry Nathan carefully—not that he cared in the slightest about the comfort of the old man he had captured, but he wanted him in good physical condition to arrange the ransom.

As the man carrying Nathan came to a small stream he tossed Nathan over his shoulder like a bag of meal and waded in with the rest of the party, Zaman Khan had with him some twenty men besides the one carrying Nathan, all of his own family.

The breath was knocked out of Nathan as his stomach hit the hard shoulder on the toss-up and the jolting around as the party went straight up the hill and down again on the other side made him sick. Soon he lost consciousness completely.

Before they had gone very far he was transferred to the shoulder of another man and several times while crossing narrow native foot bridges over deep chasms he was carried by two men, one holding his feet and the other his shoulders.

As they finally came through a narrow little pass which opened into the growth of timber where the horses had been left, Zaman Khan stared—and swore lustily. There on the ground lay the bodies of the men he had left with the horses. Some party, either coming to the fight or going away from it, had run across the horse camp and promptly, in the hill custom, had slain the guards and taken the horses with them.

"May the curses and torments of the Nine Thousand and Eight Devils be forever on these thieves and their descendants!" Zaman Khan snarled. "You, Abdullah, and you with him," pointing to another man, "go as fast as you can. Get to the camp of the Saddozai, which lies back of us below the High Mountain of the Three. Get horses there and bring them back."

He sat cross-legged beside Nathan who lay stretched out at his feet, a sheepskin coat under his head. Zaman Khan was not in any way anxious over the delay, except for the possibility that some party might come along which he must either fight or give a share of the ransom.

He sat there and looked at the thin white clear-cut features of the old man lying at his feet. The attack had come at dawn and the sun now was high overhead. As its warm rays fell upon Nathan's face, he stirred, opened his eyes and sat up. Isaac Nathan of New York looked squarely into the eyes of Zaman Khan, Afghan chief and each man knew the other was unafraid.

"You have come back from the world of dreams, O man of much gold and jewels," the Afghan said in Pushtu.

Nathan smiled grimly and shook his head. "I do not understand any languages," he said gently, "but English and Hebrew."

The Afghan did not understand what Nathan said, any more than Nathan had understood him, but he knew by the shake of the head what Nathan meant.

"Do you speak Russian?" he demanded slowly in that language.

Nathan shook his head again.

Zaman Khan turned to his men who sat in a half circle behind him. "This infidel speaks no language that we can talk in. You, Mehmet, you served in India with one of the English regiments. Speak to this man."

Steel clanged on steel.

THE MAN rose and came to where he could sit cross-legged in front of Nathan. His English was the English of the barracks, and he had very little of it, but with signs to help out he managed to act as interpreter.

"Tell this man that he will be released upon the payment to me of many bags of gold and jewels."

The interpreter got that to Nathan fairly well and also Nathan's reply to Zaman Khan, which was that he would pay whatever gold Zaman Khan asked for. The fierce old Afghan grunted approval, and having plenty of time, he thought that he would see if he could make this man show signs of fear.

"Tell him that if the gold does not come promptly, he will be boiled in oil after being beaten with whips."

The interpreter couldn't get much of that into English, but supplied other details of torture to make up for it.

Nathan smiled and answered:

"Say to the leader of fighting men that I regret that my old body will not give him much time to enjoy the spectacle. Also tell him that—"

An Afghan outpost came up.

"Two come down the path."

The entire party vanished behind rocks and fallen trees as if wiped out by a magic brush. Zaman Khan touched Nathan on the shoulder, motioned for him to follow, and slid behind a matted pile of second growth which had been trampled down by the restless horses.

There stepped from the narrow path that wound up the mountain a young man, hardly more than a boy; and just behind him there walked a girl. He was dressed in a short skirt of tanned leather, what looked like shin guards of a football player, and leather sandals; he wore some kind of metal breastplate that was embossed with metal knobs.

On his head was a helmet, its back coming down in an apron covering the back of his neck. On top of it there was a raised narrow box that held a short, thick plume like a whiskbroom cut off at the middle.

His arms were bare, as were his legs except for the shin guards. He was a slim, well-built boy, with a stern, clear-cut young face that was distinctively Hebrew. He carried himself proudly although his clothes showed signs of wear and tear and his face marks of strain and exhaustion. He carried a spear in his right hand, a straight sword hung from a sword belt across his legs in front, and on his left arm there was a round embossed shield of the same metal as his corselet or breastplate.

The girl behind him was also young, even younger than the youth. Her dress and her pretty dark face placed her. She was an Altai Mountain Tartar, and as did the boy, she carried herself with a little swagger, her head held high.

They had not taken five steps across the little clear space before they stopped as if frozen in their tracks. Out of the ground, there had arisen around them a circle of Afghans, swords in hand. The Afghan has a sense of humor and now there were smiles on the fierce hawklike faces and a shout of laughter went up at the expression on the faces of the two who had walked into the trap.

It was not an expression of fear but of utter astonishment.

The boy reacted promptly, though no more so than the girl.

He dropped his spear, drew his sword, shifted his shield in front of him and crouched a little. The girl eased the light pack from her slender shoulders, drew a long Tartar dagger with a bone hilt and stepped to the young man's back. The Afghans stood about two feet apart, their swords held loosely, the smiles of pure enjoyment still on their lips. There was no hurry as far as they were concerned. Afghan-like, they wanted to play a little, as a cat does with a mouse.

Neither the boy nor the girl was under any delusions as to the delay in attack. The boy did not know Afghans, but he knew of hill warriors in general; and the girl was a Tartar. Both knew that inside of a very few minutes at the most, they would both be dead, or what was worse than death, captured. Death on a sword point was far preferable to slavery.

ZAMAN KHAN, who stood just outside the circle with Nathan, shouted an order. "Strike his sword from his hand! You, Shere Ali! Get them alive! Shaikh, to the girl! Use care, reckless ones! If there be but a scratch on either, no share of the sale money!"

An Afghan stepped out of the circle and confronted the boy, another glided toward the girl as easily, for all his bulk, as a leopard coming in to make a kill.

There was a flash and a ring of steel on steel, a fast slicing cut, a faster parry and return and the Afghan staggered back, the sword dropping from a nerveless right hand. The boy's sword had reached his arm between elbow and shoulder and laid it open to the bone.

"Clumsy!" shouted Zaman Khan, as a shout of laughter went up from the rest of the circle. "You were too sure. You, Kaju!"

The man that stepped forward profited by the quick defeat of the first and fought more cautiously. His blade felt out that of the youth in delicate contacts and then, swung in a circle of light, changed in midswing, came down, then up against the boy's hilt with a twist that seemed to wrap his blade around the other, and the young man's sword sailed far over the heads of the Afghans. The split second it left the boy's hand, the Afghan had him in a bearlike embrace.

The girl had not lasted that long, The Afghan that came in on her was old and had played at swords long before she was born. His blade reached far out, darting back and forth a little as the tongue of a snake. It darted in a little further, the girl struck it to one side with a scornful laugh, and before the laugh was away from her full red lips, the old Afghan had struck with a *moulinet* so fast that the girl's arm was still coming back to guard after the parry when the flat of his sword struck her wrist. The blow was not a hard one, being deliberately pulled by the old Afghan, who had in mind Zaman Khan's warning about scratches. But it was hard enough to make her hand open, dropping the dagger. Like the boy, she was almost smothered against a smelly ragged sheepskin coat.

Two minutes later they sat, with their hands and feet tied, their backs to a rock. Zaman Khan had announced that in his judgment the first man, Shere Ali, was entitled to his share of the money to be derived from the sale of the two, because, though himself wounded, he had not scratched the youth, according to orders. This very diplomatic judgment quieted the wounded one and also probably averted a feud.

Nathan, his gentle old heart aching for the boy and girl who had confronted hopeless odds so gallantly, walked over to where the Afghan who had acted as interpreter stood. "What will become of them?" he asked.

"They will be sold as slaves, unless Zaman Khan wants the maiden."

Zaman Khan, who had been talking to the Tartar maiden, heard his name and at once came over to learn what Nathan and the interpreter were talking about. He was an Afghan, therefore suspicious, even when among members of his own clan.

"He asks what will be done with the youth and the maiden," said the interpreter promptly. "I told him they would be sold as slaves unless you wanted the maiden."

Zaman Khan grunted. "Do not talk to him unless I am close," he growled.

Nathan spoke. "Ask Zaman Khan if he will sell them to me."

Zaman Khan, when he heard that, smiled broadly. "With what do you intend to buy them, O man of much gold?"

The interpreter got that over all right and also Nathan's answer. "With what I have left after paying the ransom you may ask."

Zaman Khan laughed. "After paying what I will ask, you will have no gold left to buy slaves with, infidel." Then, to the interpreter, "Go over with your brothers and do not come to this man again unless ordered by me," and Zaman Khan stalked back to where the boy and girl sat.

NATHAN SAT on a log a little way from the Afghans. He felt sick again and weak. The smell of the unwashed bodies and the sheepskin, the fact that he had not eaten since the night before, the sight of the two young people, helpless in the hands of the Afghans, all combined to make Nathan feel sick. He knew that the boy was a Hebrew, but he was too sick at heart to connect that with anything. He was not afraid for himself. He sat there watching the old Afghan chief and hearing his snarling voice as he questioned the girl.

The boy spoke once in a while, too low for Nathan to hear. The girl listened, shaking her head now and then as if she were having trouble in understanding what the boy said. He would repeat and then the girl would translate into Pushtu for Zaman Khan.

From where Nathan sat he could see the beaklike profile of the Afghan chief and what expression it showed made Nathan believe that the story of the girl or rather that of the boy passed through the girl, was not believed by Zaman Khan.

Suddenly Zaman Khan leaned forward and his dagger was at the boy's throat, above the protecting breastplate. The boy paled but did not flinch a hair's breadth. The girl said something and Zaman Khan put the dagger back in its sheath. As he did he turned a little and saw Nathan. He looked at Nathan, and back at the boy; then he beckoned to the interpreter, also to Nathan.

As they came up, he motioned for them to sit down near the boy and girl.

"You two," he said to the boy and Nathan, "are of the same race. You," to Nathan, "ask this youth where he is from, and tell him if he lies he will be skinned while he lives." The interpreter explained to Nathan, and Nathan spoke to the boy in Hebrew. "This man who has captured first me and then you, asks where you are from. He also warns you to tell the truth."

The boy answered. "I am from a city far to the north in the hills. I am not afraid of this savage. But I do not want my wife to suffer. Tell him that I will do as he wishes."

Zaman Khan replied:

"Tell him that no slave has a wife. I will take the woman to my house. How far is this city from here and is it a rich one?"

The boy's eyes tightened as he was told what Zaman Khan said and he strained at the bonds around his wrists. The chieftain saw it, and laughed.

As he did, the Afghans sent for horses rode up, leading several.

"Mount and ride, Zaman Khan!" one of them shouted. "The hills are up against you! The black men beat off the attack and the hills echo with the shouts of men who say you deserted the fight after getting what you wanted. The Saddozai have turned against us. These horses we stole. Mount and ride!"

Zaman Khan knew what that meant; there was no time to spare. If the factions he had summoned had got it into their heads that he had plucked the fruit and run with it, this was no place for him to be, with fifteen or twenty men. If he could win back to his hole, he would be lucky, and he knew it well.

"To horse!" he shouted, running for one. "Throw those two slaves across a horse. One of you put the old one in front of you."

There were not enough horses to go around and each Afghan thought he was entitled to hold the reins instead of having to sit back of a man. Confusion followed, as Zaman Khan straightened out the various claims, the mounting of the boy and girl on one horse, the tying of their feet under the horse's belly, the deciding as to who would have Nathan in front of him, all thought of maintaining any kind of a guard was forgotten.

Zaman Khan shouted orders to be careful with Nathan, watched the man who lifted him to the saddle to see if his orders were obeyed, then whirled his horse and raised his sword high above his head. "Forward! We will ride down any dogs that dare snarl at us!"

CHAPTER VII

WOLVES ON THE TRAIL

THE DEAD SOLDIERS were buried with military honors, the wounded given first aid, and the camp moved back to the top of one of the foothills where no attack could succeed without heavy guns.

Lieutenant "Yaller" Coudray stood at attention before Norcross and T'ang Wang. He had been reached by several swords, but only one of the cuts had been deep. Now he stood trying to give the impression that he was as strong as ever. But his gray lips gave his efforts the lie.

"You must stay, Lieutenant," Norcross said. "I cannot go into the hills after Mr. Nathan unless I know that Mr. Landess is fully protected. The Lord T'ang Wang goes with me. This leaves you as ranking officer in full command. You will stay. Detail twenty men to go, with Sergeant Moss in command. No machine guns or heavy marching order equipment. Rifles, bayonets and Colts, that is all. Make it snappy"—here Norcross smiled at his former first sergeant—"Yaller."

Lieutenant Coudray swallowed his disappointment, and at the "Yaller" which told him how much Norcross thought of him, he grinned, highly pleased.

"I do not know how many men this Afghan has with him, T'ang Wang," Norcross went on, after Lieutenant Coudray had saluted and started for the line to pick the men. "But I think that with twenty men, plus what swordsmen you take, we can get through."

"I will take the men of my house, who are Manchu," answered T'ang Wang. "There are some thirty of them here, elder brother. With them I will guarantee that no Afghan will get through to surprise us," he added grimly.

"It was a close thing, wasn't it?" Norcross answered, as he and T'ang Wang walked toward where Landess was sitting. "It may be that the Nine Red Gods of War decided to give B Troop and myself a very expensive lesson. I am afraid that we all thought we were so good that nothing like that could happen to us. If we get Mr. Nathan back, the memory of the men who lie dead will cause us to walk very softly, for a long time. If we do not find him, I—"

T'ang Wang interrupted Norcross, for all that this was strictly against Manchu etiquette; he saw the pain in the blue eyes of the lean fighting Mississippian.

"I do not know of the gods you mention," he said courteously, "but this I know, O honorable elder brother who placed the Princess Ch'enyaun on her throne: you are in no way to blame for what has happened. My swords were outside of your lines, and should have seen the Afghans."

Norcross smiled and laid his tanned, muscular hand on T'ang Wang's arm for a moment. "Let's admit, brother of mine, that we both were a little too cocky; and then go and get Mr. Nathan."

T'ang Wang smiled also. "Yes, elder brother, we were both a little too 'cocky,' whatever that means. Now we will go and find the Lord Nathan and afterward we will be less—'cocky.'"

Sergeant Moss was having quite a little trouble in selecting the twenty men to go with Captain Norcross. The big colored men were still full of fight. Machine gunners, wounded, and all down to Cook Memphis's third assistant, promptly volunteered and began to press their claims and prowess.

"Mah Gawd," said Delicate Moss. "What's all de arg'ment 'bout? Dent wild men has all got home by dis time. Ain't nothin' but a walk in de woods. Ah needs exercise, so Ah does, dat's all. Yaller, Ah means Lieutenant, iffen dese apes doesn't git back, how can Ah pick 'em?"

Coudray had notified Delicate that he was to go, and had delegated to him the job of selecting the detail.

"**SMACK 'EM** down, dem dat is too close, an' den look 'em ovah," advised Yaller Coudray. He still wanted very badly to go himself.

"In 'bout a minute, Ah does dat," promised Delicate. "Stan' fast, Ah looks yo' ovah. De men dat Ah calls, step outa de line dat you-all bettah be formin' befo' Ah counts three. No man not in line gits to go, nohow. Hot damn, look at dem niggers line up! All right, step out, Slewfoot, Squint-eye, Skinnay Martin, Buck Foster, Happy Combes, de Mobile Kid. No, Deacon Yancey, yo' is too old to go jazzin' around mountains. Iffen yo' was ten yeahs younger, Ah'd pick yo' fust, no foolin'. Sam Lucus, Jeff Talliferro—how come, Memphis? Iffen yo' go, who does de cookin'?"

Memphis glared at the big Delicate. "Ah was a ridah in B Troop befo' yo' was dry behind de eahs. Ah goes to de cookin' school long befo' dare was a cookin' school and Ah learned to learn mah 'sistants how to cook. Ah goes—or else, does yo' come gazoopin' round mah cook tent forevah aftah, yo' gits de mop wrapped round yoah neck instead of samplin' de highah-ups' chuck."

At this dire threat, which Delicate knew was no idle one, he capitulated at once as far as Memphis went. "Doggone, Memphis! Yo' doesn't give me time to git de words outa mah mouf," he complained. "Of course yo' goes, boy. Ah was jest goin' to say 'at wid yo' erlong, don't need no mo' of dese monkey faces. Us takes 'em though for comp'ny. Step out, Livingston, Pickett, and yo', Washington Early."

So on, down the line. When the men Delicate selected were lined up, there was no doubt but that he had the most hard-boiled of a good twenty-minute-egg outfit. Delicate, being only human, had picked out his most intimate friends also.

Norcross looked them over as Sergeant Moss brought them up. Each man had his bayoneted rifle, his Colt .45, two or three cartridge belts and every pocket bulging with ammunition. Every man there had served in B troop of the 31st Cavalry, on the border of Mexico, and in France, and had been with him on his first trip to China. As his eyes went down the line, Memphis tried to make himself as inconspicuous as possible. He could put it over Delicate, but he knew better than to try it with "de Capt'n."

As Norcross reached him, after seeing the pleading look on the grim old black face, he smiled and went on to the next man. Memphis heaved a very audible sigh of relief.

Ten minutes later the tight little column slipped like timber wolves into the woods. Some of the Manchu swordsmen first, who quartered the ground ahead like hunting dogs; then Norcross and his men; then the rest of the swordsmen, all in plain sight of each other as much as possible. T'ang Wang walked with Norcross.

The Afghan prisoner had drawn a map with a dagger point on a piece of silver birchbark, and once the column got to the top of the hill from which Zaman Khan had watched, the going was easy, as far as following directions went.

Before they got halfway up, the Manchu flushed a small party of Tartars who had lingered behind in hopes of doing a little looting on their own hook if possible. They had seen the column coming and holed up in a draw. But here were no Chinese to ambush. The Manchus could play the old game in the hills, and had played it against all comers for years. The Tartars fought bravely but were cut down to the last man. The main column did not even hesitate in the ground-covering "double time" that it maintained whenever the going permitted.

As they went down the other side of the hill and turned a curve that led across a little valley, they ran head-on into one of the mullahs and his escort of fifty or more Afghans.

The fanatic leader, striding ahead of his followers, took one look at the Manchu swordsmen and the black men behind them, gave an eerie screech of joy, drew a curved sword, and charged home without waiting to see whether his escort was with him or not.

He knew without looking that they would be; and they were, to the last man.

They had quit fighting both black men and swordsmen in the main battle because the news of Zaman Khan's leaving the field had got spread around, and they, being Afghans, did not intend to hold the bag for any one. They had not quit because they had had fighting enough, or because they were afraid. An Afghan may leave a battlefield, but it is for some other reason than those.

EACH MANCHU calmly picked a man and closed with him, getting on the outside of the charge when doing it. They knew better than to stand and take the charge of the mass.

This time the Afghans were charging at men who were ready and waiting for them. The mullah went down with a bullet in his brain from Delicate Moss's Colt and his soul no doubt went to that warriors' paradise he was always preaching about.

The rest went down under the fire of the merciless black men, who had some sixty of their comrades to avenge. T'ang Wang had stepped out from beside Norcross and was a little ahead and to the right. An Afghan who had killed the Manchu opposing him, ran up to T'ang Wang, his broad-bladed Afghan knife making light blue circles as he twisted it in his hand.

T'ang Wang awaited him, his sword laid across his left forearm. The Afghan looked twice as big and heavy as the slenderly built Manchu. It was a mad buffalo charging down on a lean, striped tiger. As the Afghan came within striking distance the knife stopping twisting and darted forward, the Afghan following it with all his weight.

By now the shooting was over and the men were watching the only fight left. It did not seem possible that T'ang Wang could avoid being crushed to the ground, even if he did avoid the knife. What followed was so fast that most of the men only saw the finish, not the start. T'ang Wang's sword threw the knife up and as it did, he seemed in some way to have flitted like a shadow to one side of the Afghan and about three feet away.

The watching men saw him sway in, and some of them claimed afterward that they saw the sword go up in the deadly upward slice of the Manchu; but this claim received the scorn it deserved. They all saw the Afghan stop turning toward T'ang Wang and they all saw his head leap from the shoulders, as the razor-sharp blade sheared through the neck from the base.

T'ang Wang, his face impassive, shouted an order and the Manchus ran forward again. The column started at the double, and the incident was closed. They went through the hills, up and down, across chasms where the slender footbridges hung. Down through the little valleys, and the draws and cañons, always at the double.

Twice more they stopped and fought, once with a large party of Uzbegs, who did not stand up to it like the Afghans but ran, such as could, after the first volley. The other fight was with a mixed crowd of Cossacks, Afghans, Uzbegs and Chinese who were going toward the Altai mountains. But the Manchus had seen them going through one of the passes, and laid a pretty ambush. Some fought and some tried to run.

Twenty minutes later Norcross shouted, "All right, let's go! Save your wind, you birds, you're going to need it from now on." The double time became much more of a run. It was grueling work; no stops for rests, no easing off—just run, that was all.

Delicate, who was built for heavy action rather than foot-work, eased alongside of old Memphis, who ran lightly on the balls of his feet, his nostrils flared out a little. "Did Ah know dat Capt'n wanted runnahs 'stead of ridahs," Delicate grunted, "Ah'd of wore mah runnin' shoes."

Memphis's sardonic grin showed two rows of gleaming white teeth.

"Ain't runnin' shoes dat gits de runnin' out. Is yo' got sand in de craw, dat's de question, Del'cate. Stay wid it, big boy. Me an' Slewfoot carries yo', is yo' tired."

Delicate grunted something unprintable about what Memphis could do, instead, and forged to the front.

CHAPTER VIII

A SWIFT FIGHT

AS ZAMAN KHAN finished his command to ride, he started to lower his arm; but it remained where it was, as if paralyzed. The Afghans had risen once in a circle around the boy and the girl with smiles of enjoyment on their cruel faces, but there were no smiles on the grim fighting faces of the men who rose now in a circle around the mounted Afghans. First a black man with bayoneted rifle, then a Manchu swordsman.

For a moment there was absolute silence. Not a move was made. It was as if all were posing for an important picture. Then Norcross stepped forward, his Colt full on Zaman Khan. He raised his left hand, palm out, and shouted in Pushtu, "Dismount!"

He might just as well have shouted, "Cut loose!" Zaman Khan dropped his arm and, with sword at point, jumped his horse straight at Norcross. Every Afghan sword flashed up, and they followed him without an instant's hesitation.

Captain John Norcross shot Zaman Khan through the heart and then stepped to one side to avoid the frantic horse which dashed by him, the body of the Afghan chief dragging from one stirrup.

The man who had held Nathan in front of him, and the man who held the horse with the boy and girl slung across its

back like a couple of sacks of meal, both dropped their encum-
brances. Nathan luckily lit on his feet, out of the way of the
horses charging by him. The horse with the boy and the girl ran
toward the circle, to be caught and held by a Manchu.

The black men leveled their Springfields, and the Manchus
ran in from the sides. Afghan after Afghan was shot from his
saddle. Others went down as their horses were hamstrung by
the keen blades, to meet the same blades almost before they had
hit the ground.

Two Afghans turned their horses; and broke through the
circle where the Manchus had run in, slashing right and left.
Those two alone won through to safety. The rest went with
Zaman Khan to where the Prophet Mohammed no doubt
explained the change of plans for them.

The boy and girl were cut loose and stood on their feet,
unhurt.

Norcross went over to where Nathan was standing with an
expression on his old face that clearly indicated he was not yet
sure whether this was real.

He blinked his eyes as Norcross put an arm around him to
steady him, then he smiled. "John, I knew, I knew in some way,
that you would come. The boy and girl, John, are they hurt?"

"They are here, Mr. Nathan, and do not seem to be injured.
Sergeant Moss, bring me that first aid kit and break out that
bottle of brandy. Sit down, Mr. Nathan. We'll have you fixed up
in a minute. Mr. Landess is all right and waiting for you."

IN AN hour Nathan, under the stimulating brandy and the
efficient first aid that Norcross and the big colored men gave
him, appeared to be as fit as ever.

Memphis and the Mobile Kid had been attending to the boy
and girl, whose wrists and ankles had been bruised and cut by
the tightly drawn bonds. Memphis, gentle as a woman, clicked
his tongue in sympathy as he salved the wounds, and talked a
steady stream.

"Mah goodness! Nevah min', honey-chile, ole Memphis done

fix yo' right up. Doggone de scound'ls dat do dis way to such a prutty little lady. Is dat bettah, darlin'? Honey, yo' is a brave girl, yes, ma'am. Mah Lawdy me, look at dem bruises on dose little feet. Hol' 'em up, sugar-chile, ole Memphis ain't goin' to hu't yo'. Dog mah cats, iffen yo' isn't de split image of mah little Miss Nancy Calhoun way down yonder in Mississip'. Dare, reckon dat's bettah. Smile fo' yo' ole nigger man, little ladybird."

The Tartar girl couldn't make head or tail of what he was talking about, yet she understood, and as she stood up she smiled and patted the grim fighting Memphis on the arm.

The Mobile Kid was as gentle as Memphis, but his talk ran along different lines. The Mobile Kid was a fancy dresser himself when he was in civvies, and the clothes of the young man took his eye, even if they were torn and discolored.

"Yas, suh, colonel, jest hol' still fo' a minute—Ah cleans out de cut fu'st wid dis hot stuff what maybe-so gives yo' a little touch of high life. Dat's it—dat's de boy. Hol' fast. Yo' is got plenty of nerve, Ah kin see dat. Now, de salve dat 'll fix yo' up in no time.

"Is dat de kind of clothes what dey wears in yo' country? Mah goodness, dat is a classy lookin' what-yo'-call-'em dat yo' weahs fo' a vest. Colonel, dat 'll stop a bullet, Ah bets money. Dare, now yo' is as good as when yo' came outen de 'riginal package. Is dat a whiskbroom dat yo' carries in dat tin hat? Mah goodness, Ah sure wishes Ah had a pair of dem doggone slippers instead of dese ole heavy brogans, yes, suh, Ah sure does."

The boy didn't understand any more than the girl did; but like her, he knew it was friendly, and as he rose he smiled also.

NATHAN, LANDESS, Norcross and T'ang Wang sat with the boy in the camp in the foothills two days later.

Nathan had been carried back by the colored men in an improvised hammock swung from rifles. His weight had been nothing to the colored men who fought for the privilege. Was he not their guest of honor? Had they not lost him, then found him again?

When the hill came into sight, the march had become more

of a snake dance than an orderly advance. Norcross had smiled, his eyes a little misty as he saw Landess hurry forward, and he let the snake dance go ahead unchecked.

The Tartar girl was now sitting on an ammunition box, holding court for a laughing group of men. She was quick at languages, and already in the two days they had been back had picked up phrases and was airing them, much to her delight and theirs.

Nathan had sat apart with the boy for a long time, then walked over with him to the others.

"The ways of the Lord are past understanding," he announced, as they sat down. "This boy comes from my city in the hills."

As he spoke, his face was alight with happiness, and he held out both hands to them all.

"We are glad, Isaac," Landess answered softly. "Glad for, and with you. Tell us."

"Think," Nathan went on. "Truly the Lord God of Hosts works in His own good way. If I had not walked to the rocks, and if the Afghan had not captured me—if this boy had not come with his wife—if he had not first met her— I see you are smiling, Henry. The old smile that I always look for. See, I will calm down and tell you; no, I will ask him to tell you. I will translate. In his words there is a certainty that mine would lack."

He spoke to the youth in the sonorous Hebrew and as the boy began, translated:

"I am Zebulon, the son of Nehemiah, who is captain of a hundred in the guard of King Abner in his city of Jearim, whose corners are the four high mountains. A year ago while hunting with some of my comrades I went beyond the limits of our land. There I met the maiden, weeping at the side of her dying father, who had been forced to flee from his tribe. I loved the maiden, and she loved me.

"I took her back with me to the walls of the city of my fathers, and there she was refused admittance. No stranger may enter the city. I turned back from the gate and with her went into the hills.

We made our way south toward a tribe that she knew would be friendly, but they were gone when we came to the place where they had been. Then we went back to the hills, to be captured by the men the War Captain destroyed."

The boy stopped talking, and Nathan said simply: "It is my city of which this boy Zebulon speaks."

"There is no question of that, Isaac," answered Landess. "Have you asked him questions as to the city? Where is it from here, and how is it governed? Does he think you will be admitted? He said that no strangers are ever admitted."

"No, Henry, I have not asked him that. I was too full of joy learning that my city was not one of dreams. He was telling me of his personal affairs," Nathan added with a smile at the boy, who returned it. The good hearty food and the security had done wonders for him.

"I think if I ask him some questions it may help us," suggested Norcross. "Tell him that he need not answer, of course, if he thinks that he should not."

Nathan spoke to the boy, then told Norcross, "The youth, Zebulon, says that there is no question that he may not answer. He would not keep from us any information about the city or its people; and he asks me to say to you that you saved his wife from worse than death and he is your man if you would have it so."

"Tell him I say that is well, and that I will find some post of honor for him later," said Norcross. "First, ask him if he will guide us to the city or tell us just how to get there from here."

THE BOY answered through Nathan:

"I will guide you to the city, but I will not enter. I swore an oath that I would never again enter the city that denied me."

"If you will do that," answered Norcross, "you may return with us to the city of Ningyuan in China. There you will find peace and rest. You know why we wish to go to the city of Jearim?"

"Yes, Isaac Nathan told me that he wished to go there and be admitted to the sacred things. I do not know; he is a Jew, and may possibly be admitted, if he does not want to return to the outside world. You and your men I know will not be admitted, nor even allowed to cross the land outside the city."

"We do not wish to go further than to see Mr. Nathan safe inside the walls. How big is the city?"

"From mountain to mountain on the north wall is ten thousand cubits. The other three sides a little more."

Norcross smiled at Nathan. "I will have to have a pencil to figure that. I know that a cubit is about twenty and a half inches, at least the Egyptian cubit is."

Nathan answered, "The Hebrew cubit is less. I can tell you roughly, John: it is a little under three miles."

"Thanks, Mr. Nathan. Ask him if the city is built up all of the nine square miles inside."

"Yes," answered the boy. "All built up but the temple squares and the gardens of the king and the priests."

"What is the city built of?"

"Stone from the mountains."

"How many people?"

"Of thousands, two hundred."

"What form of government?"

"What form? What else but a king, and a high priest? We are as all other people, only we do not admit strangers."

"What kind of weapons?"

"Swords, spears, and bows and arrows, as other people have. We have none of the little fire sticks that kill with a noise. What are they made out of, and what is the noise that kills?"

"I will show you all about them," answered Norcross. "They are made by man, the same as your sword. Are the people friendly? I mean, are they at peace with each other?"

"I do not know what you mean They live as the people of Israel have always lived."

"When shall we start, John?" asked Nathan.

"Just as soon as we arrange the taking of the wounded to

Ningyuan Tell the boy that his wife may go with the party and that she will be well taken care of until he returns,"

When the youth was told that, he rose and called the girl over. She listened to what he told her, then smiled and shook her head. It was quite evident to the rest that the idea of leaving her young husband did not appeal to her in the slightest. She spoke rapidly in Pushtu, then more slowly as she saw she was talking too fast for Zebulon to understand.

After she finished, she turned and held out her little hands in a pretty gesture of appeal to Norcross.

Zebulon said, "My wife does not want to leave me. She says that she is at home in the hills, and that she will be no trouble, and she wants to go where I go."

The girl looked directly at Norcross and spoke in Pushtu. "Lord, we have been together since the day my man lifted me from my father's body and dried my tears. See, Lord! I am strong and young, as he is. If I am sent away from him, my spirit will follow him and my body will wither and grow old."

"You may go with him," Norcross answered gently. "It was only that we thought that you would like to rest in the quiet and peace of Ningyuan."

"There would be no rest without him, in the crook of whose arm I love to rest my head."

Landess queried, "John, she is asking that she may go with you to the city? Say that she may, John. Then I will be emboldened to ask that I also may go as far as the city."

Norcross laughed. "She may go; and since you have weathered one storm with us, Mr. Landess, there is no reason why you should not stick right along. Mr. Nathan, if you and Zebulon will come with the Lord T'ang Wang and me for a few minutes, we will plan the way to take you to your city."

CHAPTER IX

BEFORE THE GATES

TEN DAYS LATER Nathan, standing on a rock beside Norcross and Landess, drew a long breath, almost a sobbing one, as he looked down on a city far in the distance. He raised his arms and his face toward heaven. "God of Israel! I thank Thee for leading me to my heart's desire." He stood there and poured out his thanks and worship, Norcross and Landess standing silently until Nathan dropped his arms and turned to them. "It is my city, Henry and John. I have thanked our Lord—Jahweh as they call Him in this city—for leading me to it; and now I thank you both, also."

"We were only instruments in His hands, Isaac, as were the boy and the girl and the Afghan. Be calm, Isaac. The goal is in sight; but yet there are barriers to cross," Landess answered.

"I am calm, Henry. When shall we move down to the gates, John?"

"Well," Norcross said slowly, "there isn't any reason why we cannot start right down. But if we do, it will be dark before we reach them; and it might be better to go openly in the daytime. As soon as we reach the open places we will be seen."

"That is right, John. It will be better to start in the morning. See, Henry, how calm and collected I am, and how ready to wait? John, we might go ahead slowly now, and be closer in the morning."

Both Norcross and Landess laughed, not at Isaac Nathan, but with him.

"We will move down closer," Norcross said. "There is cover for some miles yet."

The column at dawn was at the edge of the timber which thinned out at the base of the mountain. There were about two

"To the cells with the stranger and the false king!"

miles of level country to where the wall of the city stretched between the two mountains, one at each corner. These mountains were more like high foothills, but went straight up for at least two thousand feet.

Seventy-five of the colored men, four machine guns, two of the rapid-fire two-pound rifles, and one hundred of T'ang Wang's swordsmen, including all the Manchus, comprised the column. All the rest had been sent back to Ningyuan with the wounded. The boy and the girl were very much at home now with the big, boyish black men. Norcross had ordered a tent pitched for the pair alongside his own and the ones used by Landess, Nathan and T'ang Wang.

The Hebrew youth spent all the time possible with the fighters. He had been shown the revolvers and rifles, and learned the action quickly. The colored men looked him over, listened to reports of his gameness from the men who had been in on the rescue, and with the quick intuition of the colored race had accepted him as a fighting man.

His face was deeply bronzed, and now he wore a full outfit, leggings, campaign hat, Colt .45 and all. This came about through the Mobile Kid, who had gone to Lieutenant Coudray with a proposition. Coudray had succeeded in staying with the party by a great deal of camouflaging of his wounds.

"Yaller—Ah means Lieutenant," Mobile had asked, "can Ah swap mah clothes wid de boy what us rescued?"

"Can yo' do what? Is yo' crazy? How come dat 'swap clothes' stuff? Does yo' want to weah dem shin protectahs an' dat wash-boilah instead of a shirt? Go way from me befo' Ah forgets dat Ah'm a officer an' smacks yo' down."

"Doggone hit! Ah don't want to weah dem. Ah wants to keep 'em as souv'neers. Does Ah—"

"Listen, Misto' Private Kid," interrupted Yaller firmly. "Iffen yo' doesn't fade away from heah in haste, Ah hangs one of dem souv'neers yo' is after on yo' right eye. Ah's busy gitting dis 'quip-ment ready. Git."

If it had been any one else but Yaller, the Mobile Kid would have promptly asked to have a demonstration of the speaker's ability to hang anything on his eye; but knowing Yaller full well and also knowing that there was no doubt but that he could do it on both eyes if necessary, the Mobile Kid let it go at that. But he lingered around, and finally Yaller, to get rid of him, said:

"Go ask de Capt'n can yo' trade clothes wid dat gent'mum, an' see whut *he* tells yo', monkey-face."

The Mobile Kid thought that was a brilliant idea although Yaller never had the slightest thought that his suggestion would be accepted. Yaller did not know how deep the longing for the stranger's outfit had bitten into the Mobile Kid, who at once went to find Norcross. He had observed the military rules, coming up through a sergeant to Yaller; and now he was going to headquarters.

Norcross listened gravely to the plea and then answered, just as gravely as he had listened.

"I don't see any reason why you should not swap him if he wishes, Mobile. Is your clothing allowance drawn up?"

"No, suh, Capt'n, please, suh. Ah got me eighty dollahs to go yet."

"Where are you going to get the clothes? There's no Q.M. along and you can't wear his clothes, or he yours. You are just about twice as big."

"Capt'n, please, suh, Ah can collect some extra stuff from de boys. Ah got me two shirts in mah pack and Ah knows dat Buck Foster's got him a pair of pants."

"Yeah? All right, go ahead and swap him but swap him fair. Then get some one that can sew to cut the stuff down for him. Tell Lieutenant Coudray that I said the boy was to have equipment to go with the uniform. On your way, boy."

It didn't take the Mobile Kid long to talk a complete outfit out of his friends; and as a result, the boy was soon as much B Troop as any of them.

HE CAME up to Norcross, and T'ang Wang as the dawn broke. On the ten-day march he had absorbed a lot of English, but he could not yet make them understand what he was trying to tell them. He got "If de Capt'n please," because he had heard it so often, but beyond a few more words and phrases he was sunk. They listened and tried to get it, but until Nathan came up, they were floundering as badly as the boy.

"I have brought you to the city," was the boy's message. "It lies before you. Soon the gates will be opened and the guard will come out on the inspection of the city's territory that always takes place as soon as the sun appears. If you go to meet them, let the swords stay here. The guard knows not of guns or black men and will wait to see what they are before attacking. If they saw swords, they would attack at once."

"That is good stuff, T'ang Wang," Norcross said. "I will go forward with the Lord Nathan. You and your men remain here under cover. Will you go also?" he asked Zebulon.

"No—although my father is of the guard. I swore by the sacred things that I would never enter the city again, and I will not. If this man Isaac Nathan is allowed to enter, it may be that my father will learn of my presence and come out to greet me. If so, it is well. But I remain here."

Landess joined the party. "John, if I will not be too great a burden, I would like to go with Isaac Nathan as far as possible."

"Well," answered Norcross with a grin, "I do not know just how much of a fight we may run into, but I know how you feel, Mr. Landess. Come ahead."

The little four-pointed star went slowly across the open space, Nathan and Norcross at the forward point. Landess walked in the middle of the star. The bayonets were in their sheaths and the machine guns and one of the rapid-fire two-pounders well inside the points. The rifles were carried at shoulder arms, the flaps of the holsters buttoned down over the Colts.

It seemed, as far as Norcross could make it, a peace party.

They had got about halfway across when the gates opened and a party of fifty men ran briskly out. They were dressed as the boy had been, only the leaders' corselets were more elaborate, as were their sword scabbards and helmets. They looked like a party of Roman soldiers in the time of the legions.

As they came directly toward the star, Norcross commanded a halt and he and Nathan stepped out two paces. Nathan was a little ahead of Norcross.

From the knapsack that Norcross had given him in Ningyuan, which had been carried by one of the men in addition to his own, Nathan had produced a long flowing white robe that looked more or less like a bathrobe to the colored men. He wore it now, and like the boy, he wore sandals. Delicate Moss had made them for him on the march out of the tops of a pair of puttees. Delicate had once been a shoemaker and while the sandals fitted a little loosely, they were recognizable sandals.

The men advancing came up without any hesitation or show of either fear or curiosity. They were all young men, like the boy in their clear-cut, stern young faces, and proudly carried bodies. As they came within ten feet, the leader raised his hand and they halted. He strode forward alone. As he got a good look at Nathan's face, he stopped, with a puzzled look.

"**YOU ARE** of our race," the guard leader said curtly in Hebrew. "What do you do here with these black men and this man who is of an alien race?"

"I am of your race," answered Nathan, "and I have come far, in all humility to beg that I may be allowed to enter the city of my people and remain there until I die. I am Isaac Nathan— of the tribe of Reuben. These black men, and their leader who stands beside me, are the men who have brought me in safety through the land of wicked men who would have stayed me. I come from the far place where many of the children of Israel have wandered."

The leader of the patrol, a thin-faced, tight-lipped man about thirty, who looked and carried himself like a soldier, looked at Nathan, at Norcross, and then at the big black men in the star. He looked at their rifles and equipment, at the formation of the lines, at their black, friendly faces, and then back at Nathan and Norcross.

When the star had started forward, Norcross had warned his men, "We want to make friends with these people. You birds look and act as friendly as possible. Don't slop over and make it too strong, but no hair raising along the back."

That had been plenty for the colored men, the best actors in the world. They stood there and returned the looks of the leader and the wiry, well-muscled young men behind him, with glances that told only of friendly curiosity.

"Dem's fightin' men," whispered Jeff Talliferro out of the corner of his mouth to Buck Foster, the next man to him.

"Yes, suh," agreed Buck. "Dey is dat little thing. Nevah min' de circus clothes, dem boys is scrappahs."

"Silence in de ranks!" ordered Sergeant Moss. He couldn't understand the Hebrew, but he didn't want to miss a note.

At last the leader of the patrol frowned, as if puzzled. "I do not know," he confessed. "It may be that the king will give orders that you be admitted, alone. These men with you must turn back. Await here without advancing further and I will send back a runner."

"I will await the king's command," Nathan answered gently. "And the men with me shall turn back."

The leader turned and walked back to his men and in a moment one of them turned and ran toward the gates. The rest stood silently, their eyes on the black men in calm scrutiny.

Norcross said, "I think we had better stay right where we are, Mr, Nathan, until the word comes. The less movement the better, at the moment."

Nathan stood still, but Norcross could see that his hands were quivering and that his finely molded lips were almost white with the strain put forth to keep them firm. He knew what this waiting meant to Isaac Nathan, who stood within sight of his goal.

THE LEADER of the patrol gave a curt order and his men remained as they were. Five minutes went by, then ten, then twenty. Then the runner came out of the gates. Beside him ran a man whose breastplate glittered in the sun and whose sword scabbard reflected the jewels incased in it.

When they reached the patrol, the runner halted and the newcomer strode forward, not even breathing heavily from the run. This man's face was smooth-shaved with the exception of a fringe of beard on his chin. The way he carried himself and the look in his black eyes told that he was a warrior.

He took in Isaac Nathan and the rest in one glance, then addressed Nathan. "You are Isaac Nathan of the tribe of Reuben? The king commands that you be admitted to the city. First, you are to be told that if you are admitted, you may never leave our city again. This party that has escorted you hither will turn and go back—or be driven back by the sword of Jahweh."

"I am Isaac Nathan," answered Nathan steadily, "and I shall not desire to leave the city of my fathers. The party with me will turn back. There will be no need for the sword of Jahweh to drive them. I ask for time to say good-by to the men who have been faithful to me always."

"See then that you do not make it too long," the officer answered curtly.

"It will be but a minute, O Captain of Thousands."

Nathan, with Norcross, turned and walked back to the star, which opened to admit them. Nathan had already said good-by to T'ang Wang and now he walked up to Henry Landess who stood awaiting him, a smile on his lips although his eyes were misty.

"Henry," Nathan said as he held out both hands which Landess took in his. "The king has commanded that I be admitted. You have brought me to my city as you said you would in New York. You have not failed me, Henry. You never have, in all the years. And now, with my city in sight and the gates open, I—I— Henry, if you go before me, will you await my coming, with Miriam? I will await you, Henry, if I go first. All I can say is that all my life, you—you have been always to me—Henry, you know what is in my heart."

"What is in your heart, Isaac, is the same that has always been in mine, Yes, I will await your coming, Isaac, as you will await mine. It is as if you go on a short journey. See, the gates of your city await you."

"Yes, Henry, that is it." Nathan released Landess's hands and turned to Norcross. "John," he said simply, "in New York, Henry said that you could take me to my city. You have. I—my heart is too full to talk. Henry Landess has full charge of my affairs. I would like to make your men a present, but to you, John, I can only give the thanks of an old man whom you have made happy."

"That fully repays me, Mr. Nathan," answered Norcross.

"I go, then, to my city. Good-by, Henry and John."

As he walked toward the point of the star, Norcross gave an order and the bugle blew. The lines formed in troop front. As Nathan passed, the rifles snapped to present arms, and as the

troop stood as only regulars can stand, Isaac Nathan joined the
patrol and walked toward the city gates.

CHAPTER X

TRAITORS

THE PEOPLE OF the city, the women covered from head
to heel by gorgeous silk *abbas* brocaded in gold and silver, and
the men, all but the military, in the long robes such as Nathan
wore, did not show much curiosity as Nathan was led to the
palace of the king which stood near the Temple in the middle
of the city. They looked at him, then went on with whatever
they were doing.

The city was well laid out in fairly wide streets that converged
at the Temple. The houses were of stone.

Nathan was brought as far as the palace steps and there
turned over to a palace official who came out to meet them. As
he walked slowly through the rooms, he drew a happy, quivering
breath. It was as he had seen in the paintings of life in Jerusalem
in the days of old.

The official with him made no attempt at conversation and
Nathan was only too glad to walk silently, looking at the things
he had dreamed about.

They came to a doorway curtained with heavy brocaded
drapes. The official stopped and motioned for Nathan to pass
through. Nathan parted the drapes and stepped into the presence of Abner, king of the city of Jearim.

The room was a small one and held none of the trappings of
royalty. The king sat on a plain high-backed chair over which
had been thrown a skin of some kind. The chair was on a dais
raised about a foot from the floor. Behind the chair stood two
of the guard with sheathed swords.

King Abner, a young man of about twenty-five or six, was

dressed like the guards with the exception that all his equipment was gold or gold-inlaid metal. His face was smooth-shaved and cleanly modeled. The eyes were friendly and although the molding of the lips and chin betrayed a certain hint of weakness, the king looked what he was, the sovereign of a purely bred race.

Standing beside him was a man with a hard, mean-eyed face, dressed as a commanding officer in the army. Beside him there stood another man, in priestly robes. His face also was hard and while his eyes did not hold a mean look, they were arrogant, and his smile was supercilious.

Nathan advanced to the dais and bowed. The young king smiled and bent his head a little. Neither the officer nor the priest returned Nathan's bow.

"The captain of the guard," the king said, in a kind, slightly amused voice, "told us a strange story of a man of our race who wished to enter our city. A man who had come from afar to do so. You are he?"

"Yes, O King. I am the man."

"What is your name, and where do you come from?"

The military officer spoke. "O King, there are more important matters to be discussed than finding out where a wandering vagabond comes from. Send this man to the law givers. They will—"

The young king sat up straight and his face flushed. The tone had been almost one of command, not quite, but very near.

"You have dared much, Hoshea ben Elah, commander of my army. See if you dare to go further and disobey this order: Leave me! And you also, O priest acting in the place of the High Priest as he lies sick on his couch."

There was no weakness in the voice of the young king, nor did any show in his eyes. Both the officer and the priest knew that once Abner's spirit was aroused, he would go through with the matter regardless of cost; and they both acted promptly. The priest bowed and the officer saluted as they stepped down from the dais. The officer then bowed and said: "I meant not to give an

order, O King. It was my solicitation for your health that seems
to give under the cares of your kingdom."

The king smiled. "I know your solicitation—for many things.
More perhaps than you think, O Hoshea ben Elah. Leave me."

The officer and the priest retired.

The king turned to the guards at his back. "You will walk
behind the acting High Priest and the commander of the army,
and see that they do not remain within earshot." As he gave the
order he smiled. The two guards, also young, came forward and
saluted. They smiled also and Nathan, who had stood watching
the little scene, could sense that the guards were for the king.

"Sit on the edge of the dais," the king said as soon as the
guards had gone. "You are old, and entitled to honor. I long to
be told of the far places. Tell me, from the beginning, how you
knew of my city, and of us. No stranger has entered our territory for many hundreds of years. I am the first king," he smiled,
"that would not have sent out the swords to drive away or kill
any that came."

HOSHEA BEN ELAH, his face red with passion, spoke to the
priest as they went down the palace steps.

"This youth that was made king because he was Abner of the
House of Japheth grows apace."

The priest halted and looked around to see if any were in
hearing, then, seeing that they were alone on the steps, said
softly:

"What better time than now, brave leader of the swords?"

The officer looked at him with intense scrutiny. "You mean?
Say it in words, Jehoiakim."

The priest laughed, an evil, sneering laugh, more than a little
contemptuous, although it was soft in tone. "You are afraid to
put it in words? Yet you are a man of war and I only a priest of
the Temple. I will say it. The High Priest Hasdai ben Isaac lies
stricken on his deathbed and cannot protect with his presence
this boy who sits on the throne. You want the throne for your
son, and I want the High Priesthood. What better time can

come than now? The king has admitted a stranger to the city of Jearim, and now"—the priest paused for a moment and his smile was as evil as his laugh had been—"and now, the king plots with the stranger to admit the black men who came with him, so that they may loot the city of its riches."

"That is foolish," answered the officer shortly. "Why should the king plot to do that? The people will not believe it."

"Listen, thou of little brains: Already the king has done something that no king before him has ever dared to do. He has admitted to Jearim a stranger who came backed by warriors. All the people know that. Now we tell them that the king plots with the stranger to open the gates to the stranger's men, and after that, to any that come. Why? Because the king has lost his mind in the vile orgies that he has been conducting in private. The people will not question. They will rise in their wrath, and slay."

"Yes, that is true. If the story is spread, the people will rise to protect the city. But afterward, when they become cool and examine to see what truth there is in it? What then, wise priest?"

"Then? Why then, Hoshea ben Elah, there will be no king for them to examine, no stranger, and no High Priest. Act now! Go and rouse the fighting men. You have claimed that they would follow you. I will rally the priests who are faithful to me and we will rouse the people. If we act promptly we can sweep this boy king from his throne, and the High Priest from the altar. Then your son may be king and I shall be High Priest. Say that you must seize the king's person to protect the city. Will you act with me now? If you do not, I will never again give you the opportunity."

The officer drew a long breath. It was a little fast for him. He had entered into the priest's conspiracy with others, but had not looked for more than the removal of the king after the death of his strongest protector, the High Priest whom the people loved. But he wanted his son made king. He came from a princely house, this officer, and his family had the right by blood, if they also had the might, to sit on the throne in Jearim.

"I will do as you say," he answered finally.

"Good. Go and cry out that the king plots with the stranger to open the city gates. Gather enough men to take and hold the palace. Seize the king and the stranger and cast them into the dungeons below the throne room. I will rouse the priests and they will go to the people. The House of Japheth is scattered and we can take them all before they can come together for defense. You can say that they know what the king is doing and are guilty with him. First gather soldiers and take the king. I go to the Temple."

The officer stood watching the priest run toward the Temple, then turned as if to go back up the steps. He hesitated for a moment and then ran down toward the guardhouse at the left.

CHAPTER XI

THE MOB RISES

"YOU TELL OF wonderful things," said the king to Nathan. "Things that are impossible for me to grasp. I would the High Priest Hasdai ben Isaac were here, but alas, he lies on a bed of sickness. But you are welcome to my city, and may be with the sacred things as much as you choose. I will give you a post of honor here near my person. There is not peace in the city, though, Isaac. The men of war are under the dominance of the man whom you saw me dismiss, and the young priests are—"

The two guards whom the king had sent out ran into the room.

"Guard thyself, O King!" one of them shouted as he turned to face the doorway. "Treachery! Hoshea ben Elah comes to—"

From outside the palace there came shouts.

"Down with the false king!"

"Down with the House of Japheth who would open the gates!"

"Drag him out! Kill the stranger!"

And there rose the indescribable high-pitched "hum" of a mob.

"He draws on the people! Kill! Kill! Blood has been spilled!" the mob cried as one of the king's house drew his sword to fight for his life.

The king rose from his seat and stepped down from the dais, drawing his short sword. His face was calm, his eyes steady.

As he did, a party of soldiers ran in, led by Hoshea ben Elah.

"There is the faithless king!" the commander shouted. "Seize them both!"

The two young guards ran to get in front of the king, and the three, king and guards, faced the onslaught. It was over very soon. The guards were outnumbered five to one, and went down, both of them, their young hearts stilled in death. The king sent two of the attackers to join them and then was disarmed and held.

Two other soldiers ran up to Nathan and pinioned his arms.

"To the cells!" shouted the officer, "Both of them. The king who would play his people false, and the stranger."

As the king and Nathan were being carried down a narrow flight of stone steps that led below ground from the throne room, a party of priests and people ran in. The priests were very much excited and raved about the sacrilege of admitting strangers to the city.

Some one shouted, "Crucify them!" and the shout was taken up all through the palace and out over the city, where the hunt was on for any of the house of Japheth. It had been like a spark to a powder magazine, the coming of Nathan. Already the priest and the soldier had spread baseless but quickly believed rumors of the king's debauchery and unfaithfulness to the old tenets of the faith.

The city rose as one man, and the ambitious priest Jehoiakim fanned the blaze. Those who called for the High Priest to guide them were told that he was dead. The one thing that all agreed upon was the shout of "Crucify them!"

THE PRIEST Jehoiakim came up to the officer Hoshea, and his evil smile was now one of triumph. "They are secured?"

"Yes, both the youth who was king and the stranger. You—is the High Priest—" He could not say it.

"Is he dead? No. When I went to the place where he was lying sick, I was driven back by the elders who were suspicious. I returned with enough help to handle them, but he and they were gone, also the sacred things. Some secret passage. They are hiding in the Temple. But the Temple is mine, and I will find them soon. It has gone as planned, O father of a king to be. The people cry 'Crucify!' Why wait?"

"There are many of the House of Japheth yet to be taken. The crosses must be erected on the hill. Let the city be further worked up, and when the sun's rays shine upon the temple stone we will put them on the crosses. Say that we are trying them to-night—a council of elders."

The priest laughed without friendliness. "Already you give orders as if—but you are right in this case. I will keep the city in a turmoil. See that your men of war remain steadfast to you. It is well for us that the House of Japheth had almost died out."

"My House of Hoshea is of as royal blood!" answered the officer hotly.

"More so," answered the priest placatingly as he ran toward a group of the people, shouting, "Treachery! Woe to us! Woe to us!"

The king and Nathan were carried into a dungeon whose walls were of cold, thick stone. There was no furnishing, just a pile of straw and an earthenware jug of water. The bronze door closed behind them, and they were in total darkness.

"I am afraid, O King," said Nathan, "that I brought you misfortune rather than the homage which the descendant of Japheth deserves."

"Your coming simply brought matters to a head," answered

the young king. "I have felt for a long time that this dog of the House of Hoshea was faithless; also that the priest Jehoiakim was ambitious to seize the High Priesthood. I did not think they would dare move while the High Priest lived. It would have come sooner nor later, Isaac. The men of my house may be able to win through to us, or it may be that the High Priest will arise from his bed of sickness. If he does, the people love him and will obey him."

"And if your people do not succeed and if the High Priest does not rise from the sickbed?" questioned Nathan.

"Why, then," answered the young king calmly, "it is very likely that Abner of the House of Japheth and Isaac Nathan of the tribe of Reuben will be crucified when the sun shines on the Temple."

"I am sorry—for you," said Nathan gently.

"Be sorry for yourself," answered the king sternly. "I am of the blood of Japheth, the captain of thousands, and I know how to die. I am the king!"

CHAPTER XII

A DESPERATE CHOICE

NORCROSS'S COLUMN WENT slowly back in the hills. Now all pretense of being a peace party was laid aside, and the column looked like what it was, a war party fully able to take care of itself.

The bayonets were on the rifles and the flaps of the Colt holsters were tucked back. The Manchu swordsmen were out in front and rear as well as on the sides.

It had been four hours since they had seen Isaac Nathan enter the gates of the city. Landess walked with Norcross and T'ang Wang.

"I am worried about Isaac Nathan," he said suddenly. "All my life I have had premonitions when things are not to go right. Now I feel that all is not well with Isaac. Why, I do not know; but for the last hour the feeling has been getting steadily stronger."

Norcross halted. "I think that we all feel it," he said quietly. "Look at the faces of the men."

Landess looked along the line nearest to him. The men were quiet, the usual smiles and jests were lacking. There was no talk, and they all looked like men who had brought an ex-comrade up to face the firing squad and were marching back afterward.

"John! I see it—and in your face also. You do not think that Isaac Nathan is safe there in the city?"

"I do not know that, Mr. Landess. He may be, and probably is. But in some way I feel that we should have made sure of his safety before we turned back. And yet, if we went back, we might be doing the one thing that would make him unsafe. If they thought that we were going to try to force our way into the city, they would connect him with the attempt. For all that, I feel that we should not go on."

T'ang Wang had listened, his face impassive. As Norcross finished, he smiled. "The Manchu very seldom gets what you call the—the forewarning of something that is to happen; but I had it once. That was the time I saw you first, O honorable elder brother, and asked you for protection for the Princess Ch'enyaun. I knew then as if some one had told me plainly that you would regain for her the city of Ningyuan. I did not have any forewarning about the Lord Nathan when you and he marched out to meet the men from the city; but I did send some of my swordsmen out to circle the city. There is a way up on the mountain at the south corner that leads to the top. There we would find a place that the city can be overlooked with our glasses, Lord John."

"Yeah?" drawled Norcross "Good! I think the best thing we can do is to swing around and get as near the base of that mountain as we can then you and I can do a little climbing and take a look-see. Did your swordsmen meet any one, T'ang Wang?"

"No, elder brother. The ground that the people of the city cultivate and where they graze their herds lies to the other side where there are many valleys and streams. This side is in the hills."

"We'll move up, then. Give orders that no man who sees the swordsmen or the column may be allowed to win through to the city."

The faces of the big colored men showed plainly their delight as they swung to the left.

"Hot damn!" Sergeant Moss gruntled. "Us goin' back to git Misto' Nathan. Dat wasn't no place to leave him all alone wid dem birds dat tooked him in. Dey handle dem pig-stickahs too blame careless, does yo' ask me."

"Why don't yo' go up an' tell de Capt'n dat yo' decides dat?" asked a voice behind him. "De Capt'n forget to ask yo' 'bout it."

"Yas, suh," chuckled another. "Gen'ally de Capt'n say, 'What does yo' think 'bout dis, Sergeant Moss?'"

"Ah heahs," a third took up the refrain, "dat Del'cate Moss is gwine to be made a majah. Den he fin's out iffen de place is safe. Capt'n say, 'Majah Moss, is dis place safe fo' us to be 'round?' an' den Majah Moss he say, 'No, suh. Ah'm s'prised at yo'. Take dese feeble young gals 'nother fo'ty miles back in de timbah where dey can climb trees.'"

Now the lines were happy once more and the laughter and jests went rippling up and down. Delicate Moss, secure in the knowledge that he could take any two of them apart at the same time, laughed with the rest.

AT THE base of the mountain there was a little box cañon, and twenty minutes after they arrived the outfit was in it, and the entrance was concealed. Norcross, with T'ang Wang and the swordsmen who had found the path, climbed up and leveled their glasses on the city below.

Finally Norcross lowered his glasses. T'ang Wang did the

same; and the American and the Manchu, both fighting men, looked at each other.

"The city has risen," Norcross said.

"And there are two crosses being built in front of that building which looks like a temple," went on T'ang Wang, just as quietly as Norcross. "Also, several houses are being stormed."

"The palace and the temple are quiet. Two crosses—that means that either the men responsible for Mr. Nathan's being brought into the city are to be put on them, or else that one of them is for him."

"You say that the officer that came out said that it was on command of the king that he be admitted?"

"Yes." Norcross raised his glasses again. "At least that is what he told Mr. Landess. The fighting around the houses has stopped, T'ang Wang."

"The people are not fighting the soldiers," said T'ang Wang as he brought his glasses to bear. "The soldiers stand and watch. It is not an inter-city fight, elder brother. See, they carry bodies from the houses." They both lowered their glasses.

"Mr. Nathan," Norcross said slowly, "was taken into the city and brought before the king. The people objected to his presence and rose. No, not so good. If they had, the king would have used his armed forces to quell any uprising."

"It may be that the king is a weak one, and that the army has joined with the people against the sacrilege. I do not understand the attack on the houses—unless it is that the people there would not join in whatever is going on," T'ang Wang answered.

"Whatever it is," Norcross said grimly, "it came too promptly after Mr. Nathan's arrival for it to be accidental. Mr. Nathan is concerned in it. I do not like those crosses being put up... We will go into the city of Jearim and see what they mean."

T'ang Wang smiled as they started down the path. He had studied the massive stone houses and the wide streets that teemed with people for mile after mile. He thought of his hundred Manchu swords and of Norcross's seventy-five men, and the impossibility of a surprise attack, but he smiled as he answered:

"Yes, honorable elder brother; we will go in and see what they mean."

"We can come down the mountain here and go along the wall until we are opposite the temple, then down and to it. Once we get there we can hold until we find out where Mr. Nathan is. I'll admit frankly, T'ang Wang, it has got me. It may not mean a thing as far as Mr. Nathan goes, and if we go in we may put him in the very danger we are trying to protect him from; and yet, if we don't, and see him put on one of those crosses from a point so far away that we could not do a thing—what then?"

"The fact that we attack might make them hesitate," answered T'ang Wang, "although I doubt it. I do not know this people, but I have heard and read of the Hebrews in the olden days. A thought has come to me. The crosses are not yet finished, and I think that this race only sacrifice when the sun is in the heavens. There is time to send one into the city and find out what is going on. It may be that the Lord Nathan is safe, and all of this against some other."

"That thought is a good one," said Norcross promptly. "But, T'ang Wang, whom can we send that speaks the language? The boy has sworn not to enter the city. By the wildest stretch of my imagination I cannot picture one of my men posing as a Hebrew—or your Manchus, either."

T'ang Wang laughed as they entered the cañon. "I cannot either, elder brother. It may be that we can persuade the youth to go."

Landess took the news of what was happening in the city quietly, although his face paled as Norcross told of the crosses. At the finish he asked, "What will you do, John?"

"Go in and make sure that Mr. Nathan is all right. But first, T'ang Wang has suggested that we try to send some one in that can get what is going on. We do not want to put Mr. Nathan in the very position that we think we are saving him from."

THE BOY Zebulon came up with his pretty Tartar wife. He spoke and she translated into Pushtu. "You have been up on the mountain, O War Captain?"

"Yes," answered Norcross. "We are not at ease about the man that entered."

Norcross spoke slowly and used as simple words as he could. The girl Hebrew had improved as had the boy Pushtu, and Zebulon understood most of what Norcross told him.

The boy's face grew troubled as he listened and after Norcross said, "That is all we saw," the boy began:

"The king is of the House of Japheth, who founded the city many thousand years ago. This house of the royal blood is dying out, and has only a few men left. When, three years ago King Abner was elevated to the throne there was much discontent in the city. One named Hoshea ben Elah, who commands the fighting men, came to my father and hinted that my father should join him in unseating the king. My father scorned him— and was reduced to Captain of the Guard. It is possible that this man Hoshea has taken the arrival of a stranger in the city as an excuse to rebel. That would explain why the soldiers did not interfere—and also the two crosses. One is for the stranger, and the other, for the king."

"For the king?" asked Norcross. "Do your people execute their kings?"

"My people," answered the young man proudly, "slay any and all that play them false. The priests must be with whoever it is that has raised the people."

"This king," Norcross went on, "did he not know the danger of admitting a stranger?"

"He must have. But this king, who is Abner of the House of Japheth, does as he wishes. He has flouted the rules laid down by the elders before. Twice, when he was younger, he went far beyond the limit of the territory commanded by the city. Once," the boy smiled, "I was with him."

"I see," Norcross answered. "Will you go into the city and find out for us what is happening?"

The boy studied for a moment, then shook his head slowly.

"I dare not," he said frankly. "I swore by the sacred things of the temple. If I broke the oath, I would die by the torments I invoke on myself. Only the High Priest can relieve me of the oath. I am not afraid to die," he went on proudly. "Test me with a sword or with the little guns. It is because I have sworn an oath."

"We understand," Norcross said, "and we will not ask you to break it… I think, T'ang Wang, the best thing to do is to go in— all together, and openly. We can shoot a way in to the temple if we have to. The boy has probably told just what is happening, and Mr. Nathan is being used as a cat's-paw by this whatever-his-name-is."

The girl had questioned the boy, and then had proposed something to him.

The boy shook his head, but the girl insisted; finally she turned to Norcross.

"I will go into the city, wearing my man's clothes that one of your men now owns. It will be dark, and I can speak enough of his language so that I will not be an object of suspicion. I will bandage my face as if wounded. I will seek out the captain of the guard, my man's father, and tell him that his son awaits him here."

Norcross shook his head. "And he would turn you over to be crucified also. You forget that you are a stranger also, and have already been refused admission to the city—refused by him."

"But now, O War Captain," insisted the girl, "it is different. See, my man has told that his father would not join the one who conspired. I am of the Altai Mountain Tartars, who also conspire. I know that those who do not join will gladly do anything to outplay those who do join. I will tell him that his son is here with enough men to stop anything that is going on, and that these men will swear that they will leave the city afterward. While I stand here, O War Captain of fighting men, the lord that you brought to the city may be in danger," she added with a woman's wile.

Norcross smiled as he caught it.

"If your man permits," he answered, "you may go, O Maiden of the Tartars, who can plan as well as fight. If you do, and return with the news or the captain of the guard, you may name the reward you will be entitled to."

"You rescued us and you have been good to us," she answered. "We owe you more than we can ever repay. Order the man who has the clothes to bring them to my tent."

THE MOBILE Kid was brought up, and Norcross gravely explained the matter to him. The Mobile Kid promptly volunteered to get the clothes.

"Yes, suh, Capt'n. Ah gits dem right away. Ah done lost de tin hat wid de clothesbrush stickin' up to Skinnay Martin—Ah means to Private Martin—shootin' craps. Mah goodness, Ah nevah seed de luck dat—yes, suh, Capt'n, Ah buys it back and brings it along wid de rest to de lady's tent."

"May I speak to Private Mobile, John?" asked Landess, with a smile.

"Certainly," answered Norcross. "Speak to any of them, any time, Mr. Landess. This no-'count scoundrel of a Mobile Kid isn't worth talking to, though. Some day I'm going to skin him and nail his hide up on the barn door. He can't make the galloping ivories behave at all."

The big colored man's grin showed all of his white teeth. He had enlisted in B Troop years before, a little wild negro kid, and Norcross had made a man out of him.

"I will give you the money to buy the 'tin hat,' and when we get back to Ningyuan I will get for you a whole suit of armor, in exchange for that which you are giving up," Landess said to him.

"Mah goodness," said the shocked Mobile Kid, "dat's all right, Misto' Landess. Ah thanks yo' just de same, but does de Capt'n want mah skin he gits it widout—"

"I'm going to start taking it also," interrupted Norcross sternly, although there was a smile in his eyes. "Right now, if one bird I know of isn't on his way, *muy pronto*. Move out, boy."

"Yes, suh, Capt'n. Ah'm gone." And the Mobile Kid started after a snappy salute.

And so, shortly afterward, the girl came out of the tent, dressed in her husband's clothes. She was not quite as broad-shouldered, but was very nearly his size otherwise, and if it had not been for her pretty dark face, might have been the boy's twin brother. She allowed Yaller Coudray to fix a most artistic bandage that came down over one eye and covered most of her little straight nose. Yaller was assisted by all of the men who could get close enough to watch the proceedings. That is, he was assisted, or hindered, by suggestions, the colored men dearly loving anything that even hinted at a masquerade.

"Dat don't look natural widout no blood on it," insisted Slew-foot. "Git Memphis to smear some of dat raw meat on it."

"Dat's what Ah says," agreed Buck Foster. "How come dat she git a— Ah means, dat he git a wallop on de haid wid dat trench hat to protect it? Answer me dat!"

Yaller looked around in deep disgust. "Does Ah heah much mo' from all you apes dat is helpin', Ah stops fixin' dis and shows some of yo' big-motif niggers how yo' gets a wallop wid a hat on. Ah gets de bandage on fust, den Ah chiefs it up aftah; am dat satisfactory to yo'-all?"

When the Tartar girl was pronounced ready for Norcross's inspection, she certainly looked like a wounded soldier. Her face had been whitened by some of Memphis's flour well rubbed in; there was dried blood caked on her face and on what part of her slim legs that showed above the "shinguards," and on her arms. Yaller and his chief assistant, Delicate Moss, stood off and admired their handiwork. Just enough of her nose showed to allow her to breathe.

"You is done, lady-chile," announced Yaller, who admired the slender, game little Tartar girl. "Go show de Capt'n and

Misto' T'ang Wang and Misto' Landess. Walk careful, honey, so dat yo' don't shake off de cam'flage."

The girl didn't know what that meant, but she walked carefully just the same.

AT DUSK she was taken up the mountain, then down to the wall, and lowered to the ground of the city, about thirty feet by a rope made of gunslings. There were no guards on the wall, although an empty guardhouse was within fifty feet, and another stood where the narrow one-man footbridge connected the mountain with the wall, perhaps a hundred feet away.

This bridge could be dropped into a chasm by lifting the two ends off the metal posts that secured it on the wall side. This evidently was done every night as the ropes by which it could be pulled up again were hanging in readiness. It was evident that whatever was going on in the city had left at least this part of the wall unguarded.

The girl had received instructions from her husband as to the route to take to find his father, and as soon as her little feet touched the ground, she started confidently off, the round shield held as the boy had held it.

Norcross, T'ang Wang, Yaller Coudray and Delicate Moss went slowly back to the camp in the cañon. Norcross walked silently, and finally T'ang Wang, as if reading his thoughts said, "She was the one to go, O elder brother."

"I reckon that you are right," answered Norcross. "But she is a girl. She goes into deadly danger for us, a Manchu War Lord and an American who commands men."

"She goes because she wished to go," answered T'ang Wang, softly. "It is not for us, Lord John, it is for the Lord Nathan. You and I could not have gone, unless we went at the head of our men. See, now I have what you and the Lord Landess had, a forewarning. She will return safely and will bring with her the captain of the guard."

T'ang Wang's forewarning proved correct. Three hours later,

Nehemiah, captain of the guard, stood facing Norcross and T'ang Wang in the cañon.

As he approached, his son had come forward and knelt at his feet. Nehemiah had raised the boy up and after one long look deep into the boy's eyes, had kissed him, murmuring, "My son—oh, my son."

He was the officer who had come out with the runner. He spoke first: "This woman, who is the wife of my son, found me in the city. She has told me of you and what you wish to do. I am loyal to King Abner. But he is a captive, as is the man who entered the city this morning."

The girl translated, the boy helping her. Norcross and T'ang Wang both spoke Pushtu, T'ang Wang better than Norcross; and while the Hebrew lost quite a little of its directness, the meaning of the captain of the guard's speech reached them.

"Ask him what happened after the stranger entered," Norcross directed.

"**I DO** not know all," said Nehemiah. "I took the stranger to the king and left him. Soon the commander of the army runs up to the guards and the soldiers in the barracks and shouts that the king plots with the stranger to open the gates of the city. The priests, led by Jehoiakim who would be High Priest, run about, also, shouting the same thing; and the city rises. It does not take much," he added grimly, "and most of the people believe the priests and such of the fighting men as are with Hoshea ben Elah, the commander. The king and the stranger were taken and cast into the cells below the palace.

"The priests have spread tales of long plotting on the king's part, and stories of his wild orgies—which are lies. But once roused, the people are anxious to believe anything. Most of the House of Japheth are already dead. Hoshea ben Elah dare not attack us of the guard who are faithful to the king, as yet. He knows that the people love us and would not allow it. That is all I can tell you—you who have brought a stranger to the walls of our city to make trouble."

"Ask him what the crosses are for," Norcross said.

"To crucify the king and the stranger, when the sun comes to the temple to-morrow," answered Nehemiah curtly. "What would you of me?"

"This," answered Norcross, just as curtly. "We are going in to get the stranger and in doing it we can also rescue the king. Help us and we will set the king back on his throne, then leave the city."

The captain of the guard looked around the camp. "Where are the tens of thousands that it would take to do that?"

Norcross pointed to the ammunition cases. "In there," he answered calmly. "We will come in whether you help us or not. If you will, the king will sit once more on his throne, we will give you this commander and the priest to do with as you wish; and then we will leave your city and go back to our own."

Nehemiah, never having seen guns or ammunition cases, did not understand, and laughed scornfully. "You could not get fifty feet inside the wall. The swords of Jearim would slay you all. And yet—and yet, in the rally for the attack on you, I might gather men and rescue the king. Yes, all the swords of Hoshea would come to drive you out and slay."

Both Norcross and T'ang Wang smiled at this calmly spoken plan to throw them to the lions while the king was being rescued, but they hid their mirth from Nehemiah as he looked up.

"This I will do, then," Nehemiah went on. "There is a way into the city from the south, that comes up into a house close to the palace. It is known only to the men of my house who were entrusted with it a thousand years ago when the city was built. It is the way that was left open for the king to escape from the city if need arose. To what better purpose could it be put than to help the king now?

"I will, then, lead you and your men to it and through into the house. There at dawn you may attempt to rescue the stranger— or do whatever you see fit to do. This I will tell you in fairness: I am only doing this so that I may, in the confusion that will follow the attack on you, rescue the king. Once that is done, I will help put you to the sword. Now, show me a man!"

John Norcross, ex-Army captain, now leader of seventy-five men, and T'ang Wang, Manchu War Lord, and leader of one hundred, smiled at the invitation to put themselves in the middle of a city numbering two hundred thousand.

T'ang Wang spoke, "We will go with you, O captain of the guard of the king. It may be, as you say, that in the confusion we will be able to rescue the Lord for whom we are going in; and it also may be that you will find we are not easy men to put to the sword."

Nehemiah only laughed. "Come, then," he said.

The boy would not go, and once again said good-by to his father. The girl had returned the clothes to the Mobile Kid, much to his delight, and was now dressed in her own. Landess was a problem to Norcross, who knew that if a fight started in the city, their chances of ever getting out were a hundred to one. Norcross was under no delusion as to the fighting ability of the Hebrews. The streets, too, were wide, and the houses were individual forts. He did not want to take Landess, yet he knew that if he did not come back, Landess would die in the hills unless the boy and the girl took care of him—and their chances of getting through were slim. Landess sensed that Norcross was figuring what to do and came up to him.

"John, I go with you," he said quietly. "I am responsible for Isaac Nathan's being there, and I must go, John."

"All right, Mr. Landess," answered Norcross, with a smile. "We'll take you there and back, if we can. If we can't, we will all stay, with Mr. Nathan."

The boy and girl found a safe little place where they could almost literally "hole up," and were content to wait. The boy had been given a rifle, a Colt .45 and two belts of cartridges. The girl had begged for a Colt .45 also and Norcross had given her one with belt and holster.

Food enough to last them two weeks was also left; and from

the expressions on their faces as the column left, the boy and girl were more than sure of their ability to whip the world as they traveled through it. They were to wait until the next night for the column to return.

CHAPTER XIII

INVADING THE CITY

T'ANG WANG CALLED his Manchu swords in from the hills and with Nehemiah leading, the compact little party went up the mountain.

He led them far around after they came to where the footbridge still swung unguarded across the chasm. They finally went down the side of the mountain through a draw, then up a smaller hill. He pulled away a clump of second growth and disclosed what looked like a fox hole.

"Doggone mah hide," announced Delicate, as he got down on his knees to peek in. "Ah hopes Ah don't meet no polecats."

"Tell 'em who yo' is and dey gives yo' de fust shot," offered Slewfoot behind him, when Yaller interrupted with, "Git in, git in. Does yo' git stuck, us shoots yo' loose. Hurry up, dese guns gotta git through."

The hole widened out once they were inside, much to Delicate's relief; for he was not built to do much crawling. Finally it became a stone-lined passageway after it reached the level. An hour was spent thus; at last Nehemiah led the way up some stone steps, into a cellar, then up and into a big room on the ground floor. It was pitch dark and no one could tell whether there were any windows or not.

"You are in the house of a man who died some time ago," he announced from the darkness. "It is directly across from the place where the crosses stand. When the light comes you will be able to see from the windows. This I have done for the king.

Do not try to return through the tunnel—I go now to flood it. This I will tell you also. The man you will try to take from the city will be brought out with the king when the sun shines on the temple steps. Attack then, or when you please. I go now and when we meet again, guard yourselves well, men of an alien race, for I will come as the captain of the king's guard, to slay you."

He had forgotten that the girl was no longer with them to translate, and no one understood what he was saying. Norcross and T'ang Wang felt that he was saying good-by and warning them about something; but what it was, they could not understand, so they kept still, listening to his retreating footsteps.

One or two of the men stirred a little uneasily. This absolute darkness was not so good. Norcross heard the rustle and laughed an amused little laugh. Then he drawled, "Stand fast, you no-'count scoundrels. Ease off, but don't let anything clink. I'm going to put a flash light on the floor and locate the walls. Then the men on the outside step up to them and feel for windows."

The men, at the sound of his easy, natural voice, came out of their tenseness. The little flash light played on the floor, then went to the walls starting slowly up from the floor. There were windows, or rather openings shuttered with solid board blinds.

"All right," Norcross went on, "spread out a little and sit down. No talking above a whisper. It will be light pretty soon and then we'll step out a little. We'll get Mr. Nathan and then go home. Any man that snores will get nine million years K.P. and then six more. The Lord T'ang Wang and I will stand guard."

The big colored men, afraid of nothing that they could see, but like most colored people more or less apprehensive of "ha'nts" in the absolute darkness, settled down perfectly content. T'ang Wang spoke softly to the Manchu swordsmen and from then until dawn there was silence in "the house of a man who died."

DAWN CAME and the sky was clear of clouds. Norcross found, by easing one of the shutters open a little, that the windows on one side faced the blank wall of another house about ten feet away. These windows were promptly opened; and the ones in front, facing the palace, were opened enough to allow a small observation slit at each of them.

The men rose, stretched, and contentedly turned to their emergency rations. The fact that they were in the heart of a hostile city far in the Kuen Lun range, did not make the slightest difference to them. The "Capt'n" was along, and that was enough for them.

Landess had kept up with the rest, helped over the rough spots by Norcross and T'ang Wang. Once in the house, as the captain of the guard, Nehemiah, was speaking, Norcross and T'ang Wang had taken off their tunics and laid them on the floor. Landess had first sat down on them, then before the Captain had finished, stretched out and gone sound asleep. When the light came in the windows, he was still asleep, as calmly as if in his bedroom in New York.

Both Norcross and T'ang Wang stood for a moment, looking down on the thin scholarly face and frail form.

"The body of the Lord Landess," said T'ang Wang, softly, "is old and worn; but the spirit that it contains shines with the light of youth and courage. When it goes On High it will go with all honor, O honorable elder brother."

"Yes," answered Norcross, proudly, "it will go with all honor, as you say, T'ang Wang, if it comes to a fight—and I do not see how it can be avoided—I am going to ask you to do something for me. I want you to put Mr. Landess in the middle of your swords, and as I shoot a road for you, take him out of the city and to Ningyuan. This I ask, brother that I love, in memory of past days. You have said that you were in my debt. You are a Manchu Lord.

"I ask you to do this for me as one asks a Manchu Lord for payment of a debt."

T'ang Wang's face lost its impassiveness for a moment. He loved Norcross, and he also knew what that meant. It meant that Norcross would try with every means in his power to clear the way, and in doing that, he would die, if necessary, he and his men.

"And the Lord Nathan, John?" T'ang Wang asked quietly.

"I do not think that there will be much of a fight in getting him. The surprise will be in our favor, if the captain of the guard has played fair. I think he will, up to that point, so that he can get to the king. If we get Mr. Nathan, then he goes with Mr. Landess. My thought is this, T'ang Wang. Once we have them both, or have learned that Mr. Nathan is already dead, we cannot put up nearly as good an argument if we are making a running fight. But I can take a position on the palace or temple roof and cover you all the way to the wall and over."

"Then, because I will still be in the city, the attack will come to me, instead of following you."

"I will do as you demand, John. You have asked me to do it as a Manchu, paying a debt. Now let me ask you a question, as my elder brother. Why cannot we take the Lord Nathan and win our way to this house, and go once more through the tunnel?"

"Listen," answered Norcross. "Do you hear the water running in beneath the floor? That must have been what the guard captain was trying to tell us. The tunnel is being flooded to prevent our using it, T'ang Wang."

T'ang Wang listened for a moment. "I hear it, Lord John. When you give the order, I will take the Lords Landess and Nathan out of the city and to Ningyuan, or die with them."

"Once you are clear," Norcross said with a smile, "and in the hills, I'll try to do a little of that getting out thing, myself. T'ang Wang, for the first time since I have been in this game I hate to give the order to fire. This is their city, and they are of Nathan's race, and he wished to find peace here among what he calls the sacred things. I— As God is my judge, T'ang Wang, I cannot turn this city into a bloody shambles."

The Manchu showed in T'ang Wang's eyes—the spirit of the Manchus who had cut their way through a hostile China with their swords, and had ridden with bodies as a carpet for their horses' feet. But he answered courteously:

"I regret that I cannot feel as you, honorable elder brother.

No doubt it is because my eyes do not see as yours. It may be that these people will not attack. If they do, it will be an attack by men whose trade is war. That attack must be met."

SLEWFOOT, WHO had been stationed at one of the slits, rose and announced, "People comin' out by dem crosses, and de army is marchin' 'round de block."

"All right," Norcross answered. "Keep your positions, you birds. We'll let them do all the marching they wish. Now is a good time to tell you all what I want done. We are going in to get Mr. Nathan as soon as he appears. If he doesn't, we'll go and hunt for him. At the minute he is supposed to be in the cells under the palace. We could go right now and hunt for him, but we don't know exactly where he is, and that would take time, and they might kill him while we were hunting."

Norcross spoke slowly, explaining matters rather than giving orders. The colored men listened intently, their eyes on their erect, calm-faced Mississippian leader.

"The idea is this," Norcross went on. "We brought Mr. Nathan to the city, and now all that we want to do is to see that he is safe here in it. It may be that neither cross is for him, but it's probable that one is. If it is, we will take him away from these people. The Lord T'ang Wang will put Mr. Nathan and Mr. Landess in the middle of his swordsmen and will start out with them. We will cover them with all we've got.

"Once they are safe in the hills, we will start for home ourselves. Now, I don't want any more shooting than is absolutely necessary. When we start out of here on the run, we will do it in a wedge formation. I don't know how close they will be to the house, but we will go through to Mr. Nathan. Use the butts of your rifles or the barrels of your Colts in pushing any of the people back. You are Military Police breaking up a mob, that is all.

"If there is an attack by the army in the first rush, then use your bayonets and guns, but no more than enough to drive them back. After the Lord T'ang Wang starts for the wall or the gates, we will take some high ground and shoot his way clear for him. I will make the point of the wedge with Lieutenant Coudray and Sergeant Moss. That's all. Take it easy until we start. You scoundrels with those rapid-fire guns will have a lot of work to do if it comes to a fight, so see that your trigger fingers are oiled up."

The square in front of the house gradually filled with the people of the city. There were not many soldiers in sight. One thin line was all, strung around the square, and there was a company by the two crosses. It was evident that neither people nor soldiers dreamed of alien foes being inside the city. The captain of the guard had kept faith with Norcross.

The city seemed quiet, the people unexcited. The coup of the commander and the priest had been sudden, and they appeared to have full control of the situation. What soldiers Hoshea ben Elah might have in reserve, or what the captain, Nehemiah, was doing, Norcross had no way of knowing. He could see part of the temple from the slit he was looking through, and it seemed quiet and uncrowded.

Suddenly a trumpet blew, and a company of soldiers came from the palace, marching in a hollow square. Norcross could catch an occasional glimpse of two white-robed figures in the center of the square. Another, larger company of soldiers came from the Temple. This company was led by a tall officer in resplendent trappings. As they left the Temple, a body of priests came from another part.

All three parties walked slowly toward the crosses, which had been set up in artificial mounds of dirt. Now the people began to stir, with cries of "Kill the false king! Kill the stranger! Hail to Hoshea ben Elah and the priest, Jehoiakim, who saved the city!"

Landess had risen and now was crouched beside Norcross, watching from the slit. He saw Nathan, and drew a long breath. "It is Isaac. They take him to the cross, John."

"Which he will never reach," answered Norcross, rising. "Mr. Landess, you will get in the middle of the wedge that Lieutenant Coudray is forming by the door. You will under no circumstances leave it. When we get to Mr. Nathan, T'ang Wang will throw his swordsmen around you both, and leave the city. You will go with him, both of you."

Norcross's tone was that of an officer giving orders to be obeyed without question.

Landess looked at him for a moment, then answered gently, "I will obey orders, John. If— John, to me you have always been as a son. I know what you are going to do, my son. Good-by, John—and thank you."

Landess held out his hand, which Norcross took.

"I am glad to be called your son," he said, as he pressed the slim blue-veined hand gently before releasing it. "Get in the wedge, Mr. Landess… All right!" as he ran to the door that Yaller Coudray was ready to open.

THE DOOR came open and the wedge started. About thirty feet away stood the line of swordsmen of the city of Jearim. They turned to see what was running toward them. Norcross, who was carrying a rifle, swung the stock up from his hip and caught the soldier in front of him under the chin. He went down, as did the two that were on either side of him as Coudray and Delicate Moss did the same. The line, as far as the wedge reached, went down like dominoes as the big colored men hit it.

T'ang Wang and his swords formed another wedge just behind, but their swords were not needed to go through the first line. The people were more or less massed in front of the soldiers, and at the first shock of the charge, and at the hearing of the clang as the metal of the armor hit the ground, they turned also.

In a Chinese city there would have been a wail of fear, then a frantic rush to get out of the way. But in the city of Jearim there was no panic, not even at the sight of black men whom they had never seen before. Those directly in the path of the wedge gave way sullenly, and more than one sword flashed out from under the long robes.

The soldiers in the line that had not been reached were already charging in, their round shields in front of their bodies, their short straight swords out of the sheaths. The rush had taken the colored men past them, and they met the Manchu swords of T'ang Wang. The soldiers were all young men, built and dressed as the boy had been, and swordsmen all. But they met better blades, which were wielded with no thought of mercy; and those who closed with the Manchus went down. Not all of them fell without carrying Manchus down with them, but by the time that Norcross had forced his way through the crowd there were no soldiers on that side of the square.

The colored men used the butts of their guns or pushed the people back with their rifles held in both hands. And they had to do it to the faces of the men against them. None turned to run. But the wedge went through and into the open space.

The company of soldiers that had the king and Nathan in its center had formed now in company front. The king and Nathan behind the line, held by four men. The other company, the one led by Hoshea ben Elah, was charging straight across at the wedge. The priests had halted.

The reaction to the surprise was instantaneous. These people were fighters, whose ancestors had been also fighters, and all they saw or thought about was that strangers were in the city with some kind of weapons in their hands, and that the thing to do was to kill them.

Norcross saw that rifle butts against ready swords would result in some of his men getting killed without an even break; and in the final analysis, of course, he thought far more of them than he did of the lives of the people of this city.

"Bayonets!" he shouted as they closed.

Bayoneted Springfields in the hands of big men with a long reach are deadly things, especially when hacked with the weight of the said big men in a running charge. The wedge went through the Jearim company line so fast that Norcross and Yaller Coudray and Delicate Moss almost knocked the king and Nathan down as they came through.

The men holding them had let go to draw their swords. The

men in the wedge just behind the three leaders parried the guards' cuts, then literally lifted them from the ground on their bayonets.

As Landess put his arms around Nathan, Norcross turned and shouted to his troopers, "Fan out! Fan out! On the left!"

He ran to the left of the spreading wedge with Coudray and Moss beside him. The charge of Hoshea ben Elah had almost arrived.

But so had T'ang Wang's swords, and the company of soldiers was caught between the swords and the bayonets, either of which would have been enough to face. Hoshea ben Elah saw the danger in time, and shouted an order.

His company ran swiftly to the right and won clear. No sooner had it done so than, as one man, it whirled around and stood at attention, awaiting the order to charge.

Hoshea ben Elah, no matter what kind of a conspirator he was, was brave, and a leader of warriors. He saw other soldiers coming into the square from all sides, while the people were being sent out of the way by the captains of tens and hundreds. He could also see the young King Abner, standing with the stranger and another.

The wedge of the black men had disappeared now, and he thought that by a direct charge he could pierce the line in which the black men now stood, and regain the person of the king or slay him.

He raised his sword and opened his mouth to order the charge—only to stand transfixed as he beheld what was transpiring.

COMPANY AFTER company of Hebrew soldiers, those that he had seen coming in, formed into a compact regiment in the square, which was now cleared of the people. He saw Nehemiah, the captain of the guard, was their leader; and he knew then that his attempt to gain the throne had failed.

The company that had been bringing the king and Nathan to the crosses had ceased to exist. Of the line of soldiers that had been around the square, those that still lived had formed with the regiment.

Now, in the square, the black men were drawn up as a four-pointed star with little brown tubes that pointed out. Inside the star were the king, Nathan, and Landess. Just back of the star, formed out from the south point, there was still a wedge; this was composed of Manchu swordsmen. T'ang Wang was ready to receive the men he had promised Norcross to take to Ningyuan.

The body of priests stood as they had been when the charge began. The flat roofs on all sides were covered with people. There was absolutely no noise. The men behind Hoshea ben Elah, who were his own picked followers, stood silently, waiting.

The priest Jehoiakim broke the silence. He ran toward Nehemiah's regiment, shouting, "Dare you go against the orders of the High Priest? Destroy these black dogs who have entered the sacred city, and then crucify the false king who brought them! Follow me! I, the High—"

There was the sound of many trumpets from the Temple, and the priest Jehoiakim stopped as if frozen, his face telling of utter consternation and dread.

As the soldiers of Nehemiah's regiment heard it, they stopped advancing; the people on the roofs knelt; the body of priests that had come with Jehoiakim wavered a moment, as if not knowing which way to turn, then they followed suit and knelt also.

"What de hell now?" muttered Delicate Moss. "Sounds like dat ole *ump-pa-pa, ump-de-zoom-boom* dat de band play when dey is buryin' some one."

"Wish dey git to de fightin' part," complained the Mobile Kid almost querulously. "Ah nevah liked dat kind of music, nohow. Hot damn, Del'cate! Look comin' down de steps. Reg'lar procession of de 'Ah Aims to Rise' society!"

He did not need to tell Delicate Moss to look. Delicate was already doing so, along with every one else in the square and on the roofs. Down the steps there marched four trumpeters, then several priests with long flowing white beards, then one old, old man whose beard almost touched the ground.

His priestly robes blazed with jewels and insignia, and on his head was the cap of the High Priest.

Back of him, carried on platforms, were the sacred things of the Temple, then behind them more priests. It was the High Priest Hasdai ben Isaac. He had been securely hidden from those that sought him in a secret chamber of the Temple, and he had with him the sacred things. Jehoiakim and his men had searched long but vainly, finally deciding that they could find him at their leisure, and that he would probably be dead anyway. But the High Priest had been given a new lease of life in this emergency, and now had come to do justice.

As he walked slowly forward, the soldiers knelt also, and from the roofs came the shouts of a glad people who worshiped their God through him, the High Priest.

In all the square the only men on their feet were the men of John Norcross and T'ang Wang and their leaders. Landess stood, too; but Nathan, as he saw what the bearers were carrying, had knelt.

The king walked forward to meet the High Priest and knelt at his feet. The procession halted, and the High Priest, after touching the king's head with his hand, stooped and raised the king to his feet. The king spoke to him, and the High Priest listened calmly, then answered; and the king spoke again.

The High Priest raised his hand, and two of the priests with him ran up. The High Priest gave an order, and the priests ran to Nehemiah, to Hoshea ben Elah, to Jehoiakim. The three rose in turn and came up to where the High Priest stood, then knelt again. From where Norcross, T'ang Wang, and Landess stood, they could see that the High Priest was speaking, and that the kneeling men answered.

"Holding court," Norcross said with a grave smile. "After he decides their case he'll take up ours. Better get ready to move, T'ang Wang. We will fall back to the temple steps. That will give us a line of retreat down that street to the right where we can cover—"

Norcross stopped talking. The men in front of the High Priest had risen. The High Priest was pointing to the walls of the city, and Hoshea ben Elah and the priest Jehoiakim were already walking slowly toward the wall, their heads down.

"BANISHED," SAID Norcross. "Look at Captain Nehemiah greeting the king!"

The High Priest looked at the strangers that stood in the square and spoke; and the captain of the guard walked over to where Norcross stood. He said something in a curt voice and pointed to Nathan, who rose.

"John! Henry!" old Isaac Nathan cried. "He has sent for me! I—I pray that he may allow me to stay. See, the sacred things! At last! At last I see them."

His body was shaking as with chills, but his face was lighted with happiness. Landess made a movement as if to go to him, but Norcross touched his arm and Landess, in quick understanding, nodded.

Nathan walked beside the guard captain, and the eyes of the men in the square followed him. Now there was silence again on the roofs. The High Priest would judge of the fitness of this stranger who was of their race; and the High Priest's judgment would be final. Already the too-ambitious commander of the army, and the priest who had lied, were forgotten.

Nathan knelt in front of the old man, who was much older than even he. The High Priest spoke, Nathan answered. For one, two, three minutes it went on. Question and answer, question and answer.

Then the High Priest did to Isaac Nathan what he had done to the king. He touched him on the head with his hand, and stooped a little to help him to rise.

Nathan stood up, his face working with happiness. He held out both hands toward Norcross and Landess. "Henry! John!" he called and they heard him clearly. "I may stay! I may stay in my city with the sacred things! I may help guard them always. I must go with them now back to the Temple. Good-by, Henry! Good-by, John!"

He turned again and walked to where the priests were carrying the things that to him and them were sacred; and with them he entered the Temple, all else forgotten for the moment.

Landess watched him as long as he could, then said, softly, "Good-by, Isaac."

The High Priest looked once more at the formation in the square and spoke to the king and the captain of the guard.

"All right, you birds," drawled Norcross. "Get your umbrellas up, it's going to rain in a minute. No use fooling, now. Just shoot out of the way anything that gets in it."

But it did not rain, in the sense that Norcross meant. It may be that what Nathan had told the king and the High Priest, and what the king had told him, had something to do with it. The captain of the guard once more strode up. He had grasped by this time that his speech was not understood, so he used gestures. He pointed to them, to the gates that could be seen in the wall, to the hills and waved his hand in an all-comprehensive gesture.

Norcross shouted an order and the star moved forward toward the gates that men were already running to open. The High Priest, the king, the captain of the guard, the regiment in the square—still on its knees—and the kneeling people on the roofs did not move as the big colored men, knowing that Norcross's back was to them, swaggered by. Their rifles were carried at right shoulder arms, and as cockily as possible.

THE COLORED fighters would have dearly loved to have hurled a few choice insults into the impassive faces as they went by, all of them being honestly disappointed in not getting a fight; but they knew that Norcross could hear them if he couldn't see them. So they took it out by making faces and stuck their noses in the air as high as possible.

The fact that through some miracle they were getting out of a city that held some two hundred thousand fighters, and that they were extremely lucky to be on their feet at all, never occurred to them.

The march to the gates was through deserted streets to the open place in front of the walls. As they entered the timberland, going toward where the boy and girl were waiting, Landess said to Norcross and T'ang Wang:

"Do you know, John, and you also, Lord T'ang Wang, this time I feel as if I were going home once more after a hard day's work, but a happy one because it was successful. Isaac Nathan is safe with the sacred things in his city."

Norcross and T'ang Wang both smiled and nodded their heads.

But in the ranks there was not so much of the feeling of a successful day.

"Doggone," grumbled some one, "us could have mopped up on dem birds. Comin' all dis way an' gittin' only one fight."

"Ah'll see dat dem wild men meets up wid yo'," consoled the Mobile Kid. "Ah s'pose dat yo' could lick nine million of dem wid one han' tied behind yo', huh? Boy, you is lucky to be headin' fo' home on dem numbah elevens of yoahs instead of pushin' up de daisies, like a lot of good men are doin' dis minute."

"Ain't dat de truf," agreed the first. And the happy-go-lucky column began to sing,

"Oh, de boat am comin' 'round de bend,
Good-by, mah lovah, good-by."

THE GUNS OF THE AMERICAN

*When Captain Norcross and his Manchu ally
refused to yield their mountain kingdom to Young
China's ambitious War Lords, they knew they
were starting a fierce and unforgiving fight*

CHAPTER I

"MANCHUS DO NOT THREATEN"

IN THE GARDENS of the Mandarin Len Yu at Peking sat Kai-shek, Mandarin of the First Military Class, War Lord of Hankau, to the west; and Fung-yang, also a Mandarin of the First Military Class, War Lord of the Sungar, to the north. They and Len Yu wore the uniform of a general. All were smooth-shaven, with impassive faces and eyes.

In front of them was a teakwood table on which rested price-less china teacups and saucers. Facing the mandarins on the other side of the table sat Captain John Norcross, lean-flanked, broad-shouldered, calm-eyed Mississippian, and T'ang Wang, Manchu noble of the House of Nurhachu. Their expressions were as calm as those of the mandarins opposite.

Len Yu was speaking in English so that Captain Norcross could understand. He ended with: "And so, we ask that you hold for us the territory from the Thian Shan range to the Indian border and as far east as the Pichen river."

T'ang Wang came to his feet, and as he did, Norcross rose also.

"No," T'ang Wang answered levelly. "We hold the Thian Shan range and the cities of Ningyuan and Taiyaun and the territory around them for the Princess Ch'enyaun of the House of Nurhachu. The Princess Ch'enyaun does not desire other cities or more territory and will join in no attempt to seize control of the north. The Manchu House of Nurhachu has held the Thian

"Capt'n! Look out! We is took!"

Shan range for a thousand years and will continue to hold it, irrespective of who rules in China."

"It may be, O Lord T'ang Wang, leader of swords for the Princess Ch'enyaun," Len Yu suggested smoothly, "that if we succeed in gaining control of the north without the help of the Princess Ch'enyaun, that the Manchu House of Nurhachu may, shall I say, find difficulty in retaining the cities and territory."

T'ang Wang smiled. "It may be, Lord Len Yu, leader of an army. Manchu swords and the guns of my honorable elder brother who stands at my side will do what they can to smooth any difficulty away."

"You threaten, Lord T'ang Wang?" asked the War Lord of the Sungar.

"Manchus do not threaten, Lord Fung-yang," answered T'ang Wang, indifferently. "I but replied to a threat."

"It was not meant as a threat," Len Yu said suavely. "I but pointed out a possibility, Lord T'ang Wang. You refuse to join us—on any terms?"

"Yes, on any terms, Lord Len Yu."

"The Lord T'ang Wang speaks also for you, Captain Norcross?"

"Yes, suh, the Lord T'ang Wang speaks for me," Norcross answered courteously.

"Will you rest here in my unsightly gardens before returning to Shanghai?"

"To rest here in your magnificent gardens which are the envy of the world," answered T'ang Wang, "would be a boon to be remembered always. But we must leave at once for Shanghai. The business that called us from the north was finished just as we received your request to come to Peking."

Fung-yang, who had been studying the bronzed, clean-shaven face of the American captain, leaned a little forward in his chair. "It has been told me, Captain Norcross, that you command black men. Many tales have come to us about them. How many of them have you?"

Norcross smiled. "When I first came to China I brought with me some one hundred and fifty, Lord Fung-yang. After we had been here a little while quite a few of them were killed and later others went back to the United States. But more have come out from the States at various times, so right now I reckon I've some three hundred and fifty odd."

"A third of a regiment! Truly they must be fighting men, captain. It may be that some day the gods will grant that I see them in action. Word came of their almost incredible skill with machine guns and rifles as well as their revolvers."

"I am sorry that we cannot see them fighting at our side," Len Yu said, rising. "If you must depart, allow me to escort you to the gates of my insignificant hovel."

AS THE Mandarin Len Yu walked away with T'ang Wang and Norcross, the War Lord of Hankau said softly to the Lord of the Sungar, "If the proud Manchu and the American captain were to suffer some misfortune on the way to Ningyuan it might be that the taking of the Princess Ch'enyaun's cities and territory would be less difficult. Would the Manchu swords fight as well, or the black men either, if the Lord T'ang Wang and Captain Norcross were not there to lead them?"

"When Len Yu comes back, we will ask him the question," answered the War Lord of the Sungar blandly.

Len Yu returned. His face was still impassive, but now his eyes looked as if a film had spread over them.

"We cannot hold the north," he said somberly as he sat down. "The other Manchu War Lords will not act with us unless T'ang Wang advises it. Even if we did take the northeast, the northwest would be a threat always hanging over us."

"You say 'unless T'ang Wang advises it,' O Len Yu," said Kai-shek. "To do that he must be in Ningyuan or in the north—which is a long journey from Peking or Shanghai. Also, the American captain is here. If something happened to them on the way, O Len Yu, who would advise the Manchu War Lords or lead the famous black men? The Princess Ch'enyaun, without them to counsel her, would be very apt to throw her swords against our guns."

Len Yu looked first at Kai-shek and then at Fung-yang.

"Speak plainly, War Brothers."

"This, then," Kai-shek answered. "Why allow T'ang Wang and Captain Norcross to go back to Ningyuan? We will seize them. Then we will demand the surrender of Ningyuan and Taiyaun as the price of their liberty. If the Princess Ch'enyaun does not accept, we will send the haughty Manchu and the American captain on high, and take the cities. Once we have those cities and the territory they command, the other Manchu War Lords will meet our terms or be destroyed."

Len Yu smiled grimly. "Truly it is a bold plan, War Brothers. And yet—the only one. We go to the end in this matter?"

"Yes, to the end," Kai-shek answered.

"Yes, to the end," repeated Fung-yang. "We may be able to seize them here in Peking or in Shanghai before they get to their planes. If they do, I also have flyers."

Len Yu raised his right hand and an officer of his bodyguard, who had been standing fifty-odd feet away, came forward and saluted.

"Colonel Shao Wu to report at once," Len Yu ordered curtly.

CHAPTER II

IN A WAR LORD'S POWER

THE LITTLE INN at Jen-jen on the western slope of the Khinggan mountains was nothing to boast of as far as inns went, even in China, but to "Skinnay" Martin and "Buck" Foster, two ex-troopers of the Thirty-first Regular Cavalry, U.S.A., it looked very good indeed.

The two big colored men had come with Captain Norcross, not so much as orderlies or bodyguard, but more as a reward for a brilliant little piece of scouting work they had done a little while before.

T'ang Wang had with him two Manchu swordsmen, who also were being rewarded for achievements in mountain warfare. The party of six had for three days been traveling day and night on swift horses furnished by a friend of T'ang Wang.

Skinnay and Buck didn't mind the riding, having spent most of their lives in the saddle, but they did mind the not stopping for food. Both were noted trenchermen in an outfit made up of what "Memphis," the chief cook, had justly called "mighty handsome eatahs."

"Dog-gone," Buck had grunted as they dismounted. "Ah hopes de Capt'n stays right heah to-night. Ah ain't had me nothin' to eat fo' twenty-nine days." As a matter of fact Buck had eaten a fairly substantial meal the night before, but his stomach felt as if twenty-nine days had indeed gone by.

"An' so does Ah hope it," agreed Skinnay. "Mah stomach thinks mah throat am cut, no foolin'... Ah seed a chicken run 'round de cornah when us come in."

"Yo' did! Git de saddle off dat horse, boy. Us gits him fo' suppah no mattah how good a runnah he is."

Inside, Norcross and T'ang Wang sat in the inn's one room.

"When we reach the Shamo desert, honorable elder brother," T'ang Wang said, "we can get fresh mounts from Sin-fan, who is Lord of the Shamo. He is in my debt and will forward us on our way. This is the longest way home, but I think the safest for us to travel."

"I think so too," Norcross answered with a smile. "Especially after seeing the look in Len Yu's eyes as he said good-by. I doubt very much if we would have reached Shanghai, T'ang Wang."

T'ang Wang smiled grimly. "We flew from Ningyuan in thirty-six hours; but now we ride—and it may be, walk—back."

"Which is a good deal better than remaining in Peking or Shanghai permanently, T'ang Wang," answered Norcross. "If this Len Yu is as powerful as you say, both in Shanghai and Peking, and if he planned to stop us as we both suspect, the first thing he would do would be to locate and watch our planes. He might have figured on taking us in Peking, but we outplayed him by moving out as fast as we did. He figures now that we are *en route* to Shanghai. If the planes tried to take off on receipt of an order he would know that they were going to meet us."

"Yes, elder brother. Even if he did not intercept the order which he could readily do."

"Then he would hold the planes on some pretext, or have them followed by others. This way we have a good chance of making Ningyuan, even if it does take us longer."

THERE WAS a sudden commotion outside in the compound, the sound of running feet, the ring and clash of equipment. Skinnay Martin's voice shouted: "Capt'n, Capt'n! Us is took! Look out!" The shout died away in a gurgle.

Norcross and T'ang Wang sprang to their feet, and as they did, an officer stepped in the doorway.

Norcross's right hand went to the butt of his holstered Colt .45. The officer spoke in English: "No, Captain Norcross! Do not draw your revolver. I am Colonel Shao Wu. My regiment surrounds this inn. You cannot fight your way through one thousand men. Your blacks are already captured, and your swordsmen also, Lord T'ang Wang. You are my prisoners, gentlemen. Put your side arms on the table."

"You say you are Colonel Shao Wu," T'ang Wang asked suavely. "Of what army?"

"Of the Army of the North, commanded by General Len Yu," Colonel Shao Wu said curtly. "Put your side arms on the table."

Norcross and T'ang Wang obeyed without a word, Norcross taking off his cartridge belt from which hung the holstered Colt and T'ang Wang removing his sword belt. Colonel Shao Wu stepped to one side and several Chinese officers came in.

To one of them Colonel Shao Wu said: "You will escort these prisoners, who are the Manchu Lord T'ang Wang and the American Captain Norcross, to the war junk at Stramuren and deliver them to Captain Li. Take also the two black men and the two Manchu swordsmen. Captain Li will receipt for them. Rejoin your command as rapidly as possible. Take them out."

CAPTAIN LI of the war junk signed the receipt for the six prisoners delivered to him, and then, after the colonel and his men left the junk, ordered the lines cast off. As the junk gathered way, Li turned and looked curiously at the six men standing aft near the great steering oar. His junk carried a crew of some fifty men and most of them were crowding close to the prisoners, looking at the two big colored men who returned the looks with contemptuous stares.

"Ah wish Ah had mah Colt," Buck Foster muttered. "Ah shuah would scattah dese apes."

Norcross heard it. "Steady, Buck," he drawled. "Easy does it for the moment. Don't either of you scoundrels make a play until—"

The captain of the junk came up and gave an order. Four of the crew came forward with lengths of rope.

"That is not necessary, captain," T'ang Wang said smoothly. "We do not intend to—"

"Bind them and carry them below," the junk captain snarled. "I do not care what you do or do not intend, Manchu."

One of T'ang Wang's Manchu nobles, whose old wounds were painful, stepped up to the junk captain and thrust his sword-scarred face close.

"You snarl, pariah cur? Your mean spirit will truly howl in the outer coldness before many days have gone by. If you order ropes for a Manchu, you will be hunted down like the jackal you—"

The junk captain stepped back. As he did he drew his sword and shouted an order. A rifle butt crashed against the Manchu's head and he went down. As he did, Captain Norcross stepped in and seized the wrist of the junk captain. The sword had been poised to slash down at the fallen Manchu.

A Chinaman to the right of the junk captain and behind Norcross, raised his rifle. As he did, Skinnay Martin made a flying tackle and the yellow man went to the deck as if hit by a twelve-inch shell.

Buck Foster shouted, "Mop up, B Troop!" and jumped at the nearest Chinese, his big hands outstretched to get hold of any weapon they came in contact with. The fact that there were only two of B Troop present, outside of Captain Norcross, didn't make any difference to Buck.

In a split second there was a mad swirl of fighting, T'ang Wang and the other Manchu closing with the men closest to them.

It was an unequal fight, the crew outnumbering them eight to one.

"Do not kill!" the junk captain yelled, remembering now the orders he had forgotten when in his fury he had raised his sword. "Beat them down!"

Captain Norcross went down, then T'ang Wang and the Manchu. Skinnay Martin and Buck Foster, trying to get to "de Capt'n," lasted a little longer, being so covered by Chinese that the rifle butts could not reach them. Before they too were stretched out on the deck several of the crew had reeled back with broken arms or fallen with twisted necks.

"Now, bind the dogs," the junk captain ordered, "and throw

them in the forward hold. Before we reach Peking they will pay for what they have done."

LIEUTENANT-COLONEL CHUNG looked up from some maps as Shao Wu entered the tent.

"Sit down, War Brother," he said, pushing the maps to one side. "There is an explanation to be made to me. Why were the Manchu Lord T'ang Wang and the American Captain Norcross turned over to the captain of the war junk? Our orders were to bring them to Peking—and the orders of Len Yu are not lightly be disobeyed."

"You speak as my War Brother. Chung? Or as the second in command of the regiment?"

"As your War Brother, Shao Wu."

"Then as my War Brother I will tell you. The time has come that I have been waiting for. We strike for ourselves, Chung."

"With one thousand men! Truly, your honorable wounds have caused your clever brain to be unsteady."

"No, listen, War Brother. The Manchu Lord T'ang Wang and the American captain will be taken to Peking very slowly. The captain of the war junk is in my pay and will delay as much as possible. Once there, Len Yu will endeavor to persuade T'ang Wang to surrender Ningyuan and the Thian Shan Range."

"And at the same time, once the junk arrives, he will issue the order for our arrest," Chung said grimly.

"Long before the order arrives here we will be well on our way to the Irenkha-birga, War Brother. Our regiment will follow me. The Manchus of the northwest, once it is known that the Lord T'ang Wang is held in Peking by Len Yu, will not make any move until they see what happens. They are scattered, and long before they could concentrate, even if they acted without their leader, the men of the War Lord of the Irenkha will be between them and the city of Ningyuan. We will take Ningyuan and—"

"You rave, Shao Wu. You talk of the Irenkha joining us. Does the saber-toothed tiger consort with wolves? You say, we will take Ningyuan. With one thousand men? There are ten thousand Manchu swords in Ningyuan, and the black men of the American captain. The blacks alone could destroy us with their machine guns. We had better overtake the junk and return to Peking."

"I know that we could not take Ningyuan, even if we had ten times as many men. The tiger, the War Lord of the Irenkha will take it for us. No, do not interrupt, Chung. The time has come for which I have waited. In Ningyuan there is the treasure of the ancient Manchu Chieftain Nurhachu, T'ang Wang's ancestor. All that he gathered when he led the Manchu hordes to the Peacock Throne of China. And for a thousand years it has been added to until now it fills a room many times the size of this tent. If we can secure this treasure we can rule the north after defeating our late master Len Yu and his allies. Think of the men it would buy, the ships, the power it—"

Chung laughed. "Wait, War Brother. We have not as yet secured it. At the moment we are sitting here, having disobeyed orders given by one with whom disobedience means death. All men know that the treasure is there—and also that it is guarded by Manchu swords. The city of Ningyuan is built inside a mountain."

"I know how the city is built. I also know what is in the city besides the treasure. And to secure that something, the War Lord of the Irenkha will become our ally."

"Something that will make the great Chia Wang of the Irenkha our ally! Lie down and rest, War Brother. You rave as if you were under the knives of Ling-chih!"

"No, I am sane. As you say, it is like the tiger taking wolves as allies. Yet, if the wolf can point the way to a kill for the tiger, will not the tiger heed—and it may be, let the wolf have a bone?"

"It may be. But who will be the wolf to approach the tiger of the Irenkha? That one is very liable to be bitten in two by Chia Wang before he can speak!"

"I will be the wolf," answered Shao Wu, more calmly than he felt. "If I win, unlimited gold with which to buy power is mine.

If I fail, I will ascend on the dragon's back to join my venerable ancestors. I say that the War Lord of the Irenkha will take the city of Ningyuan for us. We will lead the regiment to the north at once."

"And if he does, will he give us the treasure? Or will the Head of the House of Chia, War Lord of the Irenkha Mountains, merely laugh and add it to his own? Speak plainly, Shao Wu. I do not understand."

"Chia Wang will agree before the city is taken that he is to take the one thing he covets and that the rest belongs to us. He is old and desires no more treasure or cities to rule over."

Chung smiled. "You are a colonel and I a lieutenant-colonel of a line regiment—and we go to make the War Lord of the Irenkha our ally in taking cities. And yet—it may be that the gods will smile upon us. Tell me of this wonderful tiling that will make the tiger and the wolf allies and ward off the tiger's teeth. I, your War Brother, am with you in this matter."

CHAPTER III

THE FENCE OF LEAD

A TIGHT, COMPACT column of Altai Mountain Tartars rode down one of the passes of the Thian Shan Range. They were big men, dressed in sheepskin mostly, and their mounts were shaggy mountain ponies. With them were the women and children of the tribe.

They rode warily, with scouts far ahead and on the sides. A rear guard trotted some hundred yards behind the main column. All of them carried swords, some lances and some had carbines in their saddle boots. They rode ready to receive or offer an attack, and there was no fear in the eagle-beaked faces or in the keen eyes.

The Tartar *haduagy*, or chief captain, knew that he was getting close to where others had been halted by machine gun fire; and he called in his advance patrols. He did not want to run the chance that any of them would suddenly come on the defenders of the pass and kill or get killed. That would start a blood feud, which was the last thing in the world he wanted—at this particular minute.

As the patrols joined the main column, a well-built, lithe colored man with the silver bar of a first lieutenant on the shoulder of his tunic, stood up from where he had been crouching beside a machine gun, looking down at the column through narrowed lids.

"All right, Squint-eye," he ordered. "Put de fence up for de gent'mum."

"An' Ah hopes to de good Lawd dat dey tries to jump it," muttered the machine gunner as he pressed the trigger of a Browning. "We ain't had no fight since—"

A line of dust, dirt and small pebbles jumped up about fifty feet ahead of the Tartars, as straight across the pass as if laid down with a ruler, from where the steep hills came down on one side to the other. It ordered, in language known to fighting men the world over, "Halt!"

The Tartar leader held up his right arm, pulling in his pony as his arm went up. The column behind him promptly reined in their mounts, their eyes searching the side of the hill ahead on the right to see where the *rat-tat-tat-tat!* was coming from.

"Cease firin'," commanded First Lieutenant Coudray, who had been first sergeant of Troop B in the Thirty-first U.S. Cavalry. "Yo', Squint-eye! Does yo' heah me? Quit wastin' dat ammunition or Ah busts yo' in de jaw!" Most of the time "Yaller" Coudray forgot that he was a lieutenant, reverting back to his sergeant days. He was called "Yaller" because of his color and not because of his nerve, which was chilled steel.

Squint-eye reluctantly released the trigger. "Ah nevah did see such a bunch of quittahs," he grumbled. "Only ones dat will be 'commodatin' enough to give us a fight is de Afghan gent'mum."

"Yo' collects all de fight yo' is lookin' for, monkey-face," Yaller announced, "and dat frum me, don't yo' git at de cleanin' of dat gun. Dog-gone, dare goes a flag of truce. Now Ah got to go down dis hill. Come on, Sergeant Moss, and yo', Troopah Johnson, and yo', Happy. Us goes down and says 'howdy' to de wild men."

"Ask 'em iffen de barbahs is all on strike wheah dey lives," said Squint-eye, still fussy because the Tartar column would not obligingly charge up against his machine gun. "Ah nevah did see such whiskahs in mah life."

"Dat's because yo' ain't been no-wheah, Misto' Squint-eye," some one answered from the next gun and the colored men within hearing laughed.

They had gladly left whatever they had been doing since "gittin' out of de army" to serve under the lean, blue-eyed Mississippian, who to them was "de Capt'n." They never forgot that they were cavalry, and the non-coms wore the yellow stripes. All bugle calls were cavalry calls and no matter how much they fought on foot, it was always "Troop mount" when Highnote the bugler sounded off.

YALLER, WITH the two troopers and Sergeant Moss, who was called "Delicate" because he was almost as big and strong as an elephant, walked up to within fifty feet of the head of the Tartar column, then halted. As they did, machine guns on both left and right hills sent a line of steel-jacketed bullets along the column, not a foot out from the elbows of the horsemen on the outside. It was a polite reminder that treachery of any kind would be promptly punished.

The leader of the Tartars with two others, spurred their ponies forward until within three feet, then halted. The *haduagy* was an old man, and so was one of his companions. The third was much younger. They stared at the colored men whose exploits were talked of around a thousand hill-country camp fires; and the Tartars were looking at them as one fighting man looks at another. Finally the old leader grunted and said something in Pushtu, the universal language of the border.

"Ah don't understand much of dat talk," Yaller answered. "Us don't speak nothin' but 'Merican, Misto' Wildman." The tone was courteous.

The Tartar turned to the young man and snarled an order. The young man had been looking at the holstered .45s and Springfield rifles.

"I spike—spooch—I say Engleesh," he announced, "weeth Engleesh army in the Hind. The *haduagy* of the Altai Mountain Tartars, Vyatka, weesh to—ask if you am—is—if you be men of the Lady Anna Guilai, who was—is child of Colonel Ladislaw Guilai, *haduagy* of all Tartars?"

"If us is whut? Dog-gone iffen Ah can understand him; can yo', Del'cate?"

"Certainly Ah understand de gent'mum. Where is yo' understandin' gone, Yaller—Ah mean, Lieutenant? He say is us Miss Anna's men? Yo' has forgot dat Miss Anna was named dat Gill-somepin' before she married de Capt'n."

"Dogged iffen Ah didn't... Yes, suh, Misto' Wildman. Us is Miss Anna's men and proud of it. Whut-all can us do for yo'?"

The young man translated that and got a curt answer from the Tartar *haduagy*.

"The *haduagy* weesh to be taken in—he weeshed to be taken to the Lady Anna Guilai. It is for—I cannot say eet—it is—the Lady Anna came—once—was once lived weeth thees tribe, and the *haduagy* weesh to see her who was hees—the child of hees foster brother."

"Well, dog-gone! Is yo' Miss Anna's fostah brothahs, Misto' Wildman? Yo' is sure welcome. Yes, suh, Miss Anna done told us about de days when she was a little bitty baby wid de Tartahs. Is yo' de gent'mum dat taught her de saber and how to ride?"

The interpreter didn't get more than a third of that but he did understand enough to tell Vyatka that the big colored men were friendly and would lead him to the Lady Anna. The old Tartar grunted and said something.

"He wishes to know eef his people can also—came—ride weeth him—or will they remain here?"

"Tell him to bring 'em along iffen he wants to," answered Yaller royally. "Maybe-so Miss Anna like to see dem again. But tell him dis, an' be shuah dat yo' gets it right, boy. Tell him us knows dat yo' is wildmen. And tell him dat us is wildah, even doesn't us wear whiskahs. Tell him to give ordahs dat his men keep dare hands away frum dare pig-stickahs, 'cause us gets awful wild and bites, does us see wildmen doin' dat."

The interpreter was sunk long before Yaller got through and was blinking his eyes, but he caught the idea that the big colored men was warning them not to start anything.

The *haduagy* grunted as he heard the translation, then nodded.

"Fair enough," Yaller said. "Tell him to move his outfit to dat little creek yondah and wait fo' us. Ah sends an escort wid him to Miss Anna."

CHAPTER IV

THE TARTAR EMBASSY

ANNA GUILAI NORCROSS sat on a rug placed on the concrete top of a machine gun "pill-box." She was beautiful, with the pure-blooded Magyar type of beauty. Her bronzed hair, parted in the middle, almost concealed two perfect little ears. Her skin was the texture and richness in color of a magnolia blossom. Her eyes were gray-blue and her faultless body tapered down to slender ankles and little arched feet.

Her eyes proved that she ran true to the spirit of the Magyars also. They showed firmness of character, common sense, and the undaunted courage of her race.

Anna had greeted the Tartars with a great feast and had

made much of them. Now, as Vyatka finished a long oration, she answered promptly:

"I speak for my Lord Captain John Norcross as well as for myself. I say that an offer of assistance from the Altai Tartars is one that honors the one receiving it. Six hundred Altai swords are better than ten times that many thousand of any other race. My Lord John will be glad that the women and children of the Altai are here with me, so that the Tartar swords may fight joyfully, knowing that if they fall their loved ones are safe.

"The Lord John is in Shanghai with the Manchu Lord T'ang Wang. When he returns he will say as I say, and welcome you as one fighting man welcomes another whom he honors. I will send for Lieutenant Coudray and give orders that quarters be prepared for you."

There was a sentry pacing back and forth near one of the guns, and Anna called, "Mose!"

The big, lean colored man whirled around, his rifle dropping from his shoulder to "ready."

"Yas, ma'am, Miss Anna."

"Mose, pass the word, Lieutenant Coudray to report to me here."

"Yas, ma'am, Miss Anna," and Mose Dinwiddie Early double-timed it to the end of his beat. When he got there he began shouting, "Co'p'ral of de guard! Co'p'ral of de guard! Post numbah nine, co'p'ral of de guard!"

The Tartars listened as call after call went up from places where they could see no men.

"Co'p'ral of de guard, post numbah nine!"

The eyes of the Tartar Khan and his sub-chiefs who sat with him were wide. Anna's exquisite lips curved up a little as she saw the Tartars look at every inch of the returning Mose and his equipment. She knew they were sizing him up as a fighting man. Finally Vyatka grunted and asked:

"How many men has your Lord such as those who led us here and this one?"

"Three hundred."

"Are they his slaves?"

"No, *haduagy*. They are free men who once served under him when he was a captain in the army of his country, America."

"America? I have heard of that country."

Anna added, "My Lord commanded horsemen in a regiment composed of black men led by officers who were white men. See, *haduagy*, these black men are those who served under him, and afterwards, when my Lord had resigned from the army, came with him to China."

"COULD THEY leave the army at will?" asked the Tartar Nogai, who was a noted foray leader.

"No. Their service had expired, those who came first. Others came when they were free. See, brother, they must serve a certain number of years—afterwards they may do as they wish. My Lord John's men came with him because they love him. It is as if—it may be that this will paint the picture for you, you who know of the Manchus. The Lord John is to them as the Head of their House."

"They maintain their army discipline?" Nogai went on. He had become very much interested in the way the colored men had conducted themselves on the march and when they arrived at the mountain.

"Yes, brother. In all ways the same as if they were still in the army. They receive pay and at their homes is deposited a certain sum of money to be paid to their relations if they fall. At any time they may return to America." Anna smiled as she added, "But very few of them have gone back. It is harder for my Lord John to prevent others from Troop B and the rest of the troops of his regiment from coming over here. They love a fight as the Altai Tartars do—can I say more, O fathers and brothers?"

The Tartars smiled grimly. There was no necessity of Anna's saying more.

"We have heard of how they fight," answered Vyatka. "Did

your Lord bring them here to conquer China? If he did, we of the Altai will ride stirrup to stirrup with them."

"No. He brought them with him to shoot his way to something he was asked to get by one of the most powerful War Lords in the world—the great American millionaire Henry Landess."

"Did he get it?" asked Nogai.

"Yes—and also helped put the Manchu Princess Ch'enyaun back on her throne. In Ningyuan he met me, your little one, and there we were married. Since then he has helped defend this territory from all who came to take it."

Vyatka grunted and said, "Now we of the Altai will help him do it."

Anna knew after Vyatka said that that she had led them from the position of asking a favor to that of offering assistance.

"It is only just that you should," she answered solemnly. "I am the much honored and loved wife of this War Lord of America, and I also am of the Altai Tartars. To whom could I turn for help in time of need but to my foster fathers and brothers? And to whom should the Altai Tartars render it more quickly than to me, the daughter of their *haduagy*, who now looks down from where he rests with the gods and smiles as he sees the ones he led to battle flash their shining swords between her and the curs who press close?"

"Our swords will ring you with steel, little daughter," shouted Vyatka, rising as did the rest. Now they had forgotten that they came seeking asylum for their loved ones, just as Anna Norcross had meant that they should. They were happy, bound to her with the chains of loyalty and praise. Blood, the world over, is indeed thicker than water.

"Now may I once more smile and be at ease," Anna answered solemnly.

CHAPTER V

A MANCHU NEVER FORGETS

THE HOLD OF the junk was dark, almost without air, evil-smelling and slimy with dirty river water that seeped through rotten timbers.

The blow that had sent Captain Norcross to the deck had been a glancing one. Hard enough to put him out but not delivered so as to cut his head. The Chinaman who used the rifle had not cared whether it cut or fractured the skull; it was only by chance that the rifle butt slanted up.

Now, as Captain Norcross opened his eyes and stirred, he heard a whisper close to his right ear: "Is de Capt'n 'wake?"

"Yes," he answered softly. "Is that you, Skinnay?"

"Yes, suh. Mah goodness, Ah'm glad dat de Capt'n ain't—"

"Hold it, boy. Are you hurt?"

"No, suh, Capt'n. Mah haid is sore, dat's all."

"Where are the rest?"

"Right heah, Capt'n. Ah been rollin' 'round an' Ah felt 'em. Troopah Fostah am still out. Dat boy shuah took him some beatin' wid dem rifle butts, Capt'n."

"Are they all tied?"

"Yas, suh. Misto' T'ang Wang spoke to me when Ah rolled ovah by—"

"I am awake, elder brother," T'ang Wang said from the darkness. "Speak softly. There are four guarding."

"Are you hurt, T'ang Wang?" Norcross said quickly.

"No, not seriously. My head is cut but I do not think badly."

"Can you see the guards?"

"Dimly, John. They sit on the steps that lead down here."

"How far away, T'ang Wang?"

"About twenty feet, elder brother. I have been watching them for some time. They have been smoking opium and are relaxed."

There was a ship's lantern hanging near the steps but the light it gave out was very feeble. It had not been cleaned nor had the wick been trimmed for a long time. The guards could not see as far as the prisoners, but they knew that the only way out was up the steps and they also knew the men they guarded were bound, so they sat on the steps at ease, swords across their laps.

"Ease down behind me, Skinnay," Norcross ordered, "and bite the rope apart that binds my hands."

"Yas, suh, Capt'n, mah teeth am—"

"Show me what they are. Get busy, boy."

T'ang Wang smiled in the darkness, "We take the junk, honorable elder brother?"

"We'll make a try for it," answered Norcross, sensing the smile and returning it, although he could not see T'ang Wang's face.

Buck Foster's head was lying close to where Skinnay Martin was chewing on the rope. He came to, tried to sit up, couldn't make it, and slumped back. As his brain cleared, he heard Skinnay's muffled remarks to the rope as his firm white teeth went into it:

"Ah gits yo', Misto' Rope. Come heah to me. Dat does fo' yo'. Mah Lord, how yo' does taste. An' dat does for *yo*'," as the strands parted.

Buck inched over. "Whut de dickens is yo' doin', Skinnay?"

"Hush dat bellow, yo' big ape. Ah'm bitin' de Capt'n free," and Skinnay continued the operation.

"Dog-gone! Wheah-at is us, Skinnay? Git away an' gimme a bite. Ah bites it through in one bite."

"Quiet, Buck," Norcross whispered. "Lie still."

Skinnay chewed a little more and then Captain Norcross brought his hands around, free.

"**ROLL CLOSER** to me, T'ang Wang," he ordered. "No— wait a minute until I get some blood circulating in my hands."

"May I speak and live?" he asked the War Lord.

"Capt'n, please, suh," Skinnay Martin whispered, trying to clear his mouth of shreds of the rope at the same time, "Ah got mah razah undah mah left arm in a sheath. Dem Chinks didn't find it, 'cause Ah can still feel it. If de Capt'n reach undah mah shirt, de Capt'n can reach it. Dog-gone de taste of dat dog-gone rope in mah—"

"Silence. Turn to the right a little. You'll get nine million years K.P. for packing a razor, you no-'count scoundrel," but there was that in Norcross's voice that made Skinnay grin joyously.

"Quiet for a minute," T'ang Wang warned. "One of the guards rises and looks this way."

They froze. The Manchu who had gone down first, struggled to a half-sitting position and began to babble about green fields and snow-clad mountain tops.

The guard walked over to where the light stopped and listened. "So it was you I heard, Manchu wolf. Where is your sharp sword, O master swordsman of the world? Why do you not get up and slay me? Your claws have been clipped, wolf, and your fangs drawn. Soon I will listen to your screams as we flay you. Be still, dog of the North, or my sword will cut the tongue from your mouth."

He went back to the steps as the Manchu sank back to the deck. "I thought I heard a voice," the guard said to his fellows as he sat down.

In a few minutes Norcross touched T'ang Wang who turned over on his stomach. The keen razor blade severed his bonds, then those of Skinnay Martin and Buck Foster. As Norcross eased back T'ang Wang whispered, "Hand me the razor, John. I can reach my little brothers."

"Better not loosen the one who is delirious," Norcross answered softly as he guided T'ang Wang's hand to the razor. "He might start—"

"It was a Manchu trick, John. He is sane. Both of them are ready as soon as the ropes are cut. Will you give the word? Once we gain the deck with swords in our hands we will lesson these mongrels in spite of their rifles."

"What is Chinese for 'I am the demon-god,' T'ang Wang?"

"What is—has your clever brain gone into the far places?"

"No. Skinnay Martin had a box of sulphur matches in his shirt pocket. I felt them reaching for the razor. I'm going to rub the phosphorus on my face and hands, and be the demon-god. It may jar them loose from their swords. Tell me the Chinese. No—wait, as I rise and rush forward, you shout 'I am the demon-god and have come for you.'"

The guards were sitting on the third and fourth steps, two men to a step. They were awake, but not at all alert. There was no way of telling time in the hold, and Captain Norcross and the rest did not know whether it was day or night, or how long they had been there. As a matter of fact it was about two o'clock in the morning. Since the Manchu who had babbled of snow-clad hills had become quiet, the guards had not even looked toward the place where the prisoners lay.

Suddenly a snarling, rasping voice shouted from the darkness: "I am the demon-god come to take your foul spirits to the lowest hell!"

THE GUARDS looked up and saw in the darkness a face and a pair of hands that glowed with unearthly fire. And the face and hands were coming straight at them.

Braver men than the opium-addled Chinese would have dropped whatever they were holding at the shock of it. The Chinese rose, their swords falling from their laps, and as one man tried to get up the steps. One made it, the rest falling back down, jabbering in an ecstasy of terror. Before they landed at the bottom of the steps, iron hands closed mercilessly around their throats.

The one guard who made the deck ran to the side and jumped overboard, screaming as he did, "The demon-god comes! The demon-god comes!"

Most of the crew were on deck, two at the steering oar, a good many asleep near the mast, some more in the bow, and some scattered around the deck.

Their rifles were in racks at the mast and along the sides. Most of them had swords hanging from belts or tucked in sashes. It was fairly dark, not as dark as it was in the hold, but far from light. The yells of the man who had jumped overboard woke the majority of them up and they got to their feet.

Those in the bow, who had been near the companionway leading below, had no time even to draw their swords before the three Manchus were on them. T'ang Wang, best swordsman in the Orient, was a little ahead, then the other two, both master swordsmen.

Behind them came a figure whose hands and face seemed made of flames. And back of the weird figure were the two big black men who had wrought so much damage before they were laid unconscious on the deck.

The Chinese had little time left to see anything. Three swords flashed left and right, in the death-dealing upward stroke of the Manchu. The men in the bow of the junk died before they could even start to defend themselves.

T'ang Wang had said, as Captain Norcross started up the

steps: "Let us go first, elder brother. There is an insult to be wiped out."

Norcross had stepped back and T'ang Wang and the two Manchus had gone first. Now, as the Chinese fell away and those amidships drew their swords or ran to the rifle racks, he stepped up into line with the Manchus. As he did, Skinnay Martin and Buck Foster stooped and drew the swords from the belts of two of the dead men. Captain Norcross was a good man with a saber and both Skinnay and Buck had the saber manual at their finger-tips.

"Spread out," Norcross shouted. "Across the deck! You birds stay in line. Come on!"

They charged straight aft, T'ang Wang and Norcross in the center, the two Manchus on T'ang Wang's right and the two colored men on Captain Norcross's left. The junk was not very large, having about a twenty-foot beam and a hundred feet of length. The deck was more or less cluttered up with different things, including five or six old muzzle-loading cannon.

Some of the crew stood to meet the charge and others fled, seeking refuge behind the cannon or behind anything else they could reach. Here were no weaponless men to beat down with rifle butts, but Manchus with swords in their hands and the big black men whose grip was like that of a brown bear. And the figure whose face and hands were made of fire must be a demon called up by the dreaded Manchus.

The men who had run to the rifle racks fumbled with the catches and only one or two succeeded in getting the rifles loose. Before they could use them the two colored men were on top of them.

SKINNAY MARTIN dropped the sword and picked up a rifle. "Dis am mah dish," he crowed as he clubbed it.

The captain of the junk had been below when it started and now came on deck with two of the junk's officers.

T'ang Wang and the two Manchus broke the line and ran to meet them. More Chinese were jumping overboard, the river being no more than half a mile wide. Norcross with Skinnay and Buck went through to the steering oar, the two Chinese there unloading the second they saw what was coming.

T'ang Wang stopped as he neared the captain of the junk, his bloody sword held point down and seemingly loose in his hand.

"You mentioned that you did not care what I intended to do, jackal," the Manchu said smoothly. "I now intend to send your base spirit down!"

The captain saw that his junk had been taken and knew that unless he could also win to the side he would die.

"At them!" he yelled, raising his sword and rushing at T'ang Wang. "If we slay them we may—*aie!*"

T'ang Wang's body had swerved to the right and as it did, the sword that had been pointed down, came up in a half circle. The junk captain fell, half cut in two. The two ship's officers closed in and there was a flurry of sword-blades for a moment. They were good swordsmen, but that was not enough to be when standing up to Manchu swordplay. They fell across the captain of the junk as Norcross reached the steering oar.

T'ang Wang went over to a wounded man and lifted him to his feet. "Where are we, mongrel?" he snarled.

"Off Ho-ka-san, mighty one," the man gasped. "See—the lights still show."

T'ang Wang eased him back on the deck and walked to where Norcross was standing.

"The lights on shore are those of Ho-ka-san, elder brother. One of the House of Nurhachu is War Lord of the city. It may be that I can steer this junk in. If any live they are now hiding and can be found after we arrive."

"Capt'n, please, suh, can Ah hold de oar?" Skinnay asked. "Ah can steer dis boat. Ah used to sail all de time down in South Ca'lina."

"Ah steered many a boat, Capt'n, please, suh," Buck Foster announced, glaring at Skinnay. "Long befo' Troopah Martin evah—"

"Both of you no-'count scoundrels get on it," Norcross said. "It takes two men. T'ang Wang, I don't know how you feel, but I'm right sick. It may be this phosphorus."

T'ang Wang had been looking at the two Manchus who were searching the deck like a couple of fox terriers after rats in a woodshed. He turned and smiled at Norcross.

"I will arrange a place so that you may lie down, John." Skinnay Martin watched the proud Manchu noble arrange a spare sail that had been lying on the deck.

"Misto' T'ang Wang think a lot of de Capt'n, don't he?" Skinnay muttered.

"Why shouldn't he, monkey-face?" Buck retorted. "Ain't yo' heahed yet dat de Capt'n is Misto' T'ang Wang's honahble eldah brothah? Yo' don't know nothin'—yo' nevah did know nothin'—an' you' nevah will know—Bear to de right! To de right! Mah goodness, did yo' evah see a boat befo'?"

By dint of much maneuvering and telling each other what to do and what not to do, Skinnay and Buck finally brought the junk alongside a little pier at Ho-ka-san. They had found out in a very few moments after taking hold of the steering oar that sailing a catboat or a bugeye in Southern waters, and making an unwieldy old junk hold its course, was something else again.

ON THE pier was drawn up a company of soldiers, officers standing close to where the junk would touch. As it scraped along the side one of the officers, a young man of about twenty-one or two, shouted:

"Do not cast lines over! There is nothing here for you dogs but hot lead and cold steel."

Then he saw T'ang Wang who had come to the side.

"You, elder brother? Ho! An honor guard for the leader of swords for the Princess Ch'enyaun! It is the Lord T'ang Wang of the House of Nurhachu," and without waiting for the junk to be made fast or the honor guard formed, he ran forward and jumped on board.

When he got to T'ang Wang, he halted and bowed very low,

hand on swordhilt. He was Taio K'ai, War Lord of Ho-ka-san. A man of Young China, educated in Germany, full of modern methods and ways from the top of his close-cropped head to the tips of his toes, incased in riding boots.

He was in modern uniform with Sam Browne belt and all— yet the moment he saw the blood-caked head of T'ang Wang, all his training sloughed away instantly, and he became Taio K'ai, not a War Lord in command of a city, but a cadet of the House of Nurhachu. A cadet greeting a noble of his House who stood second only to the Head. Training is good and modern ways may be better, but once a Manchu, always a Manchu, and Taio K'ai ran true to blood.

"If you can find in the unbounded charity of your resplendent heart forgiveness for the manner in which I greeted you, O honorable elder brother," he said as he straightened up, "it will be but another instance of your magnificent graciousness."

"I forgive you, little brother," T'ang Wang answered gravely. "You did not know that I was here, worthy cadet of the House of Nurhachu. Word has come to us in the north of your excellent swordplay. Call my attention to the matter before I depart so that I may witness it."

The honor guard led by all the officers had come on board and this last from T'ang Wang was deliberate praise for Taio K'ai in front of his men.

The young Manchu bowed again and tried to keep his face impassive. He succeeded with his lips, but could not shut the joy out of his eyes. He knew, and was aware that his officers knew, that the Manchu Lord T'ang Wang was the best swordsman in the Orient where swordsmen are many and that a word of praise from him meant much, even if this were now the day of "Young China."

Captain Norcross had stepped back as Taio K'ai bowed to T'ang Wang. Now T'ang Wang turned to him and said formally: "Captain Norcross, may I have the honor of presenting Taio K'ai, a cadet and noble of the House of Nurhachu? Taio K'ai, this gentleman is Captain John Norcross who is to the Princess Ch'enyaun and myself, our honorable elder brother. The House of Nurhachu is deep in the debt of Captain Norcross."

Both Norcross and Taio K'ai bowed. Norcross had been able to get some of the phosphorus off his face and hands, but not all of it, and was still a little ill, but there was a smile on his lips and in his blue eyes as he bowed to Taio K'ai.

"One came from Ningyuan, elder brother, with many tales of your prowess and that of the men who fight under you," said the officer. "I am honored far beyond my deserts by the privilege granted me to bow before you."

"You may also have the honor of escorting us to your palace without further ceremony," T'ang Wang said with a smile. "We are very much in need of rest and—other things."

WHEN THE junk reached the pier it was about four o'clock in the morning and it was noon when Norcross and T'ang Wang, after baths and the putting on of clean clothes, sat with Taio K'ai at a table. The soft-footed servants had cleared it and now it held wines and liquors. T'ang Wang had told Taio K'ai of the escape from Peking, the capture at the inn, and what had happened on the junk.

"So that is why a detachment of Len Yu's men stopped here some days ago," Taio-K'ai said. "The officer told of the search for some fleeing men. It was well for him that he did not mention names, elder brothers. I would have lessoned him in regard to searching for Manchus. He told of a party being traced from Peking through spies of Len Yu at the gates."

"It may be that the House of Nurhachu will be able to call his attention to it at some future time," T'ang Wang answered smoothly. "At the moment there are more important matters to discuss, Taio K'ai. We flew from Ningyuan to Shanghai in airships sent to Captain Norcross by one in America who is in his debt. It is in my mind that we may now go to Shanghai with sufficient men to meet any attempt by Len Yu to stop us."

"There are here in Ho-ka-san," Taio K'ai said, his eyes shining, "some three hundred of Manchu blood. Truly, elder brother, we can go to Shanghai and retake the planes if Len Yu has them."

"He probably only posted a guard at the air field," Norcross said, "and on word arriving of our capture, withdrew that. His agents were instructed to stop us taking off in some way. If we can reach Shanghai, now we know what he is up to, we won't have much trouble getting the planes."

"No, John," T'ang Wang said softly. "There will be—no—trouble… And soon we will—fly back to—Ning—"

Norcross had turned in his chair to look at T'ang Wang, and now he caught him in his arms as the Manchu pitched face foremost to the table.

Tenderly they carried him to the private apartments of Taio K'ai. The brave Manchu had been hit harder than perhaps even he realized. The best physicians of Ho-ka-san saw that T'ang Wang lay at death's door.

"If he dies," the cadet of the House of Nurhachu warned them coldly, "he does not die alone."

But the utmost skill of the physicians could do no more than keep life in his body. For days, weeks, T'ang Wang lay there between life and death, with John Norcross and Taio K'ai constant attendants at his bedside. Every day increased the danger that the Mandarin Len Yu would find and attack them, or would hopelessly block their plans to regain the airplanes. But Norcross had no thought of that, as he sat beside the elaborate silken coverings over T'ang Wang's body.

CHAPTER VI

THE SLEEPING TIGER WAKES

THE HEREDITARY PRINCE of the House of Chia, War Lord of the Irenkha-birga Mountains, did not look much like a War Lord. Chia Wang looked more like a nice, fat old gentle-man who loved to eat sweets and to take many naps.

But Colonel Shao Wu, who had finally reached the dais on which sat that War Lord of the west, was not at all misled by appearances. He knew that at Chia Wang's command fifty thou-sand men could and would take the field—men who obeyed him as their "elder brother."

There were no men who fought for the War Lord of the Irenkha as mercenaries. They fought at his command because he was the Head of the House of Chia, even as their ancestors had fought for his for a thousand years B.C., and ever since. They held in a ring of steel the vast territory of the Irenkha range and the miles that reached to the river Tarim—and Chia Wang dozed at will or ate gingered candy and listened to the singing girls.

"You have my permission to speak, little brother," Chia Wang said sleepily as he reached for a piece of candy.

"May I speak frankly and live, O Head of the all-powerful House of Chia?" asked Shao Wu with a low bow.

"You may," answered Chia Wang courteously.

"It is this: I have learned where the Scroll of your House is."

Old Chia Wang came awake with a suddenness that belied his sleepiness. It vanished from his face and eyes. Now he was all Chinese War Lord. "What did you say?" he snarled.

"I said, O mighty one, that I know where the Scroll of your unequaled House is now resting among the trophies in the palace of a Manchu."

"You dare mention, in my presence, the Scroll of the House of Chia?" snarled Chia Wang. "Truly this Young China is made up of fools. Know that here in the northwest we still have the knives to give Ling-chih and the oil to boil. What is to prevent my ordering that you be sent to the House of Punishment?"

"There is nothing that I could do that could prevent it, leader of millions," Shao Wu answered, a good deal more calmly than he felt. "I came in all friendliness, trusting to your known honor and justness."

"It is not well to trust too far, O Shao Wu. I let you live until I question you. How long you will live afterward depends upon your answers."

Chia Wang leaned back in his chair, his face once more impassive. There was silence in the room for a full minute. Shao Wu stood at attention. It spoke well for his courage that he stood with face as impassive as Chia.

FINALLY THE old War Lord spoke, as if beginning a story:

"Many years ago, the Manchu Prince Yuan Szu, the father of the Princess Ch'enyaun who now rules Ningyuan, attacked me in my city of Pingyang. It was because of a fancied insult. I was forced to flee hurriedly because I had not enough men there to withstand the charge of the Manchu swords. In the flight the ones entrusted with the safety of the golden Scroll of my House were slain and the Scroll was taken to the Prince Yuan Szu. This I tell you because of your statement, that you may be able to regain the scroll for me. If you fail, no matter where you may hide, the Irenkha-birga will reach out and bring you here for the torturers to play with. Is that plain to you, little brother?"

"Yes," Shao Wu answered. "It is very plain, all-powerful one."

"You of Young China," Chia Wang went on grimly, "seem to know nothing of the sacred things; but this you must know. The golden Scroll of a House is as the heart is to the body."

"I know, magnificent one," Shao Wu said softly. "Although of Young China, I know."

"Twice I sent my army against Ningyuan," Chia Wang went on, "and twice I was beaten back by Manchu swords. Never yet have the War Lords of the Irenkha been able to prevail against them. Against any War Lord in China, yes—but against the Manchu, no. Then I tried to regain the Scroll, offering cities and treasure for it, but always the Prince Yuan Szu replied that he had nothing for sale and if I wanted the Scroll, to cut my way to it. That the insult given him remained dim while the Scroll rested in Ningyuan.

"The Manchu never forgets, little brother. Never forgets an injury or a favor. To the end of time he and his will avenge or repay. Against any other I could have prevailed. My little brothers are many and their lives belong to me. Truly these Manchus are born devils. Again and again have I tried to regain the Scroll by stealth, but each time I have been thwarted.

"This I tell you, O Shao Wu, to explain why the order was issued that to speak of the Scroll meant death by torture. To you, little brother, I am but a fat, sleepy old man, content to sit and eat and sleep the hours away—No, do not interrupt me. That is another bad habit of Young China. It is true that I am fat, and it is true that I sleep to forget.

"But know this, neat little child who wears the uniform of the new soldier!" he burst out. "Inside this gross body there dwells a fierce hungry tiger, crouched always, tensed to spring. This I say to you: Show me the way to restore the Scroll of my House to its rightful place, and—you may name the reward. If you wish cities to rule over—gold and jewels—regiments to fight for you—or all of them, they are yours. I cannot say on the honor of my House because until the Scroll is regained, where is the honor of the House of Chia?"

"What you have deigned to tell me, O venerable one, has sunk deep into my heart," answered Shao Wu. "If you will allow, all-powerful one, I will tell you how you may regain the Scroll of the House of Chia."

"Speak—and to the point."

"MY WAR Brother Chung and I have one thousand trained men that we can use to train others. Men trained in the new rules of the war game. Men armed with the latest rifles whose bullets are propelled by high explosive powder. Men who will answer shot for shot the black men of the American who fights for the Princess Ch'enyaun.

"Then why have you come to the North, to me?" Chia Wang asked blandly.

"For this, War Lord: we have not men enough to hold

the lines that must reach from the Thian Shan Range below Ningyuan, around that city, and around Taiyaun, then to the mountain of Szu and back up the Thian Shan. These besieging lines must be strong enough to prevent reënforcements reaching the Princess Ch'enyaun from other Manchu War Lords in the south and east, if they come to her assistance. The Lord T'ang Wang and the American Captain Norcross are now in Peking, held as prisoners by the Mandarin Len Yu. He plans to make them surrender the Thian Shan and the cities. If he does, the Irenkha-birga will pay heavily for anything he finds there."

"That is true. Now is indeed the time to strike. This person Len Yu who calls himself a general will find his way to the north barred by the Irenkha."

"We need heavy guns and airplanes that can drop bombs. That is why I have come to you, War Lord of the Irenkha. Give us your men to form the lines, and money for heavier guns and planes—and we will take Ningyuan for you."

"I will take the field once more with my little brothers. You may send to me the men who know the war game as it is played to-day, and my little brothers will obey them. I will form the lines and hold them and also will furnish men to take the city of Ningyuan. You may have as many heavy guns and ships that fly as you wish. I want to ride into Ningyuan at the head of the men of my House. After I have secured the Scroll, you may do as you wish with the city."

"It shall be as you order," answered Shao Wu, his eyes shining.

"And if you do not take the city—with the trained men, the new guns, and ships of the air—then I, Chia Wang, War Lord of the Irenkha-birga, will place you on a high scaffold and give you Ling-chih so that all may see what happens to boasters."

"That also shall be as you order, Lord."

"Truly it will, little brother. Return to me here in the morning, and we will plan. You have my permission to go."

CHAPTER VII

THE TROOP RIDES

THE LOVELY MAGYAR wife of Captain John Norcross sat at breakfast on one of the balconies of the stone house built on top of their Mountain of Szu. The mountain was a big one, miles in circumference at its base and even at the top, where, as Anna had said, "it looks as if there were great castles built by the heroes of old."

There was over a mile where the massive rocks lifted their heads. Norcross had connected many of them with concrete and between two of them a stone house had been built. Henry Landess, the millionaire for whom Norcross had first come to China, loved Norcross as a son, and he also loved the beautiful Magyar girl Norcross had married. On his return to the States after his second visit to China, Landess had sent shipload after shipload of everything he could think of that would add to the comfort and modernization of the Mountain of Szu—and also its impregnability against attack.

With the Lady Anne were several of the little Tartar children. When first Vyatka's Altai Mountain tribe had come to the Mountain of Szu, to seek the protection of Lady Anna, the children had regarded the big black men out of solemn, wide-opened eyes, their little hands clutching their mothers' skirts. It did not last long, this half-terrified wonder.

The Tartar tents had been pitched in the valleys and cañons where clear springs came from the ground, and now the children ran all over the place, if they were not perched on the shoulders of Troop B or carried in the crook of big black arms.

It was hard work keeping the Tartar boys away from the guns and finally Anna had ordered Lieutenant Coudray to detail several of the troopers as instructors and gave them a machine gun and a rapid fire one pound gun. It was amusing to see the lithe, keen-eyed little Tartars try to swagger along as the "ridahs" did, and to imitate them in other ways. Prompt demand had been made for khaki uniforms. Anna had smiled and ordered the troop tailor to make them. The tailor became the busiest man on the mountain—so much so that he had to have quite a few assistants.

The Tartars, once their women and children were safe, kept mostly in the lower reaches of the mountain, sallying gayly out on forays. Anna did not try to stop them. It was the only life they knew and now they led it without any gnawing fear in their hearts as to what was happening to their loved ones. The Tartar women had settled down, quite content, accepting what Anna Norcross did for them in the same spirit that they themselves had given her food and shelter in days gone by.

One of the little Tartar girls finished eating and climbed down from her chair. As she did so she announced: "When I am old, as you are now, Lady Anna, I will find me such a mountain as this, and also many black men to be my bodyguard."

"It may be that I can help you find it, O pearl of price," Anna answered gravely.

As she spoke, Yaller Coudray came out on the balcony. He halted and came to attention, then saluted.

"At ease, lieutenant," Anna said with a friendly little smile. Yaller would have had hard work maintaining his military attitude under any circumstances as the little Tartar girls threw themselves on him with little gurgles of delight. To them he was a wonderful playmate to be manhandled and petted or teased as they saw fit.

"Mah goodness, chillums," Yaller protested as two of them started to climb up his legs and others jumped from their chairs, catching hold wherever they lit on him, "quit dat, doggone it. Leggo mah eah! Ah turns into a big ol' bear in 'bout a minute and den Ah bites."

THE LITTLE girls didn't understand him and would have

paid no attention if they had. They were not in the slightest degree afraid of Yaller Coudray, former first sergeant of B Troop in the Regulars and now first lieutenant for Captain John Norcross. Yaller, who packed one hundred and eighty pounds of chilled steel body and who would fight anything at any time, was putty in the hands of a child, as were the rest of the Troop for that matter.

It was fully five minutes before any kind of order could be restored. And then it took a flash of genius on Anna's part to do it.

"Oh, I forgot to tell you, maidens of the Altai. The one who wears a white square cap and long white covering in front is making the candy that pulls out in long yellow ropes. It may be if you hurry the youths will not have eaten it all."

She meant Memphis, the ebony cook of the outfit. He had come to China with Norcross in the first contingent and had stayed there ever since—Memphis, long, lean, with a grim, saturnine old face, who carried himself and acted like a Zulu chieftain, and who would stop cooking any time to join in a fight. If no other weapon was handy, Memphis would meet the hurtling charge of Afghan or any other tribesman with a cleaver.

After the arrival of the Tartar children he had spent most of his time making molasses candy for them, delegating the cooking for the Troop to assistants.

The little girls knew whom she meant and the balcony cleared as if by magic.

"Mah goodness! Dem chillums is mighty quick wid dare— Ah begs Miss Anna's pardon," and Yaller came to attention again.

"It is granted. At ease, lieutenant. What is it that you wish to see me about?"

"Yes, ma'am, Miss Anna," Yaller answered as he relaxed. To all of Troop B "Miss Anna" was a friend at court and was to be loved and honored and obeyed, not only because she was "de

Capt'n's lady," but because they knew to the last man that Anna Norcross felt toward them as Captain John Norcross did.

"Dare is an officer from Ningyuan wid a message fo' yo', Miss Anna. Ah told him dat Ah would see will Miss Anna 'ceive him."

"Why, of course I will, lieutenant. Bring him in here."

Yaller saluted and left the balcony and as he did Anna smiled as she thought of the way the little Tartar girls had looked deep under the steel exterior and seen the warm heart—warm at least for them. Yaller was not noted very much in Troop B for being warm-hearted or soft-hearted, either.

In about five minutes, he came back with a young Manchu officer.

"Oh, it is you, Colonel Tu-tzu?" Anna greeted him with a smile as he made the ceremonious bow. "No, Lieutenant Coudray, do not go. It may be a matter that requires your attention. You have a message for me, Colonel Tu-tzu?"

"Yes, Lady of the Magyars and honored wife of the Lord Norcross. From the Princess Ch'enyaun, War Lord of Ningyuan and Taiyaun."

He bowed again as he handed Anna an envelope.

"I will read the message in your presence, Colonel Tu-tzu, and in yours, Lieutenant Coudray." As Anna read, her delicate nostrils flared out and her dainty lips tightened. Then as she looked at the impassive Manchu officer she asked, "You know of this matter, Colonel Tu-tzu?"

"Yes, resplendent one. I am of the Higher Council."

"I will read it to you, Lieutenant Coudray. 'The War Lord of the Irenkha-birga moves all his forces to attack. Already they have reached the River Tarim. Our Lords are away. Come with Troop B and help me drive the curs back to their northern kennels.'"

Yaller Coudray's eyes sparkled as he came to attention and saluted. "If Miss Anna gives de ordah, de Troop moves in an hour."

"My Tartars also. You will return to Ningyuan, Colonel

Tu-tzu, and deliver this message to the Princess Ch'enyaun: 'Anna Norcross will lead Troop B and the Altai Mountain Tartars to Ningyuan before the sun goes down to rest behind the hills.' You may depart, colonel."

The Manchu officer saluted and as he left the balcony Yaller Coudray walked with him to the doorway. There was a sentry on guard just outside and Yaller ordered: "De colonel is to be 'scorted to wheah-at his men am waiting." Then he came back to where Anna now stood.

"HOW MANY of Troop B must be left here to hold the mountain?" Anna asked. In her veins there ran the blood of conquerors, as in the veins of the Princess Ch'enyaun, and now she was a military chieftainess.

"To man de guns necessary to hold de paths leadin' up de mountain, thirty troopahs—wid de Chink 'munition carryahs. Dat don't mean holdin' de pass at de rivah, Miss Anna. Dat means dat no one can git up de mountain, is dare a millyun of dem."

"I see. How many of Troop B are fit for duty, not counting the thirty?"

"If Miss Anna please, dare am two hundred an' eight of dem—dat is, countin' de ones dat is in de guardhouse fo' diff'runt things."

"And in Ningyuan?"

"Fifty, Miss Anna. Dem dat de Capt'n detailed on de guns whut Misto' Landess sent."

"And in Taiyaun?"

"Twenty-five wid Brownin's and one-pound rapid-fiah guns, Miss Anna."

"Very well, lieutenant. We will leave thirty men here. I also will leave two hundred of my Tartars. How much ammunition is stored at Ningyuan?

"All de last shipload dat come when de guns did, Miss

Anna. Us don't need whut-all dare is dare to smack down dis Irene-Bridget dat is comin'— Ah begs Miss Anna's pardon."

"You have it, lieutenant," and Anna smiled a little. "I will leave the details to you, as my Lord John does. We will move as soon as you are ready. Will it be necessary to take any machine guns?"

"No, ma'am, Miss Anna. Dare is plenty at Ningyuan," he answered. "In one hour us will be ready, Miss Anna," and Lieutenant Coudray saluted.

Troop B rode toward Ningyuan through the Thian Shan range, two hundred and eight big colored men in perfect condition. Their khaki uniforms and equipment were the same as when they had served in the regular cavalry of the United States, even to the McClellan saddles. Their sabers were hooked on the left side of the saddle, their Springfield carbines in the carbine boot at right rear. There were army rifles with bayonets in the armories and when "de Troop" went on foot those were carried. But they were by training cavalry and they disdained bayonets when sabers were to be had. Each man rode with full cartridge belts from which hung the holstered Colts.

Leading the troop rode Anna Norcross. In their proper places rode First Lieutenant Yaller Coudray and Second Lieutenant Alabam' Norton. When the men that had originally come with Captain Norcross to China had been increased by later arrivals to some three hundred, Yaller had been promoted to first lieutenant and Norton to second.

Incidentally word had gone out all over the States where ex-members of the 31st were living, via the grapevine telegraph: "Capt'n Norcross of Troop B is in China wheah-at dem Chinks live. And wid him is his ol' top-cuttah Yaller Coudray an' most of de apes dat was B Troop when us whup de world. Del'cate Moss am dare, an' de Mobile Buck an' Slewfoot an' Skinnay Martin an' all of dem scoundrels. Man howdy, all dey do is to eat and fight and drink wine. Yes, suh, dey gits dem five dollahs each an' every day, an' does dey git killed, dare folks git ten thousand mo'.'"

NOW, AS the troop rode at ease, a second-file man announced:

"Ah dreamed last night dat us was scrappin' wid de cannon-bubbles again, an' de bullets jest dribbled outta mah gun and dropped to de ground. Mah bay'nets was made of cheese and dey was comin' in on me wid speahs."

"Dog-gone," Slewfoot answered, "is dat why yo' was hollah-hin', 'Save me! Save me! Misto Slewfoot, please, suh, save me!'"

"Dat's de reason, Slewfoot," said the man next to him. "Ah nevah did see a boy so scared as dis Jeff. Yes, suh, he was hollahin' fo' his Uncle Mose to come an' save him."

"An' den Jeff he hollah fo' his sweetie to come wid a razah an' cut dem cannonbubbles offen him," some one else chimed in.

"Dat's right, Ah heah him doin' it, no foolin'."

"Ain't no cannonbubbles gwine to eat yo', Jeff. Yo' is too tough and stringy, boy. Next time yo' sees dem, hollah fo' me. Ah protects yo'."

The answer that Jeff made to all that was something scorching.

The four hundred Tartars were riding far out on either side and also acting as van and rear guard. Troop B had not cared very much about having any outfit ride ahead of them, but Anna Norcross had explained to Yaller Coudray, loud enough for the front rank men to hear:

"I send my Tartars ahead, lieutenant, so that I might ride with Troop B. If I did not, it might be that the Tartars would think I should ride surrounded by their swords."

That was passed down the line and the colored men grinned, delighted at the joke "Miss Anna" was playing on the Tartars.

CHAPTER VIII

GUARDS OF THE AIRPORT

THE MANDARIN LEN Yu heard the story of one of the crew of the junk, one of those who had gone over the side unwounded.

At the finish he commanded that the man be paid a thousand taels, then hurried to Kai-shek, to whom he was closer than to the War Lord of the Sangar.

Once alone with him, Len Yu lost no time in exchanging the flowery Chinese compliments.

"Colonel Shao Wu has turned traitor," he said curtly, "and fled to the north with his regiment. For what purpose I do not know. The dog biting the hand that fed him, has turned the Manchu Lord T'ang Wang and the American captain over to the captain of one of my war junks to bring to me. Why he did not take them with him I do not as yet know, but will as soon as Shao Wu is captured. This junk captain instead of treating them with courtesy, ordered ropes to bind them and—"

"Ropes! For a Manchu noble! Truly this captain of yours is a fool."

"In the fight that followed," Len Yu went on, ignoring the interruption, although he noticed a perhaps unconscious turn of Kai-shek's phrasing, "both the Lord T'ang Wang and the American captain were beaten down to the deck by rifle butts and then bound and thrown into the hold of the junk."

"I do not care about the American captain. That war junk captain of yours has ordered a Manchu noble bound and then has beaten him to the deck with rifle butts. Truly an unfortunate circumstance for you, O Lord Len Yu."

Len Yu had caught the "captain of yours," and now the "Lord Len Yu" instead of "War Brother." He knew that Kai-shek was promptly separating himself from what had happened. Neither of them had any illusions as to how the Manchus of all China would look upon an insult to one of them—an insult of that nature, especially to the Manchu Lord T'ang Wang, who was of the pure blood and stood for all they held in reverence.

"Later," Len Yu went on, "in some manner they loosened the ropes that bound them and took the junk."

"They took the junk! Then they are at liberty and now the Manchus are gathering!"

There was nothing left of Kai-shek's usual impassiveness which a Chinaman tries to maintain under all circumstances. "If this colonel were mine, both he and the junk captain would shortly be boiling in oil. Where was the junk when this happened?"

"Near Ho-ka-san. The captain is dead and Shao Wu is not yet captured. When he is, both he and his War Brother Chung will answer to me."

"You say Ho-ka-san, Lord Len Yu? That is the city of Taio K'ai who received his education in Germany and—is not Taio K'ai a cadet of the House of Nurhachu? Our plans have failed because of a war junk captain. I leave for the Sangar at once to join Fung-yang. It may be that we two can defend ourselves there."

"You joined in the plan to seize the Lord T'ang Wang," Len Yu said, smoothly, "and swore to go to the end, O Lord Kai-shek."

"That is true; and the end has come. I joined in the plans to hold the Lord T'ang Wang prisoner, but in no plans that included a dishonorable assault on his person."

"Yet we were to send him on high if necessary?"

"That also is true. But not in public. There are a thousand ways he could have died secretly without blame being attached to us. Now we have antagonized all Manchus before we even get started. No. I leave for the Sangar with all my men."

"You withdraw as my ally?"

"Yes. In this matter you stand alone. Fung-yang and I will endeavor to explain to the Manchus that we are guiltless. Surely you know that now there is no chance of your controlling the north—or of doing anything but defending yourself as best you may."

"The game is not yet ended. They are still in Ho-ka-san. If we hurled all our men against it, it may be that we could take it quickly."

"What good that, when word has gone out of the insult? Truly, your clever brain is failing you, Len Yu. Get to your territory and prepare to defend yourself. I leave at once for the Sangar."

"You withdraw from all our plans, Kai-shek? Then I will carry the matter forward alone—or until I gain other allies who are not so much afraid of the Manchus."

"Yes. From all plans, I withdraw. I will offer prayers to the gods that you will be successful in the matter—but without my help; and, knowing the War Lord of the Sangar as I do, I will say, without his help also."

"It may that some day I can show you that you acted hastily," Len Yu said, grimly.

"In the meantime may I suggest that you give the Manchus a little thought?" asked Kai-shek blandly, as Len Yu went out after a curt salute.

ONCE BACK in his palace, Len Yu sent for an officer who was of his family. "Send spies to Ho-ka-san. I wish to report on whether the Lord T'ang Wang and the American captain are still there. If they are let all their movements be reported on. Establish a line of communications so that all in detail may reach me quickly—very quickly if those in the line wish to continue living."

It did not take very long for Len Yu to get the information that the Manchu Lord T'ang Wang lay on a sick bed, and that the American captain was attending him.

When Len Yu learned that, he smiled and called his second in command. "I leave for the south on a secret mission for the eastern War Lords. Order matters until I return."

Where he went was Shanghai, to confer with an old War Brother who, he knew, was not afraid of anything. The conference ended with Len Yu's decision:

"We will watch there and send planes to wait in hiding in case they take off from Ho-ka-san. But I do not think they will. I think that once the Manchu is well they will come to Shanghai with Taio K'ai and his men. We will await them here. The planes are as they were?"

"Yes, War Brother of my youth, just as when left in the hangar."

"There has been no attempt to move them?"

"No. Not in any way."

"There is plenty of time to arrange matters. Now I will rest and listen to the singing girls."

AT THE airport in Shanghai were the planes; three of them, that had been flown east from Ningyuan by three young Chinese pilots who had been trained by a former German ace. The airport was a semi-private one belonging to a transportation company that had failed. The owners were very glad to make a little money by offering its facilities to private owners of airplanes.

It had been a simple matter for Len Yu to take it over, and now, while there did not seem to be more than the usual number of guards around, and other private planes came and went as ever, the place literally swarmed with Len Yu's men. On the edges of the field there was a good deal of construction work going on—at least it looked like *bona fide* construction work; and in the houses surrounding the field there were concealed riflemen.

After learning that T'ang Wang and Captain Norcross were still at Ho-ka-san with Taio K'ai, Len Yu thought that a Manchu force would be rallied and brought to Shanghai to make a direct attack on the airport. That was what the Manchus generally did when they wanted something, irrespective of where it was or how well defended.

As day after day went by and no attack came, the tension naturally slacked off a little. Not much, because Len Yu's men all knew what it meant to them to be caught napping, but enough so that rifles and swords were not so close to nervous hands, nor were eyes always fixed on the hangar.

It was sixty days before T'ang Wang opened his eyes and smiled up with full, sane understanding, at Captain John Norcross. And down in Shanghai, for some time the guards had been taking things more or less as a matter of course.

"Truly," one of Len Yu's young lieutenants yawned one morning, as he got up, "it seems as if those for whom we wait have vanished into the blue sky. I wish that I could get transferred back to Shanghai. This watching a rat hole every minute, when the rat does not appear, is becoming tiresome."

Another young officer smiled. "Shanghai is but five miles away, O mighty leader of armies. You go there always when not on duty. I am satisfied here; there is no drilling to do."

"That is right—and also nothing else to do. Here are fifty men crowded into one small house."

"Would you like to stand on a platform all by yourself, then? If the Lord Len Yu thought for a moment that you were not quite satisfied, there is no doubt but that he would arrange matters for you."

"You know I but jest, Tzu-lu," the young lieutenant answered hurriedly. "I speak only for your ears to hear."

"I know that. See, I speak for your ears also. I am tired of the sameness. I also long for the lights of Shanghai. Now we see them only for a few hours once in a weary while."

"It may be that we can bring the lights to us for a little while."

"Bring the lights? What do you mean, Foo?"

"Yesterday I met one whom I have known for a long time. He has inherited all his family's wealth and is burning to spend it—in the proper way. Truly he dripped gold, Tzu-lu. He wished me to go with him and show him the way."

"Which you could without any trouble or teaching," said Tzu-lu.

"You also, O spendthrift of spendthrifts. I told him that it would take many days to do it properly and that I had only a few hours now and then. I was afraid that if he got started and I had to leave him to come back to this accursed place, something might happen to him in the meantime."

"You mean that some one else might get hold of him. May the curse of the nine thousand and six devils be on this razor. I have sharpened it a—"

"Pay attention to what I am saying and there will be many razors for both of us."

"Yes? See, I am all attention, O clever one. I bow to you."

"WHEN I said that I could not guide him," Foo continued, "he did not like it. We were youths together, and always he looked up to me. To be brief, since the double-cursed inspection is near, he said that he would take a house on the edge of the field—the big one to the north that was used by the airport managers—and would fill it with… whatever I suggested, and live there until I could arrange a transfer."

"And you named among other things, wine and singing girls. All joking aside, Foo, did you dream this last night?"

"Does that look like dream money?" Foo took from his pocket a handful of gold. "I borrowed that from him in case he disappeared in thin air. No, he is real, Tzu-lu. As real as this money."

"Why do you tell me this?" asked Tzu-lu, shrewdly. "You are not in the habit of sharing things—with me."

Foo, as he adjusted his belt, smiled. "That is true because most of the time you have nothing to share back. But this time I need you."

"You need me to help spend money? You are as the mad-head of Ch'u."

"Not to spend it but to clear the way so that I may spend it. Of all the regiment you are closest to our colonel, Wen Chin. To him you are the stars and moon. He also likes wine and the singing girls, but if *I* were to approach him he would be afraid of the Mandarin Len Yu, and would—"

Tzu-lu laughed. "You need not finish. I know what he would do. So that is it: I am to bring him to the house of mirth so that you may continue there, is that it?"

"So that you also may, don't forget that, Tzu-lu. I thought this: I will introduce you to my rich friend, then shortly afterward you bring Colonel Wen Chin there. I will not be there or any of the junior officers. He will accept your invitation—as I know he has done before when you found a place to his liking.

After he has been there several times, with some of the majors and captains, then it will be established; and—"

"And you and the rest of us that you pick out can go when they are away, is that it?"

"You speak with the wisdom of the master K'ung Foo-tze. It brings the lights to us. There will be many singing girls and much good wine that will not be shown to those above us."

"And I share with you in the spoils?" asked Tzu-lu, his eyes shining.

"Yes, at least to some extent."

"Introduce your friend to me, then. Once the house is ready I will guarantee that Colonel Wen Chin gives it the stamp of his august approval."

The house of Foo's friend truly was a house of lights. From the outside it was a somber, square stone house, more like a warehouse than a residence. Inside it was the last word in luxury.

By day or night there was always ready entertainment for the officers of Colonel Wen Chin's regiment that guarded the airport for Len Yu. At first the colonel and the higher officers went over only once in a while, and then stayed only a brief time, being careful to leave fully sober or with only one or two drinks. But little by little their caution relaxed and one night, after an inspection by Len Yu in the afternoon, all of the officers above the rank of first lieutenant slipped over there and "unbelted" for a regular party.

About three o'clock in the morning, when they were all more or less intoxicated, sitting on cushions against the wall as they watched the dancing girls, there was a sudden stir at the door of the room and the sound of servants' voices. The officers looked up to see a man in the uniform of a colonel of staff in the Army of the North, stride haughtily into the room. He hooked his thumbs in his belt as he came to a halt and ignored the salutes as the officers in the room got to their feet.

"You are Colonel Wen Chin?" he snarled.

"Yes, colonel. I am Wen Chin."

"Your regiment is to be relieved at once. Assemble all of it on the field. General Len Yu orders that after the other regiment is placed that you march your men to the outskirts of the city and camp there. General Len Yu orders that all officers above the rank of lieutenant report after the camp is made to him at the palace of the Mandarin Chitaio.

"Those are the orders, Colonel Wen Chin. Now, as I am speaking to officers, I will add that this house is known of, and—I would suggest that all haste is made in regaining control of yourselves and framing an explanation that will excuse your presence here. I await the forming of your regiment before handing over the written command—and I await also the clearing of your brains."

After he said it, the staff colonel turned curtly on his heel and left the room and the house.

THE COLONEL and his fellow-officers looked at each other with horrified eyes, each trying to clear away the fumes of the wine. To be sitting comfortably against the wall on a soft cushion, leaning back and with half closed eyes watching the graceful forms that swayed back and forth—then suddenly to be confronted with a rasping command and the knowledge that their debauchery while on duty was known to Len Yu and that they were ordered to face him! It was too much of a shock to allow them to think of anything but getting sober, and if possible unloading the blame on someone else.

The colonel was in as bad a situation as any of them, if not worse. He did not fear a death sentence, being an old and tried commander of Len Yu's; but he did fear losing his command—and thus losing face. To inspect the officer sanely and demand his written orders never came into his mind.

"Get to your commands," he snapped. "Assemble the regiment on the field. It may be that I can avert the wrath from our heads. I have fought for the Lord Len Yu for many years."

That was all that was in any of their minds as they ran to

where their companies were placed in the houses and to where the supposed laborers were camped near the construction.

The shock had sobered most of them and finally when the regiment drew up in regimental front, the officers were in their proper places, the colonel and his staff facing them.

In all they numbered some five hundred men, including the guards that were in the hangar.

The rifles were not loaded, and most of the men had bags or motley collections of belongings on their backs. It was a typical Chinese regiment about to move out.

It was just breaking dawn and the air was cold. The colonel stirred uneasily and said to his adjutant, "Where is this colonel of staff?"

From the narrow streets and the sides of the airport came a swift rush of wedge after wedge of Manchu swordsmen. The regiment had no time to load the rifles. The wedges hit the regiment, spread out, went through, met other wedges, turned and came back. It was Manchu swords at work, silent, deadly and efficient.

One great wail of terror went up from the regiment as the men in it tried to shrink back from the keen blades, but there was no place to shrink.

It was a massacre, nothing else. Colonel Wen Chin died as he tried to draw his sword, his officers with him. No one was spared; and no Manchu said a word nor was an order shouted. They killed, that was all.

No, that is not correct. There was one spared. This man, at the first rush, dropped to the ground; and when he rose after the wedges had cut through and were coming back, he had taken his tunic off. Lieutenant Foo, when he regained his feet, was in the sleeveless silk "fighting shirt" of a Manchu. The Mandarin Len Yu had neglected to find out that Foo's grandfather on his mother's side had been a Manchu noble. A little thing, and yet, like the action of the junk's captain, a big one.

Captain John Norcross and T'ang Wang, with Skinnay

Martin and Buck Foster and the Manchus who had come with them from Ningyuan, ran for the hangar. The airport was more or less isolated except from the houses that surrounded it and as yet no noise had come from the next group of houses some quarter of a mile away. Whatever they had heard, the chances were that the inhabitants were as far under their beds as they could get. It is not healthy in China to investigate sudden screams or the clashing of swords.

With them ran the three flyers and Taio K'ai.

"It was well planned, little brother," T'ang Wang said. "See that Foo is well guarded until he reaches the north."

"He will be safe, honorable elder brother. In this matter of Len Yu—should I go further into it with him at the moment? There are enough here to take the palace of the Mandarin Chitaio."

"No. I wish to make the matter more public. I will attend to it from the north. See also that our brother who took the part of the colonel of staff is rewarded. Go back, little brother of the House of Nurhachu. You have done well and I will call the attention of the Princess Ch'enyaun to it so that it may be enrolled on the Scrolls. Come to us in Ningyuan as soon as you are able to receive proper thanks."

A flyer called, "Petrol, oil and water all right."

And the other two, "Check," and "All right here."

"Try the mechanism of the guns," Norcross called, "and see if the ammunition is there."

"Right!" shouted the flyers a minute later.

Norcross smiled and came up to Taio K'ai. "We'll pull out, Taio K'ai. I heard the Lord T'ang Wang invite you to come to Ningyuan. That goes for the mountain of Szu also."

Two minutes later, three fighting planes took the air and as they did the Manchu disappeared as quickly as they had appeared, leaving the bodies of the men of Len Yu on the ground of the field they had failed to guard.

CHAPTER IX

A MAD FORAY

"**THE DOGS FALL** back," announced the Princess Ch'en-yaun coldly, as she turned from the slit cut through the solid rock over the gates of Ningyuan that led into the valley to the east. "It may be they have been lessoned enough, Hsai."

The grim old Manchu noble, whose face was seamed with swordcuts, smiled as he shook his head. "That assault was only to feel out the defense, ruler of cities. The War Lord of the Irenkha-birga has many thousands of men, and—" Two high explosive shells landed on the side of the mountain within a hundred yards of the gates. "This time he comes with heavy guns also."

The Lord Hsai had twice fought the men of Chia Wang when swords were the weapons relied upon.

"I do not care how many guns he has," declared Ch'enyaun hotly. For all her slender loveliness and the beauty of her face which was that of some exotic Oriental flower, the Princess Ch'enyaun, ruler of the cities of Ningyuan and Taiyaun and of a Territory of a hundred square miles, was a Manchu War Lord to the marrow of her bones. The Manchu do not bind the feet of the girl babies, neither do the eyes of the Manchu slant up. Ch'enyaun's little feet were perfect and her eyes of midnight darkness could be soft and warm—or cold, with the deadly cold-ness of a Manchu War Lord whose ancestors had conquered and ruled China.

"The War Lord of the Irenkha," she went on, "twice has been flogged back to his kennel by my honorable father. Now he comes again to receive the lesson that Manchu steel is as keen as ever."

Hsai smiled. "I had the honor of fighting against the Irenkha-birga both times at the side of your honorable father, O worthy daughter of a peerless leader. But this time I am afraid that they will not match their blades with ours as they tried to do twice before. Word came that his men are mostly armed with rifles and that also there are many modern cannon."

"Of what good are the rifles and the cannon if the men who fight them are cowards and will not stand? I say that when they see the flicker of our swords in the sun, they will not wait to receive the death that they know is coming for them, O Hsai."

"But first we must get close enough to charge, O Ruler of the world. It may be that the days when men charged with the sword are over. To throw a swordsman against machine guns is folly, O princess of the House of Nurhachu. You have seen what the black men of the Lord John have done to such charges."

"That is true—but my Lord John's men are men not afraid of death, and they meet charges as readily with the bayonet or their sabers. I agree that across an open space it would be folly if the rifles are concealed. But in the passes and hills, the sword still sings the death song; and so it does in close fighting. We will answer their rifles and cannons with rifles and cannons, and when they have had enough of bullets we will see if they will further await the charge of Manchu steel."

"You reason now with the clearness of your honorable father who smiles down upon you from where he sits with the heroes on high. There is no doubt, once they are thrown into confusion, but that our swords can complete the rout."

"I would that we reach them soon. Ah, the Lady Anna comes, Hsai."

NINGYUAN WAS built inside the walls of a great mountain that thousands of years before had been a raging volcano. In some frightful upheaval the volcanic matter had been blown out or overflowed, leaving the walls of the mountain. In some places near the base they were hundreds of feet thick, and even at the rim, fifty or sixty feet. In the days of the Chieftain Nurhachu, fertile earth had been brought in and the inside of the mountain became like a beautiful flower garden.

The city contained about two hundred thousand people who lived there happy and content under the firm, just rule of the little Manchu princess and her husband T'ang Wang. The mines in the territory were worked by them and the valleys farmed. Now the city's normal population was greatly increased by the country people who had come in on the approach of the Irenkha troops.

Ningyuan would be a very hard place to take even if its defenders were only armed with swords. To get in meant first battering down the gates, then fighting the way through a long tunnel which went through the mountain to turn at a sharp right angle into a street of stone houses that again turned at a hundred yards. Shells might clear the tunnel, but to advance guns and place them so as to command angle after angle would be more than difficult.

The only other way into the mountain, since one could scarcely climb the sides and come down over the rim, was through some old watercourses to the west which ran under the mountain. There massive steel gates must be destroyed before even a start could be made, and there was no cover for the guns attempting such an attack.

Captain Norcross had placed many guns at Ningyuan, and now as the War Lord of the Irenkha brought his guns to bear and threw his troops against it, Ningyuan was like a Gibraltar.

Anna Norcross, with Troop B and the Tartars, had come in through the watercourses. The attack had come on the sides of the mountain away from the hills to the west, the troops of Chia Wang not yet having completely invested the mountain. They had not expected reënforcements to come from the Thian Shan.

Shao Wu had sent two regiments into the hills, more to stop fugitives leaving Ningyuan and to report conditions than anything else. These two regiments had been strung out and the Tartars had fallen on them with wild yells of glee. Most of the

Chinese had promptly run. Those that did not were slain. The Tartars had cut them down like paper men and with Anna and Troop B had swept on to Ningyuan.

Lieutenant Coudray, as soon as he arrived, placed the Troop at the guns in time to help repulse the first attack; and now, as he announced to Sergeant Delicate Moss, he was ready "to smack ol' Misto' Irene Bridget right wheah-at he lived." Troop B were quite content at the guns—as content as cavalrymen can be off their horses—and settled down to do what Yaller called the smacking.

"I am glad you have come up here, Lady Anna," Ch'enyaun said with a smile as Anna reached her. "From here you can watch the curs try for the mountainsides."

Anna's lovely gray eyes grew troubled as she watched the pitiless machine and rapid-fire guns destroy wave after wave of the advancing men. The heavy guns in the hills were trying to lay down a barrage, but it did no good. Any shells that hit the mountain expended their force against solid rock.

"Why do they send their men to certain death?" Anna asked. "Surely this War Lord must know that they cannot climb the sides?"

Hsai smiled. "It may be, O Lady of the Magyars, that Chia Wang figures that he has men to match against our ammunition and that once it is exhausted his men could climb."

"They will meet ten thousand Manchu swords and the bayonets of Troop B when that time comes," Ch'enyaun answered calmly. "See, fresh regiments come from the Mountain of the Lower Gods. Truly, as you say, Lord Hsai, he is matching men against bullets."

"I do not like to watch it." Anna said. "If they were men charging against an equal force, it would be different. Now they have no chance—and they die as leaves fall from a tree. I will go to the palace, O Princess of the Manchu."

"I would go with you, O sister whom I love," Ch'enyaun answered gently, "but I am in command, and so must stay."

"It is only proper that you should, resplendent one," Anna answered, as she bowed to the Lord Hsai.

FOR A day and a night the attack kept up steadily. Now Shao Wu was throwing one regiment after another at the mountain and shells began dropping into the city. Not very often, as it was hard to get the range and the proper elevation to fall inside the rim.

The shells also searched out the sides of the mountain for the hidden guns that were causing so much havoc. But the defense guns had been placed in little crevices and natural depressions with heavy concrete placements that only showed a narrow slit, and only two had been wrecked.

Anna Norcross and the Princess Ch'enyaun sat just inside the water-gate tunnel. It had been hard work to persuade the Princess Ch'enyaun to take cover of any kind. But Yaller Coudray, at Anna's command, had pointed out that a shell was no respecter of persons and that she owed it to her people and to "Misto' T'ang Wang" not to take any unnecessary chances. The little princess had seen the wisdom in that, and so was sitting with Anna in a place of more or less safety.

The people of the city had been sent into the vast underground passages that ran through the base of the mountain, and about all the damage the shells were doing was the blowing up of an occasional stone house or ruining some flower garden. But the Princess Ch'enyaun did not like it at all, and she was telling Anna so.

"See, O Lady of the Magyars. Our Lords are away, and we defend the city. Are we to cower here under walls like jackals, while they are away and mongrels snap? I know that these pariah dogs will not stand up to Manchu swords. Soon I will do as my honorable father would have done at once. I will lead the swords against them. See, Anna! I have thought of a plan. You lead your Tartars. We will fall on this War Lord of the Irenkha from the rear while the guns talk in front. We will see if they do not run when they see the flash of swordblades."

Anna Norcross, true descendant of Geiza, the Magyar hero, smiled and her eyes shone as she asked: "But how, Ch'enyaun? It is what our Lords would do, surprise them in some way. But how could we take such a body of men out of the city without being seen? This War Lord of the Irenkha-birga must have spies here."

"His spies will not know, Anna. I can send the swords in, a few at a time, also your Tartars."

"In? In where, Ch'enyaun?"

"Into a deep tunnel that none know except those of my house. It opens above ground far back in the hills. Will you lead your Tartars with me and my Manchu swords?"

"But—Troop B... You know that I am not afraid, Ch'enyaun."

"Yes, I know that, little sister. In all things I count you equal to myself"—which was quite a concession for the proud little Manchu princess of the blood. There were few, very few in all the world, whom she considered her equal, at least as far as blood went. "If we can rout the army of the War Lord of the Irenkha," she went on, guilefully, "it will save many thousand of his men from the guns. If they run, Anna, we will not pursue and slay— at least not beyond my territory."

That settled it as far as Anna Norcross went. "I will go, Ch'enyaun. I have four hundred of the Altai. How many of the Manchu swords will you take?"

"Two thousand. Any more would be unwieldy. With that many we can make a wedge that will drive through these mongrels and— Anna, we will take and spike the guns that are dropping shells into my city!"

"I do not know how to—to do what you call spike guns, Ch'enyaun; and I doubt if my Tartars do, either. It may be that if we took some of Troop B, that they would know how."

"No," interrupted the warlike little princess, "this is a matter of swords only. I will have some of my officers ask Lieutenant Coudray how to do it, in a way that will not excite his suspicion. I think that you break the breech mechanism in some way. Then—we go, Lady of the Magyars?"

Anna smiled as she answered gravely, "Yes, O Princess of the House of Nurhachu, we go." And the two lovely slim women, both with the blood of fighters undiluted in their veins, smiled happily at each other as they rose.

IN THE barracks at Ningyuan, just at dawn the next morning, the Mobile Buck stretched as he got up from his bunk. "Anothah day, anothah dollah," he announced. "Ah wish dat de Troop would take de field, dog-gone it. All Ah do is go *bipty-bipty-bipty* wid mah baby up on de hill."

"Does de Troop take de field, yo' gits left behind, monkey-face," answered Happy Combes, who as sergeant of the guard had just come in. "Only ridahs gets out wid de Troop. Yo' can't ride, yo' nevah could ride, and—"

First Lieutenant Coudray came in. His face was gray, not yellow-tinted, and his lips were gray also. His upper lip was curled back like that of a snarling dog and his black eyes held little frozen flames. The first men that saw him jumped to their feet.

"Mah Gawd!" whispered one. "Whut has—"

" 'Tenshun!" Yaller snarled; and those of Troop B within hearing snapped into it. "Fall in, troop front. Come on, what is yo', a lot of tired old gent'mum? Dat's bettah. Count off!"

The line began forming, some of them with only their night-shirts on, some with pants and one sock, some without anything on at all. A long line of big colored men trained down to the minute. Now their faces were set and grim. With the unerring instinct of their race, they sensed that trouble had come to Troop B.

At the end of the "One—two—three—four," Yaller rasped: "Numbah one, two, three men—one pace forward. Heavy marchin' ordah. Eight Brownin's. Two hundred rounds of rifle ammunition. Each man to carry one-quartah box of machine gun ammunition. De Troop moves out in five minutes."

Then Yaller forgot all about his being a commissioned officer, and added as a first sergeant: "An' if dare is one of yo' apes not ready, he don't go—and Ah beats him to death when Ah gits back. Break ranks!"

Perhaps one hundred and ten men had stepped forward; and now as the line broke, the number four men began to sound off angrily.

"Whut de devil is comin' off?"

"Yaller, Ah goes, dog-gone it. Ah rode beside yo' when yo' was a co'p'ral—'membah dat."

"Ah don't give a dog-gone if yo' is a lieutenant, Yaller. 'Membah de time down in Sonora dat Ah carried yo' out of dat place on mah back when it was rainin' spig coppahs? Does de pay Ah gits fo' dat mean dat Ah stays behind?"

"Ah is de best machine gunnah in de Troop. Yo' knows dat, Yaller. How come dat Ah has to stay and—"

"Silence!" shouted Yaller. "Ah don't give a damn whut-all yo' did or is. Yo' formed de line and de men Ah called by numbah goes, dat's all. Can't all go. When us gets back Ah fights de man dat don't think it was a even break."

"Yaller—Ah means lieutenant—wheah-at is de Troop going?"

"Miss Anna snuck off wid de wild men, and de Princess Ch'enyaun snuck off wid her, wid some of de Manchu swordsmen. Dey had gone to attack the whole army of ol' Irene Bridget; dat's all Ah know—an' dat's 'nough. De Troop goes to get Miss Anna. Now get de heck outta mah way.

"De rest stays heah to fight de guns and defend de city; and doesn't Ah come back, Ah wants yo' apes to 'membah dat yo' has de honah of B Troop in yoah hands. Nevah forget dat. Yo' stays wid de men dat am at de guns now, and befo' one of dat Irene Bridget's men sets his foot in de city Ah 'spects dat yo' will all be daid. 'Membah dat—daid, yo'-all heahs me?"

"Yes, suh, Yaller, us will be daid fust, no foolin'. Does de Troop ride?"

"No, de Troop don't ride, if dat's any of yoah business. De Troop goes wid rifles and bay'nets and machine guns, to meet de same. Now get away frum me befo' Ah smacks a millyun of yo' down."

A MANCHU noble came in and bowed to First Lieutenant Coudray. "The Lord Hsai is ready to move, lieutenant."

"Mah comp'ments to Lord Hsai, and de Troop is ready, suh," and Yaller followed the Manchu out, followed by despondent mutterings:

"Of all de unlucky, dad-blamed, slew-footed apes in de world, Ah am de best."

"Ah could have been numbah three just as well as numbah fo', only dat dog-gone Mobile Buck he crowds me. Wait till Ah gets mah hands on him—dat's all Ah got to say, wait till Ah hooks mah fist to de point of his jaw."

The Lord Hsai led three rifle regiments into the hills. There were no swordsmen with the force. They were officered by Manchus, and most of the men had more or less Manchu blood—enough at any rate to make them all determined to rescue the Princess Ch'enyaun or die.

Hsai smiled grimly as Yaller Coudray came up to him. The last of the silent column of colored men had just passed. The Springfield rifles were bayoneted, the machine guns ready to set up, and every man in the column carried nearly his own weight in ammunition.

"I think they struck at the heavy guns, lieutenant," said Hsai. "I will lead the regiments through the Pass of the Sun God, which is to the left. You go as a separate unit or will you come with us?"

Yaller saluted. "Us goes as a separate unit, Misto' Hsai, suh. Iffen yo' connect, us heahs it, and iffen us does, yo' heahs it. Misto' Hsai, us loves de Princess. But us ain't got no 'thority to—to bring her back doesn't she want to come. Capt'n say, 'Take care o' Miss Anna,' so as far as she's concerned, dat lets us— Misto' Hsai, iffen de Princess Ch'enyaun doesn't want to come back, has us de— Give an ordah, Misto' Hsai, please suh."

The old Manchu noble looked at Yaller Coudray, formerly

The Manchu princess and Anna
Norcross directed the fight.

of the 31st U.S. Cavalry, then said impassively: "I, Hsai, of the House of Nurhachu, now Head of the House in the absence of the Princess Ch'enyaun and the Lord T'ang Wang, give this order to you, Lieutenant Coudray: If in your judgment the Princess Ch'enyaun is in danger and should be brought to her city of Ningyuan, you are to bring her here."

"Dat's all Ah wants to heah, suh. Us meets at de Pass of de Sun God aftah us or yo' finds dem, is dat it?"

"Yes, lieutenant, that is right."

Yaller saluted and ran to overtake the column, which was grumbling:

"Whut de heck is Yaller doin'—havin' a tea party?"

"Why don't he kiss him an' let it go at dat?"

"Yallers askin' him wheah-at to buy a pair of shoes."

"Dey is debatin' whethah to do it in Mobile or St. Louis."

"Ah hopes dey decides by dinnah, dog-gone it. Ah got nine millyun pounds of 'munition on my back."

"Ah carry it fo' yo'—like heck. Yo' ain't got halt as much on yo' back—"

Yaller arrived, and the grumbling stopped at the promise of

action. The column went forward on the double, machine guns, ammunition and all. It was rough going, and they were more than heavily laden, but any man of them would have dropped in his tracks before he allowed the next man to get one step ahead of him. And none did. For they were on their way to rescue "Miss Anna"—if she still lived.

CHAPTER X

IN A CHINESE TRAP

PRINCESS CH'ENYAUN AND Anna Norcross badly needed aid. Their forces had separated a little in the hills. The plan they evolved was that Anna's Tartars would strike at a point away from the gun placements, drawing away some of the regiments which were supposed to be on guard. In China a regiment may be anything from two hundred men to a thousand, and Ch'enyaun's spies had reported that there were ten regiments supporting the guns.

Ch'enyaun was to charge with the Manchus, spike the guns, then cut her way through to where Anna and the Tartars were. Joining forces, they would, as Ch'enyaun announced, "flog the curs back to their kennels."

It was a good plan up to a certain point. The Tartar attack, Anna ringed in by the best swords, struck hard and went deep into the Chinese ranks. The Manchu wedge utterly surprised the outer regiments around the guns, and reached the big guns without any serious loss of swords.

They went up to and over the guns, and when they turned away, the delicate breech mechanisms were destroyed. They could hear the Tartars at work, and Ch'enyaun, as near the point of the wedge as her Manchus would let her get, ordered contact made. The regiments in the path of the Manchus fled without even trying to form.

Ch'enyaun was right about one thing: that the Chinese would not stand to take a sword charge delivered by Manchus. But this only applied to those who were close enough to think that the swords would reach them personally.

The Manchus and Tartars joined, and Ch'enyaun smiled as she came up to Anna.

"Now we will commence to drive these mongrels back to the Irenkha," she announced—and as she did, withering rifle fire came from two sides. Tartars and Manchus went to the ground, long rows of them.

Colonel Shao Wu had arrived on the scene with his War Brother Chung. He had looked calmly through his glasses at the Manchus cutting their way to the Tartars, holding up his hand for quiet as Chung suggested throwing some regiments between.

"Let them get together," he said calmly. "Then we will strike. The Princess Ch'enyaun leads the Manchus. I do not know the woman with the Tartars. I have heard that the American captain married a woman of the Altai— They make it! Now, order two regiments to each of the hills, left and right. Bring up four more at the base of the hill to the north. A machine gun company on that knoll to the right. We have them in a trap, Chung. The gods are kind to us. Order that the Princess Ch'enyaun be taken alive, if possible."

Anna Norcross, as well as Ch'enyaun and the officers close to them, saw where the gunfire was coming from; and as a cross-fire began, even Ch'enyaun knew that swords were helpless.

"If we can take this hill to the right," Anna said, as calmly as though in the gardens at Ningyuan, "we can get cover from the bullets, O Manchu Princess."

Ch'enyaun looked at the hill, which was heavily timbered and cut up with draws. "We take this hill, Chou," she said to the ranking officer. And they did take it, Manchus and Tartars together. In doing it they lost many more men, and when finally they got cover, of the Manchus there were left five hundred, and of the Altai Mountain Tartars less than a hundred. It had been one of the hills that Shao Wu had fortified in case of reinforcements trying to reach Ningyuan, and on it were machine gun nests. But the Chinese were wiped out, one by one, by swordsmen.

"NOW," SHAO Wu announced with a cruel smile, "we will send in the beaters to drive the game into the open. Order that the firing cease, Chung. No use of wasting the War Lord of the Irenkha's ammunition. There are some regiments here whose officers have been arrogant and haughty. I will be glad to see them blooded. We will send them up the hill."

They went up, the men deadly afraid. It was like walking barefoot in heavy underbrush where copperheads and rattlesnakes abounded. To drive five or six hundred Manchu and Tartar swords out of that kind of cover took men who were absolutely unafraid; and the Chinese were afraid, very much so.

They would bunch together, a half or full company, and timidly advance, parting the second growth or hesitating about crossing a cleared space. Then suddenly there would be the whir of swords and an attack by ten or fifteen swordsmen who loved a fight and considered getting killed as part of it.

Shao Wu frowned as he watched regiment after regiment disappear and not return.

"Order a general assault," he commanded. "Truly these dogs must be falling into a deep cañon."

The Princess Ch'enyaun and Anna Norcross sat on a bowlder near the top of the hill, which was about two thousand feet high and a mile around at the base. The princess was still very much unconvinced as to the uselessness of her swords.

"If I had brought them all, Anna, those regiments could not have formed far enough away to shoot us down as they did."

Anna smiled. "But the swordsmen must get close… Oh! See! A company comes from the left. I wish that Troop B were here— Ah! My Tartars saw them."

"Troop B was not needed that time," answered Ch'enyaun grimly. "Swords did the work. Anna, if—if anything happens to us, I want you to know that from the first when you came to Ningyuan you have been to me always as a dearly loved sister. I love you for yourself and also because you have made my honorable elder brother Lord John happy."

Anna smiled as she answered: "And I love you, too, Ch'enyaun. It may be that we die, here on this hill. The Lord Death comes for us all, and I die happy that I have known and loved you and— Is that gunfire, Ch'enyaun?"

"Where? Yes, I hear it. Not rifle fire? It is—Anna, it is machine gun fire. See, some regiments are going to the left."

Anna Norcross stood up, very straight, her proud little head well back. "It is Troop B," she said softly. "Coming for us, Ch'enyaun."

TROOP B it was, and they were coming with all they had, which was plenty for any and all that got in front of them. The isolated machine gun fire on the hill had guided them. When Yaller first heard it, he turned a little and shouted, "Come on, yo' lead-footed apes! Whut de heck is Ah leadin', de ole men's cripple home? Git dem Brownin's up heah in front. Doesn't dey come Ah gives 'em to men whut can bring 'em. Yo' has command of dem, Del'cate. Show me somepin wid 'em when us gets dare."

The Troop came on, machine guns to the front. Delicate weighed around three hundred, but when the Troop first made contact with the Chinese, Delicate was second only to Yaller Coudray. Slewfoot, Squint-eye, the Mobile Buck, Thomas Jefferson Talliferro Johnson and the rest were as close as they dared to get.

The Troop was lucky in one thing. From where they heard the firing it was mostly downhill, and as they ran down, they struck the old dried-up bed of a river. Down it they came like a tidal wave and out into the little valley that gave them a good view of the hill up which the Chinese were charging.

"Dat's wheah-at Miss Anna is," Yaller shouted. "Get dem guns workin', yo' big elefunt or Ah does it mahself."

"Heah dey goes, lieuten—"

"To heck wid dat lieutenant stuff! Ah'm Yaller Coudray, dat's who Ah is—and dare is mah little Miss Anna up yondah on dat hill! Come wid me, monkeyfaces, till Ah gets her. Shoot dese cooties outta mah way, Del'cate."

The eight machine guns opened up. Eight Brownings, handled by men second to none in the world at the handling of them. No jamming, no hurried bursts then a pause. Just a steady, deadly, efficient *tat-tat-tat*. And after them, as the guns were picked up and advanced, came ninety-odd of the big colored men, few of whom could not wear the Distinguished Marksman badge and none who were not sharpshooters. When Yaller said "Mah little Miss Anna," he was speaking for them all. To every man in the Troop, John Norcross's wife was "Mah little Miss Anna," and the Troop was going in to get her, one man or one hundred.

Shao Wu watched the advance for a moment, then lowered his glasses. "The black men of the American captain. See the dogs of the Irenkha fall, Chung. Withdraw all regiments from the hill and throw them directly in the path."

Chung smiled grimly. He was no coward, any more than was Shao Wu, and Shao Wu knew his War Brother spoke only as an officer when he said:

"We cannot stand against them, Shao Wu. Better try for them at long range, letting the regiments retreat slowly before them until we can place others as we did with the Manchus."

"That is—" A stream of machine gun bullets *zinged* over their heads, very close, and both Shao Wu and Chung promptly fell down and rolled off the little knoll.

"They search for us, War Brother," Chung said, as he got up.

"It may be well for us that they do not find us," answered Shao Wu, with a smile as he also rose. "I go to place the regiments, Chung. Order a slow withdrawal."

There was no need to order it, the retirement had already begun and not so slow either. Chia Wang of the Irenkha had no men that would stand against the machine guns and the glistening bayonets that were now lowered.

Many of the Chinese ran without firing a shot, other companies to right and left fired, only to draw an instant fire that sent them to the ground.

"AH WISH dey would stan', dog-gone it," complained the Mobile Buck to the man next to him. "Ah run nine millyun miles wid all dis ammunition and now Ah is runnin' some mo'."

"Yo' gets yo' a chance to use it, Misto' Mobile. See whut-all is waitin' for us ovah yonder!"

Yaller, dearly loving a hand-to-hand fight with anything, had ordered the machine guns back to cover the flanks, and as the Mobile Buck started to look, he shouted: "Come on wid dem pig stickahs! Us does de rest with de bay'net!"

So the Mobile Buck didn't get a look at the regiments that were commencing to show on two of the hills to the left. The Chinese that were between Troop B and the base of the hill wavered and then some ran. Those that didn't, and were in the path, went down. It was a case of a contemptuous parry, a thrust, and the withdrawal of a red bayonet. The colored men were twice as big as the Chinese and with longer reach of arm. The regiments in place on the hills could not fire at the moment because of their own men in line.

At the base of the hill, from the shelter of a thicket, there came Anna Norcross, the Princess Ch'enyaun, and what was left of the Manchus and the Tartars. Yaller saw them and shouted an order. Troop B whirled around and confronted their foes, the machine guns swinging in a half circle of death.

"Us come to 'scort you and de Princess back to Ningyuan, Miss Anna," Yaller said with a very snappy salute.

"I am very glad you have arrived to do it, lieutenant," answered Anna with a smile.

"I also, lieutenant," Ch'enyaun said. "It looks very much as if we needed escorting."

"Yes, ma'am, Princess. Us is right heah to do dat little thing.

Ah begs de Princess's pardon. Will Miss Anna and de Princess ordah dat de swords form a tight column? Us takes de front and de reah and covahs de sides. No use in just gettin' dem killed fo' nothin'."

"I will give the order, lieutenant," Ch'enyaun said, calmly.

"I also," Anna added, as her eyes met those of Ch'enyaun. "Swords cannot win—now."

From his point of vantage, Shao Wu watched once more as the column started toward the Pass of the Sun God. "A little farther—just a little, Chung, before the order to fire is given. See, soon they will reach the angle and then—we will destroy some of the black dogs as well as the Manchus and Tartars."

But that order to fire was never given by Shao Wu or Chung. The signal was given by Hsai of the Manchu House of Nurhachu who had arrived from Ch'enyaun's city with the rifle regiments just as Troop B made the hill. Hsai's advance scouts had reported the position of the Chinese and he had got above them. Just as Shao Wu turned to Chung to give the order, Hsai gave his command. A fire poured down on Shao Wu's Chinese from all sides, and after a brief, mad milling around they ran in whatever direction gave them cover from it. It was followed by a bayonet charge that almost caught Shao Wu and Chung as they fled also. The charge carried the rifle regiments of the Princess Ch'enyaun up to the column.

Hsai, as he halted in front of her, bowed low, then with impassive face, asked, "Is it your wish, O Head of the House of Nurhachu, that I lesson these curs who have dared to snap?"

The Princess Ch'enyaun looked around, her eyes still warlike, then shook her head. "No, Hsai. See, already they are bringing up fresh regiments. We return to Ningyuan. I think we have taught the Irenkha that Manchu swords are still sharp."

"That without question is true, resplendent one," answered Hsai gravely.

"Miss Anna, please, ma'am," Yaller said after a salute, "does yo' go back wid de Princess, us acts as reah guard an' holds dem back frum comin' in de pass."

"Why, I would rather stay with—yes, lieutenant, I will return with the Princess."

The enemy made a test of whether the pass was being held in force, and in a very few minutes were convinced that it was. In that experiment, the Mobile Buck had a chance to get rid of a lot of the ammunition he had been packing, as did his fellows. It was, as he put it, "duck soup and gravy," this defending a pass. Plenty of shooting room and targets for all. During it some one called "Hey, Yaller! I ain't got no mo' shells fo' mah rifle. Can't dis onery ole Slewfoot gimme his? He is on a Brownin'."

"Where does yo' get dat Yaller stuff? When yo' talks to me on de field yo' say 'lieutenant,' yo' heah me? Whut does yo' want me to do, come ovah dare an' take it away from him? Take it yo'self, is yo' man enough."

By that the Troop knew that Lieutenant Coudray had arrived on the scene once more.

Shao Wu did not try to force the pass nor to follow up its defenders as they slowly dropped back. He knew that the War Lord of the Irenkha's men had enough for one day.

"I think," he said softly to Chung, "that I had better go and see if I can keep the tiger from using his claws and teeth on us."

CHAPTER XI

THE BOMBING OF THE CITY

THE PRINCESS CH'ENYAUN and Anna Norcross were sitting in the palace gardens at Ningyuan. There were no more shells falling in the city and the people were out once more in the open.

"At least we spiked the guns, Anna," Ch'enyaun said. "My Manchus died with swords in their hands—as did your Tartars. It was as they wished to die. It may be that—"

The hum of plane motors came to them both. Ch'enyaun

stopped talking and listened. "Our Lords have arrived home," she announced gladly.

Anna listened, then smiled. "Yes. See, Ch'enyaun, the planes come over the rim. Now they climb—see, they start down!"

"Let us go and meet our Lords. But see, they level out! Those are not our planes! Look, something drops! A bomb! They are planes of the foe. To me, Ming Li!"

A young Manchu officer of her bodyguard ran forward.

"Sound the gongs of the temples! Order all people underground. Quickly, little brother. Send Hsai to me."

There was a roaring explosion as the powerful bomb struck in the heart of the city, then a cloud of yellow and black smoke rose toward the sky and out of it hurtled the stone and timber of the ruined house.

There were three of the planes, and as each one came over, it dropped a bomb. All three landed in the crowded part of the city, killing many people before the fugitives could make any of the passages. The planes passed over and then came back dropping three more bombs.

Ch'enyaun stood erect and furious in her palace gardens, ignoring all pleas that she take cover.

"The dogs are blowing my city to pieces and killing women and children," she answered coldly. "It is fitting that I, their ruler, also die if it is the will of the gods who are ordering this."

"You can do nothing here, Ch'enyaun," answered Anna, who stood beside her. "See, the guns on the rim open up on them. Oh—no, I had thought that a shell had reached the first one."

Back came the planes, this time a little higher and faster on account of the guns on the rim. Down came three more bombs, one of which struck a temple in the palace grounds.

"The temple of my ancestor, Nurhachu," the Princess Ch'enyaun said bitterly, her eyes as cold as death. "It may be that he will look down from on high and decide the time has come to stop these dogs. Are other planes coming also?"

She looked up as did the rest of the little group that were standing with her.

Over the rim of the mountain came three more planes, higher than the first three.

None of those on the ground could distinguish any marks on them, yet Anna Norcross said, positively: "Now our Lords really come, Ch'enyaun!"

She was right. In one plane Captain John Norcross was at the machine guns on the scarf yoke. In the next, Skinnay Martin at the guns, and in the next, Buck Foster.

Later Skinnay said, "Ah was scared when dat scoundrel at de stick went zoomin' up an' Ah was worse scared when he came a bammin' down, but boy howdy, Ah shuah made dem typewrit-ahs talk turkey."

T'ang Wang and the Manchus, not being familiar with machine guns, could only be passengers, one in each plane.

THE THREE bombing planes knew instantly that enemy planes had arrived, and gave over any more bombing, to fight. Two of them were old-fashioned bombing planes, slow and unwieldy. The other was of later type with the machine guns mounted aft of the pilot. The planes that had just arrived were fast Fokkers. Norcross came over first, climbing even then to get altitude. He got it and dived down on the tail of the newest bomber, like a hawk swooping down on its prey.

The flyer in the plane below executed the upper half of a figure eight, trying to get out of the way, but as he came level again, Norcross's plane had swung the circle with him and was again coming down. The machine gun sent a burst of bullets through the bomber's fuselage, then up again. Now the Irenkha flyer was himself trying to climb, but he was out-speeded and; outplayed by the young Manchu aviator who had been an apt pupil of a German ace. The bomber could not get away, and could not get on top of that roaring engine of death that once again dived for his tail. This time the first burst of bullets tore through the Irenkha flyer's body, and the second burst fired the plane. Down the bomber came twisting around in wide spirals, crashing in the gardens of the Princess Ch'enyaun within a thousand feet of where she stood.

The other two bombers, slower by far, tried first to get altitude. One of them did for a moment, sending a stream of bullets toward the plane that was engaging it, but missing. Neither that flyer nor the man with him saw Norcross's plane coming down, so close to the ship that held Buck Foster that afterward the colored machine gunner said, feelingly:

"Ah heered something comin' like de ole L. and N. fas' express ovahdue at Birmingham. Like dis—'*Zoooom.*' Ah looks outta de cornah of mah eye. Boy, howdy, Ah seed dat big ole wing 'bout to bam me in de haid an' den Ah see de Capt'n's face an' den Ah heahs '*bippity-bippity-bippity,*' and de doggone plane was by. Ah seed de Capt'n fo' a secund and all Ah got to say is dat de Capt'n was struttin' his stuff and mad 'bout it, Ah ain't kiddin'."

The bomber that Captain Norcross had taken away from Buck Foster fell on the rim of the mountain just as Skinnay Martin lined up the pilot of the third plane with his gun sights, and cut loose. In listening to Buck tell why he had not got a scalp, Skinnay soothed with, "Yo' is too slow wid de triggah, Misto' Fostah. Capt'n see dat and say, 'Dog-gone, Ah got dat ole slow-poke of a Buck Fostah in dare. Ah got to tend to it mahself.'"

That started a fight that lasted fifteen rounds in which Buck proved that at least he was not slow with his fists.

The third plane fell outside the mountain in flames. Then the three Fokkers that had arrived barely in time to save Ningyuan from destruction, landed on the flying field that had been made by the watergates.

The attack on the mountain had kept steadily up all this time and most of Troop B were at the guns. Those that weren't lined up, troop front, as the planes landed; and with Yaller Coudray in his proper position as First Lieutenant, Troop B came to a snappy present arms as Captain Norcross's feet touched the ground.

Later that day, after he and T'ang Wang had been told what had happened, and had told in turn what had happened to them, Norcross smiled, as Anna slipped her slender hand in his.

"Well, now that we are here, it may be that we can think of something that will give this War Lord of the Irenkha-birga something else to do besides sending his men to the slaughter."

"I wish that we could, John," Anna answered, wistfully. "Already there have been many thousand poor creatures killed."

"Tell me all you know of him, Anna. You also, little sister."

"Why, the Altai Mountain Tartars have always known Chia Wang, John. I have heard tales, of course, but both Vyatka and Nogai know him well. They are here with me. Will I send for them, John?"

"Yes. It may be that we can play a game with this War Lord."

"I know him also," Ch'enyaun said grimly. "And my honorable father knew him better. Shall I tell you a tale, John, as we wait for the Tartars?"

CHAPTER XII

THE TIGER'S FANGS

SHAO WU STOOD once more in the tent of Chia Wang, War Lord of the Irenkha-birga. This time the tiger was not purring. But the face of the old tiger was calm and his voice bland as he asked, "You have come to report that the city of Ningyuan has fallen, little one who plays at being a soldier?"

Shao Wu was not misled by the tone or the calm face. He knew that the tiger was crouched to spring. There was only one thing to do if he wanted to live and that was to tell the truth, speak plainly and to the point.

"No, Lord of the North. The city is not taken. Our ships of

the air were destroyed after they had dropped a few bombs. Word has come to me that the ships that arrived carried the Lord T'ang Wang and the American Captain Norcross. The men you have given me have been slain trying to take the city, and during the sortie the Princess Ch'enyaun made with her Manchu swords."

"Your new method of lighting is proving very costly, O little brother. As costly as the way you sneered at. Truly, Manchu swords are not to be withstood."

"It is not the Manchu swords, ruler of the world, but the guns of the American!"

"You also have guns, O Shao Wu. You said that you would answer his guns with yours, shot for shot. Yet Ningyuan stands as ever. I will order the platform be made ready for you, foolish one."

"That I cannot prevent, O mighty one," answered Shao Wu steadily. "But first I ask that you, in the greatness of your mercy, deign to listen."

"I will listen," answered Chia Wang smoothly, "just as I soon will listen to your cries under the knives."

"Yes, O War Lord of the Irenkha-birga. When the uncle of the Princess Ch'enyaun held the city of Ningyuan he worked the mines also. Some of them lie fairly close to the city, on the west. I sent my miners and sappers into the nearest and they have run a tunnel that is now inside the rim of the city. The tunnel comes up close to the Temple of Ancestors near the palace square in the heart of the city. It will be completed to-night. Through it, my War Brother Chung and I will lead our men. We have plenty of machine guns, and once in, we will prove that we can answer the black dogs shot for shot. This I ask: that when we open the gates, your troops will be ready to come in. We will bring the fight to this American captain now."

CHIA WANG reached for a piece of ginger. "How many men do you need to meet the black men and the Manchu swords?"

"Three thousand. I count on the element of surprise. The black men are scattered over the city and on the rim. The Manchu swords do not count against guns. If you, O peerless one, will mass your troops as if for another assault at the given time, it will cause the black men to go to their guns on the mountain. I will take the city."

"When do you plan to do this, O Shao Wu?"

"At break of dawn to-morrow. My War Brother leads our men to the hills even now. To-night they will be in the tunnel. As the light comes we will come through the temple and take the city. If you will order that all remaining guns be concentrated against the main gates and that your troops mass as if for attack while a few go forward, it will be easier for me to take Ningyuan for you, O Head of the House of Chia."

Chia Wang studied Shao Wu, out of agate hard eyes. "You put all on one cast, little brother. What is there in Ningyuan that you want?"

"The treasure of the Chieftain Nurhachu," answered Shao Wu calmly.

Chai Wang smiled. "And with that answer, which is the truth, you have gained time to try for it. If you had lied to me, little one who holds ambition to rule China, you would have already been on your way to the platform. It is not well to come to the Irenkha with nothing but idle tales of the Red Commune. Go then and make the try. The guns will start at break of dawn. The men will be massed and some will go forward. If you take the city, the treasure of the Chieftain Nurhachu is yours. If you do not, O Shao Wu, it will be much easier for you if you die there. You have my permission to go."

Shao Wu rode through the army whose encampment stretched far out on all sides of the valley where the tents of the War Lord of the Irenkha-birga had been pitched. With him rode the officers of his staff. His eyes showed his disdain as he rode by many regiments still armed with swords and lances. He rode by some gun placements and noted lack of discipline and general looseness.

"If they were mine," he said to Chung who rode on his left, "I would send them in until there was no more ammunition left in Ningyuan to kill them with. What good are they? See what all our training has amounted to. Once we are out of sight, they go back to the old ways. It may be that once Ningyuan is taken we can also take the Irenkha. Chia Wang promised me the death of the thousand cuts. Perhaps he will stand on the platform instead."

"If you will allow Lai-chau and Hsai Hue, who lie with their men at Sangtun, to join you, elder brother, there is no question but what we can cut this army of Chia's to pieces."

Shao Wu smiled. "First we will take Ningyuan. Then we will ask them to join us—after we have secured that for which we try, little brother."

CHAPTER XIII

CATCHING TARTARS

THE OLD WAR Lord of the Irenkha-birga slept peacefully in his tent for some hours after Shao Wu left. When he woke up he was in much better humor.

An officer came in and saluted. "You have my permission to speak," Chia Wang said pleasantly.

"Two of the Altai Mountain Tartars are halted at the outposts, mighty one. The dogs demand audience with you."

Chia Wang smiled. "Always the Tartars demand, not beg. Especially the Altai Mountain Tartars. Many of them I know. Who are these, Captain Hue?"

"Vyatka, the Khan, and Nogai who leads under him, O ruler of the world."

"I know them both. Many times they have brought me sweets and wines from the land of the Turks and Persians. How many men ride with them?"

"Some ten or twelve, Lord. Back in the hills just outside our lines there are wagons and pack horses. How many men are there guarding them I know not."

"Wagons and pack horses? It may be that they have taken a caravan. Bring them to me. You have my permission to go, Captain Hue."

A half hour later Vyatka and Nogai strode into the tent. Both were armed and both carried themselves as if they commanded the Irenkha army that surrounded them, rather than the Head of the House of Chia.

They nodded curtly and Vyatka grunted in Pushtu: "Hail, Chinaman who rules the Irenkha-birga."

It may have been a relief to Chia Wang to have men in front of him who neither flattered nor feared him. At any rate he smiled as he answered, "Hail, O Tartars of the Altai. Be seated. Will you eat or drink?"

"No," answered Vyatka surlily as he and Nogai sat cross-legged on a rug. "We have eaten and drunk our fill in the hills."

"You come to explain why the Altai Mountain Tartars attacked my little brothers at Ningyuan?" asked Chia Wang blandly. He was thoroughly enjoying himself now. He knew that the Tartars were not afraid of him in the slightest, any more than he was not afraid of them. He had unbounded physical courage, this old War Lord.

Vyatka and Nogai both laughed. "Your little brothers did not stay long to receive the kiss of our swords, Chinaman. We went with Lady Anna, the daughter of our former *haduagy*. If you had been there we would have slain you also if she commanded," Nogai said.

"That," answered the old War Lord, "I fully know. You slay many of my people and yet you come to me. What is to prevent my taking your lives in payment, Tartars?"

"This," answered Nogai, drawing his sword an inch from the scabbard.

"And this," Vyatka grunted, doing the same. Neither of them made any attempt to rise, though.

"Can you take lives, Chinaman, when your own is flowing out on our swords?" demanded Nogai.

"I do not think so," answered Chia Wang, a little smile on his tight old lips. "But this I think, and know, Tartars. If I but raise the little finger of this hand"—he held out his right hand—"you will both die by bullets before it reaches the height to which I can raise it."

"We are big men," said Vyatka calmly, "and well nourished. Our swords will reach you before the bullets stay us, Chinaman. Try it and see."

CHIA LAUGHED heartily, a real laugh of enjoyment. "You make me feel young once more, Tartars. Truly you are men. See, I do not raise my finger. Take your hands from your sword hilts. The matter of the killing of my little brothers we will take up later. Tell me why you have ridden to me."

"That killing was war," answered Nogai contemptuously. "We are at war with all who would harm the daughter of Ladislaw Guilai. This is not war. We took a caravan yesterday and in it are many of the things you crave, Chinaman. We come to ask you if you desire to purchase. We of the Altai are poor men."

Again Chia Wang laughed. "I see, O Tartars. This is trade and not to be in any way confused with war. You cease killing my little brothers to come and trade. Then you resume the killing."

"Why not?" asked Nogai in real amazement. "You are getting foolish as well as old, Chinaman. Does the fact that we of the Altai fleshed our swords in your men prevent us from coming with that which you wish to buy?"

"It might," answered Chia Wang, "with many. But I have known Tartars all my life, which, as you say, is getting to be a long one. Truly you see no bar in coming to me."

"Too much talk," snarled Vyatka. "Do you want to buy, Chinaman? We have killed, yes. And we will kill again as often as we wish. You, your men, or any others. We come under no flag of truce. Raise your finger and come with us into the eternal darkness—or talk of trade."

Chia Wang's concealed riflemen, at least all who understood Pushtu, tightened their fingers on their triggers. That their Lord allowed these savages to talk like that to him could only mean that he was playing, like a cat with a mouse. Surely he would give the signal soon, which was not the raising of a finger at all. But it did not come, and trigger fingers relaxed.

"What is in the caravan?" asked Chia Wang blandly.

"The sweet wines of Persia, great cases of candied fruits and melons from Turkey. Also the sweet stuff that is made in Bokhara."

That last settled it as far as Chia Wang was concerned. He dearly loved the Bokhara sweets and had not had any for a long time, owing to the unsettled condition of the country. The fact that he had made up his mind to have all Altai Mountain Tartars executed as fast as he caught them did not show in his face or in his voice as he asked, "You have with you the goods mentioned?"

"Yes. Just beyond your lines. And in case you think you can take them without payment, Chinaman, we will tell you that if your men advance on them, there will be a bonfire and you will get nothing but Tartar swords."

"I know that," answered Chia Wang with a chuckle that shook his fat sides. "I want the sweets, not Tartar swordplay. Bring the goods in and I will examine them. Then you may name your price."

"There are fifty Tartars with them," Vyatka said as he and Nogai rose. "Give orders, Chinaman, that a lane be made for us to come through and that none step over the line. You we trust, but we have seen some unspeakable ones camped here whom we do not trust. Also give orders that the same lane be made for us to return to the hills after the purchase. We take your word that the lane will not be narrowed until we have reached the hills."

"The orders will be given, Tartars, and you have my word, on the honor of the House of Chia. How soon will the sweets be here?"

"Some time to-night. Longer, if you keep us here talking. There are many loads and the way is rough. Will we bring the goods up close to your tent, Chinaman?"

"Yes. There is space in the rear for you to camp. In the morning I will examine what you bring. Make as little noise as possible when you arrive. I do not wish to be awakened."

Both Vyatka and Nogai grunted and stalked out without even bowing.

A little later Chai Wang sent for a staff officer. "The Tartars who have just left are to return with wagons and pack horses. See that they have plenty of room on all sides to bring the goods to me. Also see that they have the same room when they leave for the hills.

"This I have agreed with them. But place a regiment in the hills to take them once they are returned to the hills. Concerning that I gave no promise. Give orders that as many as possible be taken alive and brought to me."

THE DARKNESS deepened as the moon went behind a cloud and the old War Lord slept peacefully in his tent. He had gone to sleep with a smile on his lips as he thought of the Tartar insolence and how, when he had them in his power again, he would make them pay for it.

He had not been wakened by the caravan's coming, and was sleeping soundly—so soundly that when a bugle blew from the top of one of the hills it did not wake him. It blew "Commence firing."

But what happened right afterward did wake him. It was the sound of machine gun fire; and as he sat up, there came the long-drawn-out yell of pure exultation that Manchu swordsmen send up as they start a death charge. It came from the right of the spread-out encampment; the machine gun fire from the south. As Chia Wang got to his feet a high officer ran in and saluted.

"You have my permission to speak," Chia Wang said, without a trace of agitation.

"The guns attack from the south. Lord, and the Manchu swords come from the hills!"

There was the clash of swords outside and the *pow, pow, pow!* of Colt .45s. A voice shouted in English, which both Chia Wang and the officer understood. "Hold 'em back, you birds!" The sounds of bloody conflict continued.

Into the tent came Captain John Norcross, Colt in hand. With him was T'ang Wang, his jewel-hilted sword red with the blood of the Chinese guards who had died trying to protect their War Lord. Just behind came First Lieutenant Yaller Coudray and Sergeant Delicate Moss.

The officer with Chia Wang drew his revolver, or rather started to draw it. T'ang Wang was closest to him and the Manchu sword licked out like the tongue of a snake. The officer went down.

The old War Lord of the Irenkha-birga reached for a sword that lay on a table near-by. There was no fear in his eyes as he did. He knew he had been tricked, that instead of sweets the wagons had held the black men he had said he wished to see. He thought that death had come for him, but his face was impassive.

His hand never reached the sword. Captain John Norcross stepped in and his left fist came up in an uppercut that landed squarely on the point of Chia Wang's chin. It was not a hard blow, but a well placed one. Norcross did not want to hurt the old man. He knew that the flat of a sword or the barrel of a Colt on the head would hurt him more than the blow. He wanted Chia alive, and that uppercut to the jaw seemed the most merciful way to keep him that way.

"Pick him up, Delicate," Norcross ordered swiftly. "Easy with him! Can you carry him? Give him a hand, Yaller. Put him on a horse. You two ride on either side and hold him on. Get going!"

OUT OF the tent they came with the War Lord of the Irenkha. Over from the right there came what sounded like a thousand cat-fights rolled into one. It was where the Manchu swords were at work.

Inside the Tartar wagons had come fifty of B Troop with Captain John Norcross. T'ang Wang had come also, giving the honor of leading the Manchu swords to the master of swords from the school of swordsmen, who had requested it so that he might round out an honorable career.

The big colored men had poured out of the wagons when the bugle sounded. The Tartars, as the colored men ran to the horses, had charged straight at the nearest Chinese regiment.

This charge of Altai Mountain Tartars, coming from inside their lines, coupled with the gun fire from the hills and the Manchu yell, was more than enough to throw what Chinese were already awake into a frenzy of fear. They had only one connected thought—to get out of the way of whatever was coming. It was dark and the Irenkha regiments on the sides away from the Manchu charge, were confusedly trying to form. More disciplined troops than those have been thrown into panic by a night attack, and as the Chinese regiments closest to the center ran back, they prevented other regiments from forming. Far out it was calmer, except on the side where the Manchus were and on the south where the machine gun bullets were landing. As Troop B came up on the horses, riding without saddles, the Chinese regiments under control began forcing their way through the confusion toward the attacked center.

Norcross and T'ang Wang mounted, Yaller and Delicate lifted the unconscious War Lord of the Irenkha onto a horse, mounted two other steeds that were brought up for them, and holding Chia Wang's arms in their iron hands, ran all three horses into the center of a wedge. As the wedge started in the direction of the Manchu column, the Colt .45s were issuing Troop B's defiance to all armies, no matter how big.

The Tartars, wild with glee at the success of their trick, were at the point of the wedge now, their swords rising and falling. In daylight the Tartars and the colored men would have been overwhelmed before they had got two hundred yards through the countless forces of the Irenkha, but now they cut and shot their way through the confusion to where the head of the Manchu column was still under headway.

The Manchus opened up to let the riders through, then turned as a rear guard and followed to the hills. As the Manchus opened up, Norcross shouted to a bugler who rode behind him: "Retreat."

The bugler blew the call and then disobeyed the positive orders of Highnote, his boss, who had said, "Ah'm de one dat blows de Troop song, boy. Not yo' or any of de rest of dese apes dat Ah'm learnin'. Don't forget dat. Does Ah heah yo' tryin' it, Ah busts yo' wide open."

The bugler forgot all about this order and immediately started, "Oh, they keep the pigs in the parlor."

Highnote, who was with the guns, lowered his own bugle and complained bitterly. "Does yo' heah dat? Dat baboon does 'zactly whut Ah tells him not to. When Ah gits mah—"

"Git outta de way wid dat tin horn," interrupted Second Lieutenant Norton who was in command of the guns. "Move out, boy. Tell it to dat monkey-face when us gits home. Us got to be at de fork when de Capt'n gits dare."

It had succeeded, this mad plan that Norcross had worked out with the Tartars. It was a long chance, in which many things could turn remote possibility of success into failure. But it had won, and Troop B rode toward Ningyuan with the Tartars and the Manchus, carrying the War Lord of the Irenkha-birga with them. The Chinese regiment that had been placed in the hills to stop the Tartars did not even wait to fire a shot. They had run when they heard the Manchu and Tartar yells.

The officers of Chia Wang succeeded in getting order once more, and then, with the determination of rescuing their War Lord or avenging his death if it meant the tearing down of the mountain that held the city of Ningyuan with their bare hands, they moved toward the city with all the men from the Irenkha, leaving the guns in the hills where they sat. They did not care anything about bombardments or airplanes now. They were going in to get the Head of their House and their War Lord, or die, come what might.

CHAPTER XIV

THE TUNNEL OF DEATH

PRINCESS CH'ENYAUN SAT on the dais in her audience chamber. It was two o'clock in the morning, but her officers were still coming and going with reports. A palace official entered and bowed.

"You have my permission to speak," Ch'enyaun said curtly.

"The commander of the watergates begs that he be admitted with a prisoner, mighty one."

"With a prisoner? Admit them."

Two minutes later Ch'enyaun looked down on the commander of the gates, Shi-chung, and a young Chinese dressed in the uniform of a private.

"You have my permission to speak, Shi-chung."

"This man was taken at the watergates, Lord of the world. He was trying to enter the city."

"Why bring him in front of me? Am I to be bothered by details regarding prisoners?" asked Ch'enyaun coldly.

"I was not taken, O Manchu Princess," the young Chinese said calmly. "I came to the gates so that I might be brought in front of you."

Ch'enyaun knew the Chinese and the way they acted and thought. So she said, "You have a tale to tell, little brother?"

"Yes, resplendent one. It is this. I am Major Tzu Shan of the National Army of the South, although I now wear the uniform of a private. Thirty days ago my brother, Captain Tzu Li, was ordered tortured to death for some statements he had made regarding this dog Shao Wu for whom he was fighting. I left my command when the word came and in disguise came to the north to avenge my brother. Once here I joined the regiment of Chung, the War Brother of Shao Wu, and waited until the time came. I joined Chung's regiment rather than that of Shao Wu because it might have been that one or two of the officers of Shao Wu's regiment have seen me—when I was Major Tzu Shan."

"Come to the point, little brother. What is the tale you have to tell me?"

"This, War Lord of the North. The regiment of Chung has been digging a tunnel from one of the mines that lie on the hill to the west of Ningyuan. It was told that it is a mine that your uncle the Prince Lun Yu worked for many years—"

"What is the name of this mine?" Ch'enyaun interrupted.

"On a board there I saw the name, Yao-chau, Princess."

"Go on with the tale."

"This tunnel is now beyond the rim of the mountain and under the Temple of Ancestors. It opens up into the lower hall of tablets. In the tunnel is the regiment of Chung and the regiment of Shao Wu and one other, led by them. They wait for dawn to attack and open the gates for the men of the War Lord of the Irenkha. I pretended illness and lagged behind, then made my way to the gates. This I tell you, Manchu Princess, so that my brother may be avenged."

"He will be," answered Ch'enyaun coldly. "Take Major Tzu Shan to your quarters, Shi-chung. He is to be treated with all honor."

"May I speak and live, defender of cities?" asked Tzu Shan.

"Speak quickly."

"May I be among those who receive the torturer of my brother?"

"Yes. See to it, Shi-chung. You have my permission to go."

As they bowed and backed to the door, Ch'enyaun clapped

her hands once. The heavy silk curtain behind the dais moved and an officer saluted.

"The Lord Hsai to report to me at once."

SHAO WU, standing with Chung behind a wall that had been mined away so that only a thin sheet was left, looked at his wrist watch by aid of a little flash light. Behind them in the tunnel there stretched the long column of their regiments, with bayoneted rifles.

"It is time, War Brother. Dawn has come. We go for the treasure of Nurhachu. I take the gates of the watercourse. You the gates that open into the valley. These we hold until the War Lord of the Irenkha—who will be that only a few days longer—arrives. Order that the wall be pushed down."

Some men came forward with iron bars and in a few moments; the wall fell. The men went back to the ranks and Shao Wu, Chung and the officers of their staffs behind them stepped over the rubbish into the lower hall of the Temple.

As they did, a dull rumbling *boom!* sounded far back in the tunnel behind them. Then came the rending, tearing crash of rock and earth settling. The great, dark hall became suddenly light as powerful arc lights went on. Norcross had installed several complete lighting systems in Ningyuan. His colored men had, in an hour, set one up in the hall.

Shao Wu and Chung, as well as the officers behind them, stood absolutely motionless, as if statues. Not twenty feet in front of them, in a line that reached from wall to wall, there were machine guns. And behind each gun were the grim, cold-eyed Negroes of Troop B. Back of the gunners stood others with rifles. And behind them, rank after rank of Manchu swordsmen. From the soldiers in the Chinese column who could see this, there went up a wailing cry of utter fear.

It broke the spell. And Shao Wu laughed. He laughed, as his dream of treasure and power and empire-building faded away. "We are trapped, War Brother," he said calmly, as if in his tent. "The way is blocked behind us. We will take these—"

A Manchu officer walked calmly past the machine guns toward Shao Wu and Chung. And behind him, a little to the left, came Major Tzu Shan. He was dressed as an officer now and in his right hand was a naked Manchu sword.

"You are Shao Wu and Chung?" the Manchu officer asked blandly.

"Yes, I am Shao Wu and this is my War Brother Chung. You are the Manchu Lord Hsai?"

"Yes. I am Hsai. The Princess Ch'enyaun, ruler of Ningyuan and the Thian Shan Range, orders that your men be allowed to surrender. They may put down their arms and march through the tunnel to the palace square. The Princess Ch'enyaun will spare their lives."

As Hsai said that, it was heard by the front ranks, who relayed it back along the column. Another cry went up, this time of thanksgiving, and the sound of rifles and belts dropping could be heard. Anna Norcross had asked that the men be allowed to surrender. Had it been left to Ch'enyaun, they would all have been slain in the tunnel.

"You speak of my men," Shao Wu said smoothly. "What of my officers and my War Brother and myself?"

"Your officers may surrender. Their lives will also be spared. You and your War Brother die on the platform under the knives because of what you have done—and tried to do."

Shao Wu heard behind him the dropping of the staff officers' equipment, and he knew that he and Chung stood alone.

"May I ask the priceless boon of a moment's time? I wish to say good-by to my War Brother."

"You may have it," answered Hsai suavely.

Major Tzu Shan stepped forward and gave his name. "Shao Wu, you tortured my elder brother, Captain Tzu Li. He is now avenged and smiles. It is my work, this trap. I will laugh as you are—"

Shao Wu's iron control broke and he saw through a red haze the man who taunted him.

"You dog," he snarled. "I will send your spirit to join that of your brother which howls in the outer darkness," and drew his heavy service revolver. As he did, Chung drew also.

They were fast, both of them, but the big colored men were faster. The hall seemed to rock at the detonation of the rifles that loosed off as one. Both Shao Wu and Chung were lifted up and flung back to the feet of their staff officers as if hit by a giant hammer, dead before they landed.

"You may carry the bodies that held the spirits of Shao Wu and Chung out of the Temple and prepare them for honorable burial," Hsai said suavely to the Chinese staff officers. "Now order your men forward."

Even as he spoke, Norcross, T'ang Wang, the rest of Troop B, the Tartars, and the captive War Lord of the Irenkha-birga were riding through the gates of Ningyuan.

CHAPTER XV

THE SCROLL OF THE HOUSE OF CHIA

CHIA WANG, WAR Lord of the Irenkha-birga, and Head of the House of Chia, sat in a comfortable chair in the garden of the palace at Ningyuan. On a little table close to the chair were many little dishes of sweets. He had regained consciousness during the ride, and Norcross had halted the column while a litter had been made for him to ride in. This was made with long poles cut from the timber on the hillsides, interlaced with boughs and Tartar sheepskin coats.

It was not a very easy-riding vehicle, but much better than being astride a bareback horse. Chia Wang was still a little sick from the effect of the uppercut that had put him out, but was in full possession of his faculties otherwise when he woke up.

He saw the big colored men who surrounded him, as his eyes opened, and he felt the grip of the hands that held him upright.

Yaller Coudray saw that he had come to, and asked solicitously: "Is yo' awake, gineral? How does yo' feel?"

The old War Lord of the Irenkha looked at lean, hard-boiled "Yaller" Coudray. The dawn was coming rapidly, and he could see plainly enough to know that Yaller and the big man who rode on the other side of him were regarding him with friendly eyes.

"I am awake," he answered in perfect English. "It has been many years since I sat a horse and the blow has made me sick. Loosen your grips on my arms; they hurt me."

"Mah goodness! Let go, Del'cate. Us was only holdin' yo' on, gineral. Can yo' ride widout us? See dat, yo' would fall. Us just steadies yo'. Git to the Capt'n, Tollivah, and tell him dat de gineral us took is 'wake and sick to de stomach."

Norcross had halted the column and had ordered the litter. While it was being made the old War Lord rested on the ground, his head on a pillow made by a Tartar saddle covered by Norcross's tunic. He had been given a little brandy carried by one of the first aid men who had been with the guns, and now he felt better. Norcross and T'ang Wang sat beside him and after a few minutes Chia Wang had raised himself on an elbow.

"You I know, Lord T'ang Wang," he said calmly in English. "And you are the American captain who leads the black men. What is your name?"

"I am John Norcross. Lie back, sir, and rest," answered Norcross gently.

"You are taking me to Ningyuan?"

"Yes, sir."

The War Lord of the Irenkha looked steadily at Norcross for a moment, then said: "I will take up the matter of the blow with you later, Captain Norcross—after my little brothers have taken Ningyuan." Then he lay down again.

Norcross rode once more at the head of the column with

T'ang Wang, the old War Lord now being carried in the litter. The captain grinned as he thought of the fearless old man.

T'ang Wang saw it and smiled also. "I am afraid you are scheduled to fight a duel, elder brother," the Manchu said gravely.

"It looks that way, unless I can find something that will wipe out the blow. It seemed the only thing to do. If the flat of a sword or the barrel of a Colt had connected with the old gentleman's head he would have been much worse off this morning."

"It may be that if we explain to him that the blow was meant only to save him pain, he will understand and forgive… See, the watercourses appear. We have won through, John."

THE OLD War Lord was taken to the palace and treated with all courtesy and medical skill possible. Now, as he sat in the gardens, he was as good as ever. With him sat the Princess Ch'enyaun, in the full court dress of a Manchu princess of the blood, wearing gold and jeweled headdress.

One would have thought to see them there that they were some kindly old grandfather and his pretty granddaughter enjoying the scented gardens, instead of being the Manchu Princess Ch'enyaun with her captive the War Lord of the Irenkha-birga, whose men were even then raging at the walls of her city. The sound of the guns that defied them came clearly to the gardens.

"Your little brothers die fast, O Chia Wang," Ch'enyaun said coldly.

"There are many of them, little golden flower," the Head of the House of Chia answered placidly. "So many that soon the ammunition for your guns will be exhausted. Then my little brothers, of whom there are many thousands, will take the city."

"You forget, O War Lord of the Irenkha-birga. After the ammunition is exhausted there still remain ten thousand Manchu swords and the bayonets of the Lord Norcross. Can your little brothers last until they also are exhausted?"

"That I do not know," answered Chia Wang, as he nibbled on a piece of candy.

"I do not think they will even wait to receive my swords who go to drive them back to the Irenkha as soon as the guns cease talking," Ch'enyaun said with a cold little smile.

"My little brothers fight for *me*, lotus bud… Truly this sweet I am eating must have been made by the gods."

"They will not have you to fight for much longer," Ch'enyaun said. "The platform is being erected now on top of the gates upon which you will be given Ling-chih in front of them all. Afterward my swords will send them to join your spirit on high, War Lord of the Irenkha-birga."

Chia Wang, at the mention of the death of the thousand cuts, did not even stop nibbling the candy. "Twice have I tried to take Ningyuan," he said with a sigh, "and twice have I failed. Truly the gods do not regard me with favor. With regard to the matter you have just mentioned, beautiful one, I am old and have little blood in my veins. I am afraid that I will not afford much of a spectacle for you to watch."

Ch'enyaun, brave herself, recognized the absolute courage of the old Chinaman and now really smiled as she answered: "It is done to lesson the Irenkha-birga about coming into my territory, not as a spectacle, Lord Chia Wang. It is— The guns stop! Your little brothers have fled."

"They will return," answered Chia Wang with a smile. "More and more of them, little one whose grace is that of a flower. May I finish this sweet before I go to the platform?"

"You may," answered Ch'enyaun courteously.

"**BEFORE I** go, I have a request to make, O Manchu Princess," the old War Lord said formally as he finished the candy. "I would, while I am enduring the knives, that I could hold in my hands or have held in front of me, the—" He stopped talking and rose as Norcross and T'ang Wang came up.

"The forces of the Irenkha-birga have fallen back to the hills, Princess," T'ang Wang said to his wife like an officer reporting.

"Order the swords— Wait. The War Lord of the Irenkha-birga goes to the platform first." Ch'enyaun held up her right hand and the swordsmen of her bodyguard that had been standing some twenty feet away came forward. The little princess's face and eyes were as cold as those of her ancestors had been when they led the Manchus to storm the Peacock Throne of China.

"Order that your swords halt, Ch'enyaun," Norcross said quietly.

"What? This is not the time to interfere— For what reason, John?"

"Order them back, little sister." His calm blue eyes met her black ones.

"I will not!" Ch'enyaun flamed hotly. "I am the ruler of— See, John, they shall go back. You are my elder brother." Her hand went up as she started to speak, and the swordsmen halted.

Chia Wang stood with hands folded across his big stomach, with no more expression on his face than on an idol.

"Will you give me the War Lord of the Irenkha-birga, little sister that I love?" Norcross then asked.

"Will I give you the—" Ch'enyaun looked amazedly at T'ang Wang and at Chia Wang, then back at Norcross. "Yes, honorable elder brother, I give you the War Lord of the Irenkha-birga," she said calmly.

"And also will you give me something that is here in Ningyuan?"

"Yes, John. I give you anything that is in Ningyuan."

"I knew that you would, War Lord of many swordsmen. Order that the Scroll of the House of Chia be brought from the Hall of Trophies."

"That the Scroll— John, what are you going to do?"

"Order that the Scroll be brought to me. That is the thing I want that is in Ningyuan."

Chia Wang sat down. His knees suddenly had become too weak to hold his body up.

The Princess Ch'enyaun turned and beckoned the officer of

the bodyguard forward. "You will go to the Hall of Trophies and there with all honor take from the table on which it rests, the Scroll of the House of Chia. Bring it here to the Lord John. You have my permission to go."

Norcross turned to Chia Wang, who looked up at him.

"Touching that matter of the blow, Lord Chia Wang: When I saw that you would resist capture, instead of striking you with the barrel of my gun, or having the Lord T'ang Wang strike you with the flat of his sword, either of which might have caused you serious injury, I struck you with my fist, meaning no dishonor to you. In my land of America men fight with their fists, and a blow taken or given is done so with no thought of insult. I am very sorry if you look upon it as an insult. And the next time," he added, "I assure you I will use a gun barrel."

The Princess Ch'enyaun came and stood by Norcross, her little jeweled hand taking hold of his bronzed one.

"My honorable elder brother speaks ever truly, War Lord of the Irenkha-birga," she said proudly. "I the Manchu Princess Ch'enyaun, Head of the House of Nurhachu, say to you that there was no insult in the blow."

"I also," T'ang Wang said formally. "I, T'ang Wang, Manchu noble of the House of Nurhachu. I say there was no insult in the blow."

"**I AM** not of Manchu blood," Chia Wang answered smoothly. "But I do not need the assurance, O Manchu Princess and noble of the House of Nurhachu. The words of Captain Norcross explained—and wiped away any thought of insult. The matter is forgotten. I sit in your presence only because my legs will not bear this fat old body at the moment. Will you honor me by being seated while waiting for—" He drew a long breath and in spite of his attempt to remain impassive, his hands trembled.

Coming up to Norcross was the officer of the bodyguard, followed by swordsmen with drawn swords as an honor guard. The officer bore on a silken cushion the gold pages that made up the Scroll of the House of Chia.

Chia Wang tried to rise, but could not make it, tried again, and this time succeeded by holding on to the arm of the chair with his left hand.

The officer handed the cushion to Norcross, bowed, and stepped back. Norcross took it and stepped close to the old War Lord, whose face was no longer impassive.

"I give you that for which you came, Lord of the Irenkha-birga," Norcross told him solemnly.

The old War Lord let go the chair and took the cushion in both hands. Then he bent his head for a moment over the golden pages. Once again his knees gave way and he sat down, the Scroll and cushion hugged to his breast. At that moment the guns started their snarling *bang-bang-bang!*

"Your little brothers come once more to be slain, O Chia Wang," said Ch'enyaun silkily. She was all Manchu and ran true to her blood always. Ch'enyaun had yielded to John Norcross; first because the House of Nurhachu was deeply indebted to him, and with a Manchu the paying of a debt takes precedence over everything; second, because he really was "her honorable elder brother" whom she loved.

If the matter had been left in her hands, Chia Wang would have stood on the platform and the Manchu swords sent out afterward "to lesson the Irenkha-birga."

The Head of the House of Chia looked up, brought back to the present by her voice pronouncing his name. The guns he had not even heard. "You spoke, little one? I—" He heard the guns now. "The guns talk! I ask that you order them to stop, O Princess of the House of Nurhachu. Then that I may be carried to the gates and a flag of truce waved. My little brothers do not know that I—have that for which I came."

Ch'enyaun looked up at John Norcross, who smiled.

"If you will, Ch'enyaun?" he asked.

Ch'enyaun said promptly: "I order that the guns cease. You, Chia Wang, War Lord of the Irenkha-birga, I have given to

Lord John Norcross. He will order your disposal. You have my permission to leave."

"Please, Ch'enyaun," Norcross put in gently. "See it through with me."

The proud little princess opened her mouth to say something, thought better of it, then laughed softly. "I will see it through with you, honorable elder brother."

As the city's fire stopped, one of the commanding officers of the Irenkha who was well toward the front of the troops shouted: "They have run out of ammunition! Now we will take the city. But see! The gates open and it is our Lord, alive! and carried in all honor! A flag of truce is waved... Officers forward!"

Old Chia Wang looked blandly down on his officers who halted in front of his advancing litter.

"I have regained the Scroll of the House of Chia," he announced, holding up the cushion on which it rested. "Withdraw to the Irenkha-birga, little brothers. I go with the American Captain Norcross, my War Brother, to inspect his mountain of Szu and the black men who fight under him. My War Brother's men will escort me back to the Irenkha-birga. You, Lin Lee, will detail an honor guard of one hundred officers to accompany the Scroll of our House. You have my permission to go."

The Princess Ch'enyaun smiled and said softly to Norcross: "T'ang Wang and I will go to Szu also, John, and be friends with your—War Brother of the Irenkha-birga."

A DAY or so later on the mountain of Szu, Skinnay Martin eased up to Yaller Coudray.

"Yaller—Ah means lieutenant, whut does de ol' gent'mum carry 'round wid him all de time dat he thinks so much of? Dogged if he has let go of it long enough to blow his nose since Ah seen him."

"Dat's de Scroll of his House, boy."

"Is dat so? No wondah he thinks such a lot of it... But say, lieutenant, whut-all *is* a Scroll of de House? Ah been in lots of houses an' Ah ain't never seen no Scroll yet. It looks like a gold book to me."

"Dat's whut it is, ig'runt. A Scroll is de names of all yoah ancestahs writ down from de time dat yo' had any. No wondah yo' nevah see one. Yo' ancestahs was jumpin' 'round in trees when Scrolls was started. Go on away, Ah'm busy."

"Dat's whut Ah thought it was," answered Skinnay unabashed, ignoring the remark about ancestors. "How come Miss Anna and de Capt'n makin' such a fuss ovah him? Miss Anna, she smile and pat his hand and feed him candy all de time."

"How does Ah know, boy? Ah knows dis, dat Scroll whut he packs cost plenty of lives, no foolin'. Boy, yo' should 'a' seen de way his men come bammin' ovah de plain at us when us had him at Ningyuan. Most of de time, Chinks will run aftah a little while, but dem boys was a comin' whethah or no. Dey would get killed daid, take a rest, and den come again."

"Whut did the ol' gent'mum said to de Tartahs?" asked Skinnay, who had a very large bump of inquisitiveness.

"Git away from me befo' Ah smack yo' down. Dog-gone it, yo' is de askin'est ape Ah evah saw. De ol' gent'mum, he said to de two Tartahs, de one named Vat-something and de one named No-guy: 'Yo' tricked me.' He was talkin' in dat Push-too language whut Ah am learnin' so good.

"De Tartahs laugh and de one named No-guy, he said, 'Whut of dat? Many times has yo' tricked othahs, Chinaman.' Jest like dat, proud and hostile. An' de one named Vat-somethin' he say: 'Us *did* take a caravan, Chinaman,' and his talk was jest as hostile as No-guy. Den he go on: 'And dare is sweets from Bok'—from some place—'in it. Us is holdin' dem fo' yo'. Does yo' want to buy dem, Chinaman?'"

"Dog mah cats, Yal—lieutenant, Ah mean. An' whut did de ol' gent'mum say to dat?" Skinnay asked, very much interested.

"He look at dem Tartahs for a long time, den he said: 'Ah pass ovah de mattah of de killin' of mah little brothahs, because yo' did it at de command of de golden one who stands beside me. Yo' may bring de sweets to me, Tartahs,' and den he smile at Miss Anna."

"Dog-gone! Whut did he— Ah'm on mah way, Misto' Lieutenant."

ABOUT THE AUTHOR

ANOTHER WRITER WHO makes his bow to readers is W. Wirt—a man whose life has been packed with adventures. We asked Mr. Wirt to stand up and introduce himself so that we can all get some idea of what sort of hombre can spin a salty yarn such as this. Mr. Wirt has the floor:

Born—Boston, Massachusetts, 1876.

People on both sides hard-boiled Maine and Massachusetts Presbyterians of strictly English descent. All but one—but that one was a direct descendant of one of Sir Francis Drake's captains. The King of Spain had a standing offer of one thousand golden crowns to the hombre that would present him with "That pirate devil's head." Every once in a while one of the elect breaks out. The rest of the family at once put it down to the old pirate.

My late pa was one of them, all right. I think he had more than his share of the blood. He was a special agent and one of the very few Americans who served in the Secret Service of foreign countries. He went here and there, all over the world, in the oddest places, from northern China to the South Sea Islands, from there to Alaska and way points. Sometimes for Uncle Sam in the Post Office Department; other times for other people.

My education and experience? They are part and part. If there ever was a scrambled one I had it. When I wasn't much bigger than knee-high to a grasshopper my pa began taking me along with him, whenever he could do so safely. I remem-

ber military, private, public and
every other kind of school in a
dim way. He'd leave me in one
somewhere, go and attend to his
knitting, then come back and get
me, and away we'd go again. But
the constant education I received
from him regarding the conduct
of "an officer and a gentleman"
under any and all circumstance
still remains vivid in my mind.
One month we'd be in England,
evening clothes after six as regular as clockwork, down at one of

W. Wirt

the big estates for the week-ends, then, in a month or a darn
sight less, we'd be in some "flop house" as poor broken-down
bums—I acting the part of the devoted son who wouldn't leave
his poor old ex-con father, and so forth.

After I reached eighteen I worked with him for a good many
years, and when he was called to join his venerable ancestors
I carried on alone. No matter where I was, in the Orient or
anywhere else, I missed him—with his cool laugh in the face
of death and his never failing, slow, amused drawl. His favor-
ite weapon was a sawed-off shotgun carrying buckshot. This,
of course, was for use in the places where the little yellow and
black brothers congregate mostly. I miss him yet, and always
will—and that's that.

I have been behind a badge for Uncle Sam some little time
and at present am still special agenting, but on my own, seldom
going out of the States and not hunting for any trouble at all,
having more than my share already. I've had my gun in the ribs
and ears of a few jaspers and used to say "Put 'em up!" so darn
often that my longhaired partner—now bobbed haired—every
once in a while wakes me up with a demand to know if I have
any good reason for poking my fi nger in her side and hollering
at her in the middle of the night.

Then there have been many times when the reverse English was in force and I did the reaching for the blue sky, promptly and in haste. All in all, I lived and rambled when things were wide open, no blue laws or anything, just help yourself to the mustard if you wanted any. And I am darn glad I did. Man, howdy, you could go over the mountain, in "them" days and see things—and do 'em likewise, if you wanted to.

I and Schley whipped the Spanish fleet together, I as a volunteer and Schley as a regular. There were a few others present, but we did most of it. In the late argument I did some "hush, hush" stuff.

My present standing? Well, been married seventeen years; have two children, boy and girl. Have an old place in Maryland near Washington, a police dog, three or twenty-six kittens and cats, an old "colored lady" named Medora to make the corn bread, plenty good old corn lick—I mean corn licorice—to drink and am "out of commission."

A lot of my old buddies drift through, hang their hats up behind the door and drink my said good old yellow-with-age corn licorice, eat some fried chicken and curse me in all the living and dead languages because I won't let go all holds and go wild-catting over the hills once more. They don't get a rise out of me at all. I'm like the colored man who, when asked if he wanted to make a quarter, replied: "No, suh, I done got me a quarter." All I want is peace and quiet.

1. GENIUS JONES by Lester Dent
2. WHEN TIGERS ARE HUNTING: THE COMPLETE ADVENTURES OF CORDIE, SOLDIER OF FORTUNE, VOLUME 1 by W. Wirt
3. THE SWORDSMAN OF MARS by Otis Adelbert Kline
4. THE SHERLOCK OF SAGELAND: THE COMPLETE TALES OF SHERIFF HENRY, VOLUME 1 by W.C. Tuttle
5. GONE NORTH by Charles Alden Seltzer
6. THE MASKED MASTER MIND by George F. Worts
7. BALATA by Fred MacIsaac
8. BRETWALDA by Philip Ketchum
9. DRAFT OF ETERNITY by Victor Rousseau
10. FOUR CORNERS, VOLUME 1 by Theodore Roscoe
11. CHAMPION OF LOST CAUSES by Max Brand
12. THE SCARLET BLADE: THE RAKEHELLY ADVENTURES OF CLEVE AND D'ENTREVILLE, VOLUME 1 by Murray R. Montgomery
13. DOAN AND CARSTAIRS: THEIR COMPLETE CASES by Norbert Davis
14. THE KING WHO CAME BACK by Fred MacIsaac
15. BLOOD RITUAL: THE ADVENTURES OF SCARLET AND BRADSHAW, VOLUME 1 by Theodore Roscoe
16. THE CITY OF STOLEN LIVES: THE ADVENTURES OF PETER THE BRAZEN, VOLUME 1 by Loring Brent
17. THE RADIO GUN-RUNNERS by Ralph Milne Farley
18. SABOTAGE by Cleve F. Adams
19. THE COMPLETE CABALISTIC CASES OF SEMI DUAL, THE OCCULT DETECTOR, VOLUME 2: 1912–13 by J.U. Giesy and Junius B. Smith
20. SOUTH OF FIFTY-THREE by Jack Bechdolt
21. TARZAN AND THE JEWELS OF OPAR by Edgar Rice Burroughs
22. CLOVELLY by Max Brand
23. WAR LORD OF MANY SWORDSMEN: THE ADVENTURES OF NORCOSS, VOLUME 1 by W. Wirt
24. ALIAS THE NIGHT WIND by Varick Vanardy
25. THE BLUE FIRE PEARL: THE COMPLETE ADVENTURES OF SINGAPORE SAMMY, VOLUME 1 by George F. Worts

26. THE MOON POOL & THE CONQUEST OF THE MOON POOL by Abraham Merritt

27. THE GUN-BRAND by James B. Hendryx

28. JAN OF THE JUNGLE by Otis Adelbert Kline

29. MINIONS OF THE MOON by William Grey Beyer

30. DRINK WE DEEP by Arthur Leo Zagat

31. THE VENGEANCE OF THE WAH FU TONG: THE COMPLETE CASES OF JIGGER MASTERS, VOLUME 1 by Anthony M. Rud

32. THE RUBY OF SURATAN SINGH: THE ADVENTURES OF SCARLET AND BRADSHAW, VOLUME 2 by Theodore Roscoe

33. THE SHERIFF OF TONTO TOWN: THE COMPLETE TALES OF SHERIFF HENRY, VOLUME 2 by W.C. Tuttle

34. THE DARKNESS AT WINDON MANOR by Max Brand

35. THE FLYING LEGION by George Allan England

36. THE GOLDEN CAT: THE ADVENTURES OF PETER THE BRAZEN, VOLUME 3 by Loring Brent

37. THE RADIO MENACE by Ralph Milne Farley

38. THE APES OF DEVIL'S ISLAND by John Cunningham

39. THE OPPOSING VENUS: THE COMPLETE CABALISTIC CASES OF SEMI DUAL, THE OCCULT DETECTOR by J.U. Giesy and Junius B. Smith

40. THE EXPLOITS OF BEAU QUICKSILVER by Florence M. Pettee

41. ERIC OF THE STRONG HEART by Victor Rousseau

42. MURDER ON THE HIGH SEAS AND THE DIAMOND BULLET: THE COMPLETE CASES OF GILLIAN HAZELTINE by George F. Worts

43. THE WOMAN OF THE PYRAMID AND OTHER TALES: THE PERLEY POORE SHEEHAN OMNIBUS, VOLUME 1 by Perley Poore Sheehan

44. A COLUMBUS OF SPACE AND THE MOON METAL: THE GARRETT P. SERVISS OMNIBUS, VOLUME 1 by Garrett P. Serviss

45. THE BLACK TIDE: THE COMPLETE ADVENTURES OF BELLOW BILL WILLIAMS, VOLUME 1 by Ralph R. Perry

46. THE NINE RED GODS DECIDE: THE COMPLETE ADVENTURES OF CORDIE, SOLDIER OF FORTUNE, VOLUME 2 by W. Wirt

47. A GRAVE MUST BE DEEP! by Theodore Roscoe

48. THE AMERICAN by Max Brand

49. THE COMPLETE ADVENTURES OF KOYALA, VOLUME 1 by John Charles Beecham

50. THE CULT MURDERS by Alan Forsyth

51. THE COMPLETE CASES OF THE MONGOOSE by Johnston McCulley

52. THE GIRL AND THE PEOPLE OF THE GOLDEN ATOM by Ray Cummings

53. THE GRAY DRAGON: THE ADVENTURES OF PETER THE BRAZEN, VOLUME 2 by Loring Brent

54. THE GOLDEN CITY by Ralph Milne Farley

55. THE HOUSE OF INVISIBLE BONDAGE: THE COMPLETE CABALISTIC CASES OF SEMI DUAL, THE OCCULT DETECTOR by J.U. Giesy and Junius B. Smith

56. THE SCRAP OF LACE: THE COMPLETE CASES OF MADAME STOREY, VOLUME 1 by Hulbert Footner

57. TOWER OF DEATH: THE ADVENTURES OF SCARLET AND BRADSHAW, VOLUME 3 by Theodore Roscoe

58. THE DEVIL-TREE OF EL DORADO by Frank Aubrey

59. THE FIREBRAND: THE COMPLETE ADVENTURES OF TIZZO, VOLUME 1 by Max Brand

60. MARCHING SANDS AND THE CARAVAN OF THE DEAD: THE HAROLD LAMB OMNIBUS by Harold Lamb

61. KINGDOM COME by Martin McCall

62. HENRY RIDES THE DANGER TRAIL: THE COMPLETE TALES OF SHERIFF HENRY, VOLUME 3 by W.C. Tuttle

63. Z IS FOR ZOMBIE by Theodore Roscoe

64. THE BAIT AND THE TRAP: THE COMPLETE ADVENTURES OF TIZZO, VOLUME 2 by Max Brand

65. MINIONS OF MARS by William Gray Beyer

66. SWORDS IN EXILE: THE RAKEHELLY ADVENTURES OF CLEVE AND D'ENTREVILLE, VOLUME 2 by Murray R. Montgomery

67. MEN WITH NO MASTER: THE COMPLETE ADVENTURES OF ROBIN THE BOMBARDIER by Roy de S. Horn

68. THE TORCH by Jack Bechdolt

69. KING OF CHAOS AND OTHER ADVENTURES: THE JOHNSTON MCCULLEY OMNIBUS by Johnston McCulley

70. THE BLIND SPOT by Austin Hall & Homer Eon Flint

71. SATAN'S VENGEANCE by Carroll John Daly

72. THE VIPER: THE COMPLETE CASES OF MADAME STOREY, VOLUME 2
by Hulbert Footner

73. THE SAPPHIRE SMILE: THE ADVENTURES OF PETER THE BRAZEN, VOLUME 4
by Loring Brent

74. THE CURSE OF CAPISTRANO AND OTHER ADVENTURES: THE JOHNSTON
MCCULLEY OMNIBUS, VOLUME 2 by Johnston McCulley

75. THE MAN WHO MASTERED TIME AND OTHER ADVENTURES: THE RAY
CUMMINGS OMNIBUS by Ray Cummings

76. THE GUNS OF THE AMERICAN: THE ADVENTURES OF NORCROSS, VOLUME 2
by W. Wirt

77. TRAILIN' by Max Brand

78. WAR DECLARED! by Theodore Roscoe

79. THE RETURN OF THE NIGHT WIND by Varick Vanardy

80. THE FETISH FIGHTERS AND OTHER ADVENTURES: THE F.V.W. MASON FOREIGN
LEGION STORIES OMNIBUS by F.V.W. Mason

81. THE PYTHON PIT: THE COMPLETE ADVENTURES OF SINGAPORE SAMMY,
VOLUME 2 by George F. Worts

82. A QUEEN OF ATLANTIS by Frank Aubrey

83. FOUR CORNERS, VOLUME 2 by Theodore Roscoe

84. THE STUFF OF EMPIRE: THE COMPLETE ADVENTURES OF BELLOW BILL
WILLIAMS, VOLUME 2 by Ralph R. Perry

85. GALLOPING GOLD: THE COMPLETE TALES OF SHERIFF HENRY, VOLUME 4
by W.C. Tuttle

86. JADES AND AFGHANS: THE COMPLETE ADVENTURES OF CORDIE, SOLDIER OF
FORTUNE, VOLUME 3 by W. Wirt

87. THE LEDGER OF LIFE: THE COMPLETE CABALISTIC CASES OF SEMI DUAL, THE
OCCULT DETECTOR by J.U. Giesy and Junius B. Smith

88. MINIONS OF MERCURY by William Gray Beyer

89. WHITE HEATHER WEATHER by John Frederick

90. THE FIRE FLOWER AND OTHER ADVENTURES: THE JACKSON GREGORY
OMNIBUS by Jackson Gregory

www.ingramcontent.com/pod-product-compliance
Lightning Source LLC
Chambersburg PA
CBHW030522020726
47494CB00004B/1191